SUNSHINE RIDER

Also by Ric Lynden Hardman

Fifteen Flags
The Chaplains Raid
No Other Harvest

SUNSHINE RIDER

THE FIRST VEGETARIAN WESTERN

RIC LYNDEN HARDMAN

DELACORTE PRESS

Published by
Delacorte Press
Bantam Doubleday Dell Publishing Group, Inc.
1540 Broadway
New York, New York 10036

Library of Congress Cataloging-in-Publication Data
Hardman, Ric Lynden.
    Sunshine rider : the first vegetarian western / Ric Lynden
Hardman.
       p.   cm.
    Summary: In the late 1800s while on a cattle drive which
takes him north from Texas, seventeen-year-old Wylie learns
that it is no longer necessary to run from the father he never
knew.
    ISBN 0-385-32543-6
    [1. Cattle drives—West (U.S.)—Fiction.   2. Fathers and
sons—Fiction.   3. West (U.S.)—Fiction.]   I. Title.
    PZ7.H2187Su 1998
    [Fic]—dc21   97-16244
                                                CIP
                                                AC

The text of this book is set in 12-point Adobe Garamond.
Book design by Julie E. Baker

Manufactured in the United States of America
March 1998
10 9 8 7 6 5 4 3 2 1
BVG

For my wife, Mickey, and my Pacific Northwest friends,
Dick and Jo Anne Feringer, Bill and Pat Hooper, and
Brad and Shirley Fischer, who read this tale aloud
around campfires and kitchen stoves
at Salmon la Sac and Stehekin

PORTERHOUSE STEAKS.

CHAUNCEY POTTER.

❖Raise a tripod of three stout poles about twelve feet off the ground with a rope and pulley at the crown.

❖Catch a well-fleshed steer, about eight-hundred-pound weight. Bind its rear legs, trip it off its feet, and stun by a blow to the head with a four-pound sledge, being careful not to crush the skull. Hoist the steer to the tripod and place a washtub under the head. Open the jugular vein and let the heart pump the blood until the steer is drained. Skin the steer and open the abdominal cavity, being careful not to spill the guts.

❖Concentrate fecal matter in the lower colon and tie this off in two places. Slice above and below the ties and bury. Remove the intestines and organs and place them in a washtub with blood for future use. Cleave the sternum and prop ribs open. Wipe the body cavity dry with a clean cloth and dust with pepper or powdered charcoal. Attach the forward portion (head) to the pulley so it will not fall into washtub of blood and organs when spine is severed. With a sharp butcher knife and cleaver remove the short loin. Set this on a large board to cool.

❖When the loin is sufficiently cool to take the knife (it is best to wait twenty-four hours and let the beef age if time permits), cut loin into porterhouse steaks. Heat a large skillet with lard the size of a walnut.

❖Sear the steak on one side until blood appears on the surface. Turn and fry on the other side to taste.

❖A good steer should yield twenty pounds of fine steak. Feeds fifteen men.

CHAPTER ONE

❖ ❖ ❖

For weeks cattle had been coming to Odessa from all parts of southwest Texas. The townsfolk were doing their best to outfit the drovers and get provisions for their drive to Wichita. The demand for groceries had raised prices so high that my aunt Clara was scandalized by what she had to pay for eggs.

School was out, so I was running errands for Bridges' Hardware Store, and that morning Mr. Bridges gave me a package I was to deliver to the Circle Six cook, Mr. Chauncey Potter, out on the cattle ground.

Activity in town was frantic from dawn to dark, but folks were careful about making noise because no one wanted to stampede the cattle, which could smash through Odessa and leave nothing but a pile of torn canvas and kindling wood. Everything was exciting and important, and the chance for heroism was in the air, so as I walked down the street I thought what I'd do if a thousand head of rampaging cattle came at me.

Here's Wylie Jackson plumb in the center of the road, I thought. *Women are screaming and running into buildings and that horde of beef, led by a big longhorn steer, his eyes rolling white fire, his hooves drumming death, is charging toward me.*

I know this steer is the leader of the crowd and must be put down to stem the tide of destruction. "Ho up!" *I command. The longhorn continues at me. I feel his*

3

breath in my face as I seize him by the horns and throw my weight, jabbing one horn into the dirt. The charging beast cuts a furrow in the road one foot deep and forty feet long before it falls in a neck-broke heap with a sound like a busted bass drum. Blocked by the body of their fallen leader, the stampeding cattle stumble about and grow docile. The townspeople spill into the street huzzahing me, and Mr. John Boardman, trail boss of the whole Circle Six caboodle, rides up and says: "I never seen such sand in my life. What's your name, boy?"

"Wylie Jackson, sir!"

"Who are you talkin' to?"

"You, sir."

"Wylie, will you wake up!"

I looked around and there was Alice Beck at my side with a silly smile on her face. "Who were you talking to?" she asked again.

"I wasn't talking."

"You were so!"

"I'm taking a package to one of the drovers for Mr. Bridges."

"I'm going to see Roselle."

"How many times you going to say goodbye to that dumb beast?"

"She is not dumb, and I guess that's none of your business."

Alice clouded over because I'd called her pet cattalo dumb, and we walked on together in silence.

Alice had been in my class since we started school. In times past we'd whupped each other in about equal amounts, but since she filled out we weren't so quick with our fists, which was fine with me because I could

4

never be sure Alice wouldn't get a lucky hit and leave me with a bloody nose. The last time we got really mad at each other I refused to fight, saying I couldn't strike a lady. This surprised her so much she pulled her punch, and I only got a black eye.

"A lady," she said. "Do you really think so?"

"We're not kids anymore," I said. "Dang! It's time we give over beating on each other every time we get mad."

"Every other time, then," Alice said.

Her father, Jesse Beck, is a lawyer by trade, but there wasn't much lawyering in Odessa, so he tried other things, enlisting investors when he could. "It'll make a fortune!" was his most frequent and most erroneous saying. He'd opened a stone quarry, but no one wanted the stuff. He'd invented a hay baler that didn't work. His last scheme was crossing buffalo with Texas cows. People all up and down the Pecos River laughed up their sleeves about that one, but Jesse Beck went right on ahead. He brought two bull buffalo down from Montana and tried to match them up with some Texas longhorn cows. When that didn't work he tried the reverse, and it did.

There were three cattalo offspring born. Two were sent off to demonstrate the success and advantages of the breed, and Alice fell in love with the other, a cattalo heifer she'd named Roselle after her favorite aunt, who lived in Boston. Stockmen were unenthusiastic about the breed except as carnival fodder, but Alice took her father's part. It was indecent how she went around parroting her old man. "Both breeds are indigenous to the territory," she'd say.

They used words like that in the Beck family. Big ones that always seemed unsuitable for mixed company.

Alice gave a report on cattalo in our class and about ruined her reputation.

"Cattalo embrace the best qualities of both animals," she said. "They have the stamina and grazing qualities of both breeds without having such cumbrous and dangerous horns. They pack more beef by far than the longhorn, which is a stringy beast. Mark my words, cattalo are the coming thing. Why should we import expensive European breeds to upgrade our stock when we have the makings right here? Cattalo!"

Jesse Beck spent three years on this scheme, but at last he threw in the towel. The bison he imported died of heat and lack of enthusiasm, and the longhorns made unwilling brides and grooms.

"Cattalo are very intelligent," Alice announced to me one day at school.

"Hoohaw!"

"They are! They deserve a chance!"

"To what?"

"To increase and multiply!"

"And speak French," I said.

Alice's face flamed, and she cocked her fist. I raised my guard. "Say cattalo are intelligent," she demanded.

"They're freaks of nature," I replied, whereupon she uncorked a blow that skipped under my guard and caught the point of my chin. I windmilled backward to avoid falling and blessed my stars there was no one around to witness my disgrace. I fetched up against the school wall, and Alice came up to me cocked again. She thrust her face into mine, her teeth clenched. "Say cattalo are smart," she demanded.

Just then my aunt Clara and Mr. Larkin came from the school, where they both taught.

"Cattalo are smart," I whispered, to avoid making more of a fool of myself.

Aunt Clara saw us and waved. I danced away from Alice and joined Aunt Clara and Mr. Larkin. Alice flounced off, scowling in my direction.

That was about two months ago. Alice had the goodness not to mention it, and I never again mocked her father's scheme to her face. Cattalo, of course, was a bust, and now Mr. Beck had given his last cattalo, Roselle, to be driven to Wichita for whatever price it could fetch. Alice had begged her father not to send Roselle north and abandon his dream, but Mr. Beck was fully awake and just about broke. Tears did not avail, so Alice went each day to say another farewell to Roselle and feed her an apple or some alfalfa.

When we reached the bed ground and holding pens the drovers and stockmen were making final preparations to get the herd ready to move. Stock was being trail-branded with the Circle Six brand and the tally books put in order. Alice winced at the smell of burned hide as the branding irons hit it, and turned her face away as a steer was snubbed off its feet and fell with a windy groan. Her sensitivity to such roughness made me feel bold, and maybe I swaggered a bit when I asked a drover where I could find Chauncey

Potter. This drover looked down at me from the altitude of his horse. "You talkin' to me, tyke?" he asked.

Now, *tyke* is a word I'd heard applied to infants and dogs and not one I expected to be directed at me. I saw Alice hide a smile and saw the drover share it with her. He was a rangy, whiskery poke, not more than ten years older than me. He wore a black armband, to commemorate the death of one of his recent victims, I supposed, and had a nose sharp as an Indian arrowhead. I suspected he was acting up for Alice's benefit, so I had a choice of slinging the package I was carrying in his face and being whipped to a frazzle, or repeating my question. I repeated the question.

The drover pointed to a chuck wagon beyond the holding pens and said I'd find Chauncey Potter there. I saw a fresh-killed steer hanging by its rear legs from a pole tripod and a man working at it with a butcher knife. The drover leaned forward, resting his arms on the saddle pommel, and addressed Alice, grinning at her in a way I didn't like. "Tell Chauncey that Zeb Zeff sent you," he said to her. "Tell him Zeb Zeff will be back in Odessa in about six weeks aching for pretty company."

The way Alice colored up I coulda poked her in the snout. Instead I snatched her hand and dragged her after me toward the chuck wagon.

"Don't be draggin' me!" Alice complained, trying to pull away.

"Just shut up!"

"Don't you tell me to shut up, Wylie Jackson!"

We came to the chuck wagon, and Alice jerked free. She tucked the hand I'd been holding in her armpit

8

and glowered at me. "Go find your dang critter," I said.

"Maybe I will might, maybe I won't might."

Alice had a way of making nonsense of common things, and I was trying to parse this last to muster up a suitable reply when a stringy old man came around the side of the chuck wagon with a forequarter of beef over his shoulder. He flopped this on the tailgate and spat a stream of tobacco juice in the proximity of his tattered boots.

"Are you Mr. Chauncey Potter?" I asked him.

"Be so."

I offered my package. "Package from Bridges' Hardware," I said.

Potter stripped the paper off and held up a metal crank. He grinned at it, revealing a sparse set of teeth stained the color of rawhide. "Handle fer my hash maker," he said. He fitted the handle into a meat grinder attached to the tail board and gave it a spin. "Just fits," he said. "She'll do."

Alice scowled at the meat grinder. "Well," she said.

"Well what?" I asked.

"Well!" Alice proclaimed, and she marched away. The drover I'd asked directions of rode up beside her. I saw he was talking his line of slime, and Alice was gulping it in.

I nodded toward him. "You know that drover, Mr. Potter?" I asked.

"Zeb Zeff," Potter replied. "We call him ZeeZee. John Boardman's stepson."

"John Boardman who's trail boss of this drive?" I asked.

"The one," Mr. Potter said, and he went to slashing meat.

I had an urge to follow Alice and dislodge the cootie riding at her side, but I couldn't see it was any of my business what she subjected herself to. Let her break out in a red-all-over rash as far as I cared. I headed back to town heart-sunk because all this adventure was going on and I didn't have a share of it. In two days the cattle and drovers would be gone, and Odessa would shrink into a dusty little town of clerks and schoolmarms, and I'd be there among them doing my chores and hammering through the summer reading list my aunt Clara made up for me, Sir Walter Scott, Dickens, Thackeray, *Silas Marner,* and such. All this literature was supposed to get me through the doldrums of summer and make a cultured man of me, like Eldon Larkin, who quoted poetry without provocation.

The tragedy of the Civil War was that I was only an infant when General Lee surrendered, or I might have helped stem the tide. My parents were killed in the bombardment of Vicksburg when a Union mortar collapsed the dugout in which they'd taken shelter. Sometimes I dreamed of that and woke up gasping, but I survived the collapse and was exiled to my deceased mother's sister, Clara Hampton, in Odessa. We didn't talk about it much unless Aunt Clara had a point to make, as with the reading. "Your father, Mr. Jackson, was a well-read man, Wylie, and I expect you to carry on the tradition."

Some tradition! He hadn't even been in the Confederate army! Served the Confederacy as a cotton broker, Aunt Clara said. A cotton broker! What kind of tradition is that? It made me wonder what kind of money-grubbing blood ran in my veins. I'd have swapped it all for the blood of a decent Labrador retriever rather than to be lumbered with the blood of Eliot P. "Cottonwall" Jackson, well-read or not. No wonder Alice Beck could lick me half the time.

As I came to town a tangled knot of drovers fell out the door of Casey's Billiard Parlour into the street, where they milled around, all arms, legs, and hats. In the center were two men fighting, and the others were trying to pull them apart. "Here now, Colvey! Ho up, you Lee!"

The efforts to separate the men got partisan, and where two had been fighting it got to be four, then eight, and the brawl might have swept through the whole county if a rider hadn't galloped in on a seventeen-hands-high black horse and dropped off dead center into that mass of struggling, cursing men. I knew him to be Mr. John Boardman. He wore a skirted duster and high black cavalry boots. His face was hard as the heel of a boot, and his rusty eyes drove into a person like railway spikes. His mouth was straight as a ruler, and his lips appeared to be stitched together from behind as though he never ate, or smiled.

Seeing him, the men shied back and dropped their heads, except for one who was thrashing about on the ground, groping for his pistol. He got it out and aimed it up at Mr. Boardman, who looked down at him. "Colvey," he said, "I've taken enough Yankee lead to make a full-size statue on your grave. One more chunk won't make a dent."

Colvey let his pistol flop in the dust. "Sorry, Mr. Boardman," he said. "I didn't know it was you."

"Who's been fighting?" Mr. Boardman asked.

"Him and Deter Lee," someone said.

"You two men collect your time and take this fight back where it came from. I'm not having quarrelsome men on this drive."

"That's not right!" Colvey objected. "Deter started it."

I'd never seen lava, but I knew what it looked like from Mr. Boardman's eyes. "Stand up, Mr. Colvey, if you please," he said quietly.

Colvey saw he'd made a bad mistake. He looked around at the other men, seeking their support. There was none.

"If you please," Mr. Boardman repeated.

Colvey rose, pale as a bedsheet.

Mr. Boardman looked at the drovers, and his eyes spiked one of them. "You, Mr. Lee," he said. "Will you step up here, please?"

The man addressed as Lee stepped up beside Colvey and they stood there in front of Mr. Boardman like suck-egg dogs.

"Would you gentlemen care to continue this fight?" Mr. Boardman asked softly.

"No, sir," the two men replied.

"Then you will shake hands, collect your time, and return to wherever you hail from."

Colvey and Lee shook hands. Mr. Boardman

12

swung onto his horse. He glanced in my direction, and I felt he'd read me clear through from cover to cover without having to turn a page. As he turned his horse and galloped away I saw he had a black armband on his duster.

I gaped after him. To say he galloped away is not strictly correct. He diminished is more like it. He receded, and I doubt the hooves of his horse touched the ground. "Boardman," I whispered.

When I looked around, the drovers had vanished, except for Colvey and Deter Lee, who were sulking down the street with their arms over each other's shoulders, consoling each other for having lost their billets on the drive, just as I would have done had I been in their place.

GOODBYE CHOCOLATE PECAN PIE.

AUNT CLARA.

❖My favorite. Gather three-fourths cup of sugar, half a teaspoon of salt, three eggs, a cup of black corn syrup, two tablespoons of flour, three ounces of cooking chocolate, two tablespoons of melted butter, a spoon of vanilla, and two cups of pecan halves.

❖Combine and whip sugar, syrup, salt, flour, and eggs. Add butter, vanilla, melted chocolate, and pecans and mix well. Pour into pastry shell, bake an hour in medium-hot oven. Top with whipped cream. This is sure to bring the departing home again.

Chapter Two

❖ ❖ ❖

When I finished for the day at the hardware store Mr. Bridges took a barlow knife from the display case on the counter and handed it to me. "Take this, Wylie," he said. "You'll be needing it."

I'd lost my knife a week before and was planning to buy a new one from my wages, so I thought Mr. Bridges was letting me have the knife on credit. "Thank you, Mr. Bridges. You just deduct it from my pay," I said.

"I won't do that, Wylie. Things will be slow here when the cattle leave, and I'll be able to manage the store alone."

"Oh," I said. "Well, thank you, Mr. Bridges."

I supposed it was a kind way of letting me know I was fired, but I regretted losing the job. Not that we needed the money so much. Aunt Clara had her teaching position, and the noncombatant cotton broker, Eliot P. Jackson, whose blood I reluctantly pumped, had left her an annuity, which carried us through. I needed the job to protect myself from all the literature Aunt Clara had stacked up for me to consume. Now I had no excuse not to read all day until I got four-eyed and half blind, like Eldon Larkin.

As I opened the front gate and approached the house I noticed a curious flurry of activity in the parlor windows. I came down the path between the roses, which Aunt Clara said were taken from my mother's home in Vicksburg, and I wondered if I could escape having to read my eyes out by offering to paint the house. When I stepped into the hall it was filled with silence, and I knew something had happened. I was about to call out when Aunt Clara slid back the parlor door. She had on her gray dress with the lace collar. "Hello, Wylie," she said.

I was sure someone had died, but when your parents are already gone and you have no brothers or sisters, and your only living relative is standing before you, it's hard to put on the face of grief. I hoped maybe it was Eldon Larkin because I never liked the amount of attention he paid Aunt Clara. If Larkin cashed in his chips, I'd be hard pressed to express much woe. "Hello, Aunt Clara," I said.

She stood there, and I stood there, and the silence got weighty. Then Aunt Clara laughed and opened the door wide, and behind her was a crowd all shouting "Surprise!" It wasn't my birthday, and my last report card had a C-minus in fractions. But there was Eldon Larkin grinning like I'd got an A. Mr. Beck and his wife, Ella, were there with Alice. Mr. Bridges was there and Mr. Peavey from the bank and Mr. Conrad from the livery barn and their wives.

I was dumbfounded, of course.

"Well, come in," Aunt Clara said. She took my shoulder and thrust me into the center of the crowd. The table was set with refreshments and a chocolate pecan pie. There were paper festoons hanging from the ceiling, but what caught my eye was a three-quarter single-rig saddle riding the back of Aunt Clara's horsehide rocker.

"What's this all about?" I asked.

Aunt Clara put her arm over my shoulder and hugged me. "Mr. Beck has arranged for you to go on the cattle drive, Wylie," she said. "With Mr. Boardman, to Wichita."

Suddenly my lungs were so full of something I could barely speak. "Wichita," I said.

"Mr. Beck and Mr. Boardman are old acquaintances, and Mr. Boardman has agreed to take you along as assistant cook."

"Coosie segundo," Mr. Beck put in.

"And you'll be able to look after Roselle!" Alice said.

This dumb notion further confused me. What had that fool cattalo to do with it? I must have looked funny because Aunt Clara removed her arm and looked at me closely.

"Of course you don't have to go, Wylie," she said. "Not if you don't want to." I looked at my poor aunt Clara, who had gone crazy right before my eyes. Her face swam. I felt weak. Not go?

"You do want to go, don't you, Wylie?" Aunt Clara asked with a troubled frown.

I nodded. The men all looked at one another, also troubled, no doubt thinking that my cotton-broker blood made me too timid to leave Odessa and Aunt Clara. When at last I was able to express myself, it came out as a sustained screech, which, had it been a buzz saw, would have sliced the house in half.

19

"Eeeeyiiii! Yiii! Yuiiie!"

The men laughed. The women smiled. Alice's face shone, and Aunt Clara burst out weeping, clinging to me and sopping my collar with her tears. "I'm going to miss you so much," she moaned.

"Hey, hey," I said, "I won't be gone that all-fired long."

What came to me first, of course, was that I'd ditched the literature, that I'd be doing the stuff others wrote and read about, that at last I was a live character in a living world and not just a pair of eyes roving a printed page.

Aunt Clara dried up and began distributing refreshments with the other ladies' help. I thanked Mr. Beck and asked how he knew Mr. Boardman. "Why, I did some legal work for him a time back," Mr. Beck said. "We've been in touch off and on ever since."

I examined the saddle, which was secondhand but good. Mr. Conrad said he'd taken it for an unpaid feed bill a year or so before. I thanked him and took a piece of pecan pie. The sugar went straight to my head and made me dizzy.

There was a hat on the seat of the chair, but I was so overcome with happiness I didn't bother about it. I had to get outside and be alone. No one said anything when I set my dish aside and excused myself. I expect they thought I was going to the outhouse, or maybe they knew I had to be alone.

Outside, I hopped our fence and walked to the school. It was dark by then, and cool. I thrust my hands into my pockets and stood in the schoolyard trying to catch up with myself. Overhead the stars

20

cared not a bit that I had crossed the line to man-hood. Ahead I saw the glory I was to experience, while behind was the pale ghost of the boy I had been.

I could see that ghost very clearly, a broad-faced, hazel-eyed, towheaded boy, playing in the schoolyard, running inside at the bell, twisting in his seat as he tried solving problems on his slate, but I couldn't see the man he would become. I tried some visions of my future self on for size, but these were tainted by cotton and commerce and none of them was satisfactory.

Then I remembered Mr. John Boardman looking at me after he'd put down the fight. He must have known I was coming on the drive. Half the town must have known for days and kept it a secret from me.

I heard footsteps, and Alice came out of the dark-ness. "You knew I was going on the drive," I accused.

She stopped beside me, smiling and smug. "I've known all week," she said.

"And you never told me!"

"It was to be a surprise."

"You let me suffer all week long and never told me one dang thing?"

"I didn't notice you suffering."

"You think I want to sit around Odessa reading and weeding peonies? You think if I knew something so big was about to happen to you, I'd keep it a secret?"

"Like what?"

"Why . . . why, that you were . . ."

"Going on a cattle drive?"

"Course not," I said scornfully. "There's no place for girls on a drive."

"What, then?"

"Well . . . that you were to have a new dress, for instance."

"Oh, my!"

"Or getting engaged to be married, or some fool thing."

"I'd probably be the first to know about that."

"Well, whatever surprises girls get, dang it!"

"Not many," Alice replied.

"Anyhow, you should have told me."

"If I had, you'd be barking up the other side of the tree, saying I spoiled your surprise."

"Would not."

"I know you, Wylie Jackson."

"You knew me! That's true. But you don't know me."

"Oh, excuse me! I thought I was speaking to Wylie Jackson of Odessa, Texas." Whereupon she marched back toward the house.

I was tempted to let her go, but a man has to be bigger'n a girl in matters of this kind, so I followed her. "Hold on, Alice," I called.

She turned to me, her eyes snapping in the starlight. "Your head's already too fat for your hat, which, by the way, I chose myself, and you didn't have the decency to thank me for it."

"I didn't notice it, Alice!"

"And I won't be a bit surprised if they send you home after two days on the trail, for by then they'll be mightily sick of your uppity opinion of yourself. I was going to ask you a favor, but since you probably won't last a hundred miles I'll take my request to Mr. Zeb

Zeff, who seems partial to me and is an experienced drover. . . ."

She went on with more of the like, but I knew what she was on about. It was Roselle. I remembered her calling out I could look after that blamed beast during the drive.

"Alice, why don't you just buy that critter out of the herd and keep it here?" I asked.

"Because we're going to California," Alice said, and the stars glistened in her eyes like tears.

"California!"

"Monterey, California, to open a sardine cannery! It's another of Papa's schemes. He'll practice law and can sardines."

I was tempted to say he should do the reverse, but this was no time for cracking smart. Alice was upset and angry. "Why, sure," I said lamely.

"Sure what?" Alice demanded.

"I'll watch over that cattalo heifer for you, Alice."

"Roselle is her name, in case you've forgotten."

"Yes, all right."

"What do you mean, you'll watch over her?"

"I'll see she gets to Wichita."

Alice blazed up again. "To Wichita!" she cried. "Is that what you think I want? You think I want Roselle to get to Wichita and be killed and et, or made into bully beef?"

"That's what a cattle drive is all about, Alice."

"Well, it's not what I'm all about! I've written my cousin Agnes Badgley, who lives near Enid, Oklahoma, and who says she'll take Roselle and keep her until I decide what to do."

23

"I thought your father wanted to be shut of that beast."

"Never mind. You go right near Agnes's place on the drive and can just run Roselle over to her."

Of course I didn't know Enid was fifty miles east of the trail we'd be taking, but I now suspect Alice knew it very well. "Your father know about this?" I asked.

"He doesn't like to be reminded of his failures."

"Does Mr. Boardman know?"

"Are you going to do this and keep it a secret or not, Wylie Jackson?" Alice demanded. "If not, I think Mr. Zeff will."

"You want me to steal Roselle and deliver her to your cousin."

"You are so dumb, Wylie! I'll send Agnes the money to pay for Roselle, so it won't be stealing! All that stock is for sale. Mr. Boardman will accept the money. It's an ordinary business proposition. I suppose you want to be paid for doing this."

"No, I don't."

"Well, then it's settled. Agnes will have the money and my address in Monterey in case you ever want to write me."

"Write you what?"

"If I knew what, you wouldn't have to write me!"

"I guess you do."

"Do what?"

"Know what I'd write if I wrote! Do you ever listen to anything you say, or does it just spill out?"

"I know what I'm going to say and what I mean, so I don't have to listen, unlike you, who likes so much to hear himself talk. But let's not fight. Thank you for promising to look after Roselle and take her to Enid."

Alice stuck out her hand. I hesitated, feeling I'd been roped somehow, but I shook it. "I guess you won't be here when I get back," I said.

"No, I won't be."

"I see."

"What do you see?"

"Why, that I thought you'd always be here," I said.

"Things change, Wylie," she said. Then she tipped up on her toes and kissed me on the cheek, which surprised me more than a black eye and branded me for certain as that cattalo heifer's guardian all the way from Odessa, Texas, to Enid in the Territory. "Good luck, Wylie," Alice said; then she went back to the house.

I stood a time longer, gazing at the stars, trying to imagine the weeks ahead, all the country to be seen and the people to be met. It took the edge off never seeing Alice Beck again, but I didn't really believe I wouldn't.

BREAD PUDDING.

WYLIE JACKSON.

❖Dice a panful of stale bread, about two quarts. Mix with a like amount of condensed milk and water (one to one) and add salt, two pinches. Separate and beat six egg yolks, a cup of sugar, nutmeg, two fistfuls of raisins, and a spoon of vanilla. Pour this over the bread and milk and mix. Whip the egg whites stiff and fold them into the pudding. Cook pudding in a Dutch oven until firm. Serves fifteen men.

CHAPTER THREE

❖ ❖ ❖

It was my duty to assist Mr. Chauncey Potter at the chuck wagon—not an exalted position. I'd rather have been a drover, or in charge of the remuda, as Zeb Zeff was; anything to put me up on horseback. But *coosie segundo* was a start, so next morning at dawn I shouldered my new saddle, plunked on my new hat, and trudged out to the bed ground, arriving to find that the drovers had already eaten breakfast and were out among the cattle.

Mr. Potter said nothing as I put my saddle in the wagon among the sacks of provisions and drovers' bedrolls. He did sorta snort, which scalded me some, but as the day wore on I learned he did this all the time to rearrange the hairs in his nose. I tipped my hat back (it was a danged black porkpie sort of affair with a wide brim, but I had to keep it, or risk insulting Alice Beck for all eternity) and asked Mr. Potter if he had anything particular he wanted me to do.

"Wylie Jackson, is it," he said.

"The same."

"Mr. Boardman said you was like to show up someday."

"I wasn't sure what time it all began," I said lamely.

"About four thousand B.C. according to the Book," Mr. Potter said, and he commenced slashing loaves of bread to smithereens with a butcher knife.

I deduced he was making bread pudding, one of

29

my favorite dishes, so I pitched right in and let him snort. I got the condensed milk, eggs, and sugar and began separating and whisking. Aunt Clara had never been shy of sharing the cooking with me, and I knew more than I thought I knew about it. Unlike fractions, cooking is one of those things you absorb as you go along and that sticks to your ribs. I judged by the amount of bread Mr. Potter was chopping that he intended to feed the pudding to about fifteen men and measured my ingredients accordingly. Since a good drover could manage about a hundred head of cattle I guessed the trail herd would be about fifteen hundred beeves, and since each drover had between eight and ten horses there'd be about a hundred thirty horses in the remuda.

I found the big Dutch oven and poured my ingredients in, with a slosh of vanilla. Mr. Potter added the bread, and I folded it all together with a couple of swipes of a wooden spoon.

I set the oven in the coals of the fire, then looked to see how much water was in the barrel attached to the chuck wagon. It was but half full, so I took two canvas buckets, mounted one of the wagon mules, and rode to town to fetch water from the well. It took me four trips, and whenever I spotted a chunk of dry wood I brought it with me and popped it into the coonie suspended beneath the wagon.

The beef I'd seen suspended on the tripod the day before had been cut up and stored in salted sacks and would have to be used pretty quick or it would start festering. I peeled two dozen potatoes and cubed them, then ran six pounds of fresh beef through the grinder. I put this in a big frying pan and added water, the potatoes, salt, pepper, and a touch of mustard powder. I put this on the rack near the fire to stew until along toward dinnertime, when I'd add some bacon fat and eggs to make a hash. I'd lost track of Mr. Potter, though I heard him snorting now and again.

I was rooting around in the chuck wagon for something green, but all the stuff was canned, and there was no sense using that until we were on the trail, so I told Mr. Potter I was going into town for a mess of snap beans to garnish the dinner.

"Snap beans," he said.

"They're all over town in kitchen gardens, dying on the vine," I said.

Mr. Potter colored up until I thought he'd blow. He snatched the sweat-stained hat from his head and slammed it on the ground between his feet, bobbing down as he did so.

I saw something then that about killed me. The whole top of Mr. Potter's head was bone white with a ragged red welt around where his scalp had been. I knew what had happened to him, and it jammed me up inside like I'd swallowed a cannonball.

"Snap beans!" Potter raged. "Snap beans now! Why, I expect you'll be discharging Boardman and the rest of these hands too and taking up their work. No use wasting wages on all that crowd when we got a one-man band on the premises. Why, I expect you can coax these cattle along to Wichita with a flute like the Pied damn Piper of Hamelin. No use any a us standin' in yer way. Why, take her all! Take her all,

31

boy! I never see the beat of it! Runs in here like a stampede and tramples old Chauncey in the dust. Never asks a word. Converts raisin pudding to bread pudding with no by-your-leave. Grinds up six pounds of buffalo intended for wolf bait and sets it out for hash. And now it comes to snap beans!"

All the while Potter was rampaging around, stamping on his hat and thrashing his arms in fury.

I was too stricken by the sight of his horribly scarred head to say a word or snatch my eyes back into their sockets. The word *scalped* kept drumming in my ears. *Scalped. Scalped!*

I backed away plumb into the breast of a horse behind me. I looked around, and there was Mr. John Boardman and Zeb Zeff and half a dozen other drovers staring down at me from their mounts. I gulped the cannonball and took to my heels, running blind with volleys of laughter plowing up the earth around me. If the world had been flat I'd have run to the edge and dove off. As it was I fetched up behind the billiard parlor gasping for breath, knowing my career as a cowhand was over. The drive would go, and I'd be left in Odessa with all that literature.

I flopped down, huddled and miserable, wondering who I could send to recover my saddle, not that I'd ever have any call to use it, but I could probably swap it for an eye examination and spectacles.

Alice Beck found me there about an hour later.

"Go away," I said.

"I was looking everywhere for you, Wylie!"

"Go away!"

Alice sat down beside me with her back against the wall and pulled her skirt down to her shoes.

"Would you get my saddle for me, Alice? It's in the chuck wagon."

"They were hurrahing you, Wylie," Alice said.

"What do you know about it?" I flashed.

"What Mr. Potter told me."

"You saw Potter?"

"Of course I saw him. I was looking for you. He said they'd hurrahed you pretty sizable, as he put it."

I groaned as the shame of the experience drilled into me again. "I can't go back," I said.

"Of course you can go back! You've got to go back for your own self-respect, Wylie! You're not a bunch quitter, or if you are I miss my guess! Besides, you and I have a deal, and I mean to hold you to it. So don't be a darn fool."

"You can't talk to me like that!"

"If you quit I can talk to you anyhow I darn please! If you quit over such a little thing everyone will know you had no right to go in the first place. They do that nonsense to all the new boys, Wylie! Only Mr. Potter said you invited it more than most. Damn! If I was a boy and they done that to me I'd a stood up to them instead of scrambling off like a cowed dog. Now you got to go back and brave it out. You got to, Wylie, however painful it seems. They'll respect you for it if you do, but they won't if you don't."

There was a glimmer of hope in what she said, and I hated her for it, of course.

Alice stood up and brushed her skirt straight. "Come on, Wylie," she said. "I'll go with you."

"I'm not going back there with a girl! Why, it'd make me look ridiculous!"

When Alice Beck's eyes were glacial, it was worse than fire, and her voice took on the hard edge of a hacksaw blade. "Wylie Jackson, you come now, or I am going to jerk you up by the ear, prance you back in front of all those drovers, and beat the daylights out of you if I die for it." I knew she'd try to do it. I had some doubt she would succeed, but not enough that I wanted to put it to the test. I got up and we went back.

As we walked down the street Alice began talking about how I was to care for Roselle on the drive. The thing about women, I've noticed, is once they've had their way they go right on as if nothing happened. Now she was smiling and sprightly as though she'd never threatened to disgrace me for life and there was no thought of her threat lingering in her mind. A man, on the other hand, wants to even things up someway. It always astonished me how quick Alice washed the slate clean and started all over again on a new trail.

When we came to the cattle I raised my head up and glowered at every drover who came into my view. I puffed up and stalked until Alice giggled.

"What?" I demanded.

"Don't make such a fool of yourself, Wylie," she said quietly.

Dang! I wanted to just kill her.

"There's not one of these men who couldn't tie you

34

into knots like a pretzel, so don't be scowling and flexing at them. It's pure dumb. The point is to make friends. They laughed at you and rightly so, as I understand it. Now you better learn to laugh along with them."

"You're so smart."

"About some things I am, Wylie Jackson. Now just act natural, if you know what that is."

We found Roselle lounging off to the side of the main herd, and when Alice called her name she got to her feet and trotted to us, tossing her head with pleasure.

I'd seen the cattalo critter often enough since Alice had made it her pet. It was, to my thinking, an awkward-looking beast, deep-chested with thin rear legs and a big block head. Not yet a yearling, and her horn buttons gave no clue what would emerge. She was tan-colored with a dang white face and a goatee suspended beneath her chin. She hadn't grown up to her eyes, which were enormous brown pools of what Alice said was intelligence. "Hybrids are often smarter than other cattle," she insisted. "They take the best of both breeds."

I wasn't sure Roselle hadn't taken the worst. She had a bag of tricks Alice had taught her, dumb things like standing on her hind legs and pawing the air, or lying down and rolling over. Dog tricks. She came when called. She sat down on command, which looked pretty comical. Alice said she would tap out numbers on the ground if she held up her fingers to give Roselle a clue, but I think Alice switched her fingers to match how many times Roselle tapped.

Anyway, Alice spent a good deal of time trying to get the beast accustomed to me.

"This is Wylie Jackson," she crooned. "He's going to take you to Enid with all these nice cattle. Here, pet her head, Wylie."

I did so, feeling more a fool than I already was feeling.

"There, isn't he nice, Roselle? Now, I want you to obey Wylie, unless he asks you to do something truly stupid, in which case you can set him straight."

I shot a sideways glance around, hoping none of the drovers caught me talking to this cattalo freak. Fortunately, they were all engaged at the holding pens branding late-arriving cattle. Alice told me to back off and call Roselle. I did as instructed, but the heifer did not come.

"Go on, Roselle. Go to Wylie."

She'd sooner have gone to hell. She kept looking at me, then at Alice and shaking her head.

"Call her again, Wylie."

"Here, Roselle."

"Well, put some life into it, Wylie! Not just flat like that, like you didn't care."

I didn't. "Here, Roselle."

"Go to Wylie," Alice said, and she shoved Roselle up to me. The beast gazed at me, reflecting on my existence and concluding it was of no importance.

We tried several more times, but I might as well have been a dead dog for all the attention Roselle paid to me. For a time Alice was stumped; then she got the brainstorm.

"Turn around, Wylie," she said.

By this time I was following instructions like a spring-wound toy soldier.

"Here, take these."

I raised my hand, and Alice put the article in it. It was warm. It was soft. It was embroidered. It was Alice Beck's drawers!

I about died. "What in thunder—!"

"Oh, shut up!" Alice said, backing away. "When I'm gone, she'll think you're me!"

Alice turned and ran toward town. The cattalo heifer had its attention fastened on the drawers and missed her going entirely.

I saw Zeb Zeff riding in my direction and stuffed the drawers into my shirt. "Hey, you Jackson," ZeeZee called. "Cookie wants to know where the snap beans are."

I saw a patch of pink embroidery protruding from my shirt and hunched over, clutching my stomach. "I'll get them right away, Mr. ZeeZee," I yelled, and I ran toward town with that blamed cattalo heifer cavorting after me. I zigged and zagged, but the creature wouldn't be thrown off the scent of Alice Beck's drawers.

ZeeZee rode along beside me, whooping. "By golly, that cattalo is frolicsome fond of you, Jackson. You better get yourself a saddle and let her ride!"

"Rope and hold her!" I cried. "Rope and hold her, Mr. ZeeZee, so I can pick snap beans."

ZeeZee unlimbered his rope, tossed a loop over Roselle, and dragged her, protesting and romping, to the holding pens. I skinned for town thinking I might survive the cowardly blood of the cotton broker in my veins, but if I was ever caught with Alice Beck's laundry I'd be an object of universal ridicule all the rest of my life.

SON OF A BITCH STEW.

CHAUNCEY POTTER.

❖This fare is designed to use fresh beef on the trail before the maggots get it.

❖Two pounds of beef, a pound of beef fat, four pounds of narrow gut, a pound of heart, a pound of liver, a pound of sweetbreads, one set of brains, skinned. Add seasoning. Cut meat into small particles and put in a cauldron with about four gallons of water. Hold out the brains.

❖Cook slow for four hours. Add salt, black and red pepper, and the brains. Thicken the gravy with a pint of flour mixed with water.

❖Serves fifteen men three days unless they rebel.

Chapter Four

❖　❖　❖

As the time to depart drew near I'd overcome most of my chagrin at the hurrahing, but I was still pretty tender in the crust. I spoke when spoken to and otherwise kept my mouth shut.

Chauncey Potter allowed that my hash and contribution to the bread pudding hadn't been far off the mark and that there was no such thing as using buffalo meat for wolf bait. He didn't exactly apologize for ragging me so raw or promise never to do it again, but I sensed he meant to ease things up for me. For my part I allowed I'd taken too much charge of things for a greenhorn and promised thereafter to await his instruction.

I was still curious to know which tribe had lifted Mr. Potter's hair, but I daren't ask. I did hear a tale about it, though. Burt Purple, one of the drovers, said Chauncey, who was notorious against the use of alcohol, had been invited to address the Women's Temperance Union in Chillicothe, Hardeman County, Texas. In those days he sported a raspberry-colored wig to protect the citizenry from his scarified head. On this occasion his denunciation of the demon rum was so impassioned that when he concluded, the ladies of the audience rose in ovation. Pleased to have made such a hit, Chauncey bowed all around and his rosy wig dropped from his head. At the sight of his naked skull the ladies began toppling over in faints

41

and vapors. Chauncey abandoned his wig and beat a hasty retreat.

For months afterward sales of laudanum and Hostetter's Bitters (forty percent alcohol) skyrocketed in Chillicothe, and temperance ladies were seen staggering around town in various states of medicinal inebriation as they tried to quell their nightmares of Chauncey Potter's scalp condition. Eventually they hit upon the idea of knitting Chauncey skullcaps to shield other innocent women from his disfiguration. They knit seven caps in seven colors, white for Sunday, green for Monday, blue, yellow, red, black, and brown. You could always tell the day of the week by Chauncey's skullcap. The day he hurrahed me he took the cap off to give me a fright, which he succeeded well enough in doing just as he had in Chillicothe.

I tried to get all my goodbyes said in the privacy of home. Aunt Clara seemed to understand my need to avoid sentimental displays and did not cry. I had another battle with Alice when I tried to return her drawers. "You got to keep them, Wylie, in case Roselle gets lost or confused during the drive. She'll follow those drawers anywhere!"

"I'm not taking your dang drawers clear to Wichita!"

"Of course not, Wylie. Just to Enid."

"Or to Enid! I will not do it."

"You will so!"

At last we compromised. Alice sewed her drawers into a small cotton sack, which I socked into the bottom of my saddlebag when I got to the chuck wagon.

It was either that or she was going to parade through town saying I'd swiped her drawers and make me the laughingstock of every man, woman, and child in all Odessa. Some compromise.

I wished Alice a happy life in Monterey and said I hoped her father would have good luck with the sardines. As I turned to go Alice clouded over. "Wylie?" she quavered.

"Hangfire! Now what?"

"Give Roselle a kiss goodbye for me," she said, and she tipped up and kissed me right in front of my ear.

"I will never kiss no damned cattalo, Alice Beck!" I declared.

Alice smiled like she knew better what I would or would not do. "Maybe you will might, maybe you won't might," she said, and she went into her house and shut the door.

At last the day of our departure came, July 17, 1881.

Chauncey Potter slapped leather to the chuck wagon mules, and our wheels began to roll. Behind us the drovers yipped and popped their hats against their chaps, and fifteen hundred head of mixed cattle lumbered up, lowing and clattering as they began to move.

The whole town turned out to see us off, so I sat with Potter on the wagon very straight and heroic, gazing at the far horizon, but out of the corner of my eye I could see Alice making a fool of herself, running along the face of the crowd, waving as though she expected me to notice her.

I saw Mr. Boardman ride up on his big horse and

drop to the ground to speak to some of the Odessa people. I looked around to see who it was. Mr. Boardman removed his hat and bowed, revealing my aunt Clara. She and Mr. Boardman talked a good bit. Once they laughed, and I had an attack of anxiety, imagining Aunt Clara asking Mr. Boardman to look after me, saying I was just a boy and this was my first time away from home and generally ruining my life. I watched until Mr. Boardman mounted again and galloped ahead to the point of the herd. Aunt Clara waved her handkerchief and dabbed her eyes, and I waved back, wishing she wouldn't cry and embarrass me.

We passed the outlying ranches, and at last there was nothing ahead of us except the land. Then I allowed myself to look back, but I was too late. Odessa was gone as though it had never been. There wasn't even a trace of smoke in the morning sky, and I thought my life in Odessa might have been a dream from which I was only now awakening, or that I was dreaming now and would wake up again in Odessa. It made me dizzy being so unsure of reality, and I sat very still gazing at the unbroken land ahead. So much land, I thought. So far to go.

"You sit there like a ramrod, boy. I'll need a crowbar to detach your tailbone from the seat board," Mr. Potter grumbled. He was slouched forward with the reins loose in his hands. His eyes were so tight he might have been asleep, and he was rolling a chaw of tobacco in his cheek. I wasn't certain of the uses of tobacco, except for cigarettes and cigars. The snorting, chawing sort was a mystery to me. Mr. Potter, so far as I could tell, inserted the stuff in his nose, and when it had served its purpose there it made its way through his nasal passages to his mouth, where it was masticated and finally ejected in a stream of brown spit powerful enough to warp horseshoes.

I stood up to see the herd, which was stretched back a mile and moving briskly. The idea the first day was to wear them down so they'd sleep when we came to bed ground and not take it into their heads to stampede back as they had come. Even cattle get homesick and know they're moving off to strange places. After the first day they'd be let to move slower, grazing as they went, making fifteen miles a day at best. Off to the side I could see the remounts being driven by Mr. Boardman's stepson, ZeeZee, who I envied but despised for the insinuating words he'd spoken to Alice Beck.

I sat down and asked Mr. Potter about the black armbands worn by Mr. Boardman and ZeeZee. Potter said it was because Boardman's wife had died recently down in Waycross, where the Box Z ranch was found. Her first husband, Captain Zeff, had been Boardman's adjutant during the war and was killed at Port Gibson. After the war Boardman married Captain Zeff's widow and adopted her son, Zeb.

"ZeeZee is Captain Zeff's son," I said.

"Why, you got a memory like a steel trap," Chauncey declared. "You clamp into facts as a catamount into sheep guts. I never seen the like of it. I'd better warn the boys not to load you up with too much information or you'll be toppling over by the sheer weight of your head."

He continued on in this like, which made me understand there was a line of tolerance in Potter that I ought not in the future to overstep and that any extended conversation was apt to give him constitutional fits.

The first night and the second passed without incident, as some might say. To me, of course, it was filled with incident. I kept my eyes open and did as I was asked to do, no more. I kept watch on Roselle, who always straggled in at the drag end of the herd as it came to bed ground for the night. She was shorter-legged than most and had to take more steps to keep up, but she seemed to have the stamina and always came in ten or twenty minutes after the main herd, so I quit worrying she'd get left behind. Sometimes the drag riders complained that she got frolicsome and had to be driven back into the line, but they seemed to find her amusing. To them the idea of breeding cattalo was a hoot. They concluded she would be sterile as a jackass, which I took for an insult, but I had no reason to defend Roselle on that score. All she was to me was freight en route, though I hadn't yet found an occasion to explain my agreement about her to Mr. Boardman. I expected there would be time enough for that when we crossed the Red River or the Canadian.

I hadn't much use for Potter's style of cooking. Plain fare is one thing, but the desecration of decent ingredients is another. Potter laid out a procession of gummy biscuits, half-cooked beans, and beef stews that would have strained the stomach of a grizzly bear. Under Potter's watchful eye the drovers slathered their food with varieties of bottled sauces and gulped it down. I suspected Potter was breaking the drovers in to see how much bad stuff he could play off on them before they started to complain. For their part the men tamped the stuff down in silence with faith that things might improve if they stood the punishment. About the fourth day out, having made his case as to how bad his cooking could really get, Potter began to improve the chuck and the drovers started complaining about it, but not too much because they'd been shown what could be served if they got too far out of line.

I saw from this how indirectly things tended to operate on a cattle drive. Drovers are tender of their independence. Mr. Boardman, for instance, never gave a direct order, unless it was an emergency, but laid out what he wanted done as suggestions, which the men acted upon without getting their bristles up as they might have done had they been given a direct command. Maybe some of this was because they'd objected to the orders and discipline of the war, those as had been in it, which I judged was about one third.

On the evening of the fifth day, which was Wednesday by Potter's yellow cap, we came to the place chosen for our night camp, and Potter suggested I might like to ride back with Burt Purple and bring him up some brains.

I heard the ride back part, which meant I'd be up on a horse at last; the part about the brains I thought was one of Potter's grisly jokes. "Ride back with Purple," I said.

"You can take the Sharps," Potter said.

I dug my saddle and Potter's old single-shot breech-loading Sharps carbine out of the wagon. When I hit the ground Chauncey was talking to Purple, a blocky drover whose back was as chesty as his front so you couldn't be sure if he was coming or going unless you saw his nose. There didn't seem to be any use for the collar on his shirt except to give the illusion he had a neck. His eyes were sour blue, but when he grinned he seemed easy enough. I set the Sharps on the wagon seat and tapped my hat hello.

"Chauncey says you're goin' back with me."

"Right, Mr. Purple," I replied, trying not to suck so much air as to make myself look proud.

"Saddle up and let's get it done," Purple said, and he dropped from his horse and roll-gaited over to the chuck wagon for coffee.

I lugged my saddle to the cavvy where Warren Steele and V. A. Eberhart, the point men, were talking to ZeeZee. I asked for a horse, and ZeeZee nodded to the mounts in the rope corral and went on buzzing with the drovers.

Knowing they were watching made me nervous, and I tossed four loops before I caught a horse. I hadn't been aiming for him, and I had to pretend he was the one I'd wanted all along.

"That the one you're taking?" Steele asked me as I hauled the balky horse out of the corral.

"That's it," I said.

"Boardman say?" Eberhart wanted to know.

"Chauncey Potter's orders," I replied.

"Boardman's horse," Steele said.

Then I saw I'd snagged Mr. Boardman's best cutting pony out of the cavvy. He called it Ruddy Bob for its color, a kind of rose brown. With the pony about to yank my arm off and everyone watching, I had to choose whether to be shown up for a danged fool or take the bull by the horns. ZeeZee was smirking fit to kill, and I couldn't bear to back down in front of him, so I had to take Mr. Boardman's horse.

"He hasn't been rode in a time," I said. "He needs to limber up." But the pony was demonstrating how limber he was by doing everything but somersets on the end of the rope. "Whoa down there, Ruddy Bob!" I yelled with all the bass stops out in my voice, hoping the pony would take the hint, and he did, which surprised me some. He stopped cavorting, came up to me, and winked one big brown eye like he was in on it, too. He stood patient while I laid my saddle on, and I started praying for some event to save me from Mr. Boardman's certain wrath, like lightning would strike him—not kill him, you know, just rob him of his entire memory and leave a streak of white in his hair.

As I led Ruddy Bob back to the wagon I tried rehearsing what I'd say when Mr. Boardman saw me, but it never came out better than "Ah . . . ah . . . ah!" like someone was pulling a length of barbed wire through my throat.

Purple was mounted and ready to go. When he saw the horse I'd chosen, his eyes dried up and went as dead as water holes in alkali. He tossed me the Sharps, which hit me in the chest and fell to the ground.

"You blind, or what?" Purple grumbled.

"Missed it," I said, which wasn't much excuse since the Sharps had only come about two feet through the air. I got down and picked it up. I blew the dust off and would have licked it clean if it would have taken the alkali out of Purple's eyes.

Potter brought me a fistful of shells for the Sharps, and I tucked them into my pocket.

"You got chaps?" Purple asked. "We'll be poppin' brush."

I shook my head.

Potter rummaged in the chuck wagon and produced a beat-up pair of Cheyenne chaps. "Tie these on," he said.

I did as instructed, but to keep them from falling below the soles of my boots I had to cinch them high up on my chest. Potter shook his head woefully as I mounted Ruddy Bob. "Don't forget the gunnysack," he said. He slapped a sack under the saddle cantle, and I set out after Burt Purple, who was trotting away toward the dust of the drag.

The cattle were still coming in to bed ground, and the figure of Mr. Boardman jumped out at me like I'd stuck my whole head in a spyglass. He was riding along the flank of the herd, and I wished I could reverse the flow of cattle or freeze them in position like a beef glacier instead of the ice ones I'd seen in Aunt Clara's stereopticon slides. I'd been told glaciers move only an inch or so a year, and at that rate I figured I'd have a chance to grow old and die before Mr. Boardman got to me.

But the cattle came on, their horns clattering like castanets because they were being worked so close.

There was a kind of blood beat to the sound, better than hymns or drums, I thought. I had always liked it, but now it meant that Mr. Boardman was going to catch me riding Ruddy Bob, and those horns sounded like snare drums at an execution.

STEAK AND KIDNEY PIE.

CHAUNCEY POTTER.

❖With this dish Potter took pity on the men.

❖Eight pounds of beef chuck, diced. Two steer's kidneys, trimmed and diced. A cup of suet. Four onions, chopped.

❖Fry the suet in the Dutch oven and remove the cracklings. Fry the onions. Add the beef and kidneys and stir until browned. Season with black and cayenne pepper and Worcestershire sauce. Add a bottle of steam beer. Simmer until tender. Thicken the broth with flour mixed in cold water.

❖Have a thick piecrust in a large pan. Pour meat filling into crust and cover with another. Bake until top crust is brown.

❖Serves fifteen men.

CHAPTER FIVE

❖ ❖ ❖

I saw Mr. Boardman coming my way and knew what it must have been like in *The Charge of the Light Brigade,* a poem Eldon Larkin recited every chance he got, about a bunch of English cavalrymen charging Turkish cannon. Ruddy Bob was carrying me toward Mr. Boardman, but my guts and brains wanted to be headed in the opposite direction. My hope was that Mr. Boardman would be distracted by something and I'd slide by him. I was about to do so when Mr. Boardman yelled, "Purple!" His voice was like those Turkish cannon. "Purple!"

I saw Boardman coming for us, parting cattle like Moses parted the Red Sea. All four of his horse's feet were off the ground, and I don't think they touched until he hove up beside us. He looked at me fit to fry, then at Purple. "What's *he* doin' on Ruddy Bob?"

Burt Purple's head tucked down a notch in his blocky shoulders, and he waited for me to answer.

"Ah . . . ah . . . ah!" I said, as rehearsed.

"You Jackson," Boardman boomed, "speak out."

"I . . . ah, thought he could use the exercise, sir."

"You thought."

"Best I could, sir."

Mr. Boardman swung his rusty eyes on Purple. "You let him take Ruddy Bob?"

"He took him," Purple said with a shrug that all but hid the top of his head in his shoulders.

55

Mr. Boardman spiked Ruddy Bob, then he spiked me. "He don't seem to mind," he growled.

"Who, sir?" I quavered.

"My horse, confound it. Can you manage him? I don't want you hurt."

"So far, sir."

"All right. I've never seen another ride him. He can use the exercise." Then he rode on down the flank of the herd, and I wanted to feel myself all over to make sure no vital parts were missing. Purple popped his head up, and gazing after Boardman with a puzzled expression, he motioned me to follow and began to explain our mission.

The job, as I understood it, was to back-trail over the course of the day, shoot any calves that had been born, and drive the bereaved cows to the herd bed. Since newborn calves couldn't keep up and the mother cows wouldn't leave them, this was the only way to handle it.

I could see this was so.

On short drives there was sometimes a calf wagon to collect the new calves, Purple said, but that meant more mules and men, so it got to be an expensive proposition on long drives.

"No question of it," I said.

While listening to Purple I caught sight of my shadow on the ground, and it pleased me. The sun was low and made me look tall. I raised the Sharps to cast a shadow too and judged I cut as good a figure on horseback as any man in the outfit and better than ZeeZee.

56

I didn't notice Purple had fallen silent until I looked at him.

"Like it, do you?" he asked.

"What?"

"The shadow you're ogling."

"Why, I was, ah . . . just checking."

"You're a real sunshine rider," Purple said. "When we hit town, I'll buy you a plate-glass mirror so you can admire yourself without getting a crick in your neck. Did you hear what I said?"

"About the mirror?"

Purple blew a stormy breath and said it again. "Never get near a longhorn cow in the brush when she's calved. She'll attack and kill a bear, a cat, or a wolf that comes in on her that way. They're fast and mean to protect the calf and won't leave it until it's able to walk or dies. We can't afford to lose a cow for the sake of a calf."

"So we have to shoot the calf," I volunteered.

"You're right handy," Purple said sourly. "I see you know all about it. I don't expect there's anything I can tell you. I expect you been killing chickens and such like since you was knee-high just for the joy of it."

"No, sir. But they have to be killed to be et."

"Why, that's the same as cows," Purple said. "I never seen a man try to eat a live cow. We ain't got the teeth for it, and they won't stand still and let us chew. They turn mean when we bite into them. Even chickens dislike it."

I saw he was making me out dumb, but I put up with it and absorbed the scenery.

"All right, now. When you see a set of horns in the brush, don't ride up like you was welcome. If the boys see a cow about to calve they put a marker on a stick beside the trail to show about where she'd be, like that one there."

"Where?" I asked, squinting and craning.

"Right there," Purple said, pointing to a cleft stick with a patch of cloth on it.

We rode over to the marker and scanned the brush and thickets off beyond the trail.

"You goin' to shoot, or do you want me to?"

I hefted the Sharps. "I can manage it," I said.

"Then you'd better load up."

I fished a cartridge from my pocket and had trouble loading until I solved the mechanism.

"You ever shoot one of them Sharps?" Purple asked darkly.

"Sure, plenty," I lied. "My father had one."

"He also had you," Purple grumbled. "Now the idea is to shoot and git before the cow knows what you're up to. It's a heavy bullet and it'll do the job, but don't miss, hear? I've seen longhorns cut a horse and man like butter, so kill and skedaddle. We pick up the cow on the way back when she knows it's no use waiting anymore. They're pretty quiet by then."

We walked our horses into the brush, moving cautiously.

"How many calves do we expect to find?" I whispered.

"Depends on the romance of the range, don't it."

"I suppose that's so."

"You do know how they get made, don't you?"

"Why, sure!" I said disdainfully.

"How?" Purple shot back.

"Why, the bull, you know, he mounts the cow. . . ."

"Saddles her up and gets aboard, you mean."

"No! You know what I mean. He mounts her!"

"Oh, like goin' up a set of stairs."

"With his penis!" I declared.

"Whoops!" Purple yelped. "We got a Latin scholar in the crowd. Go to the head of the class, Jackson. You get an A in geography. . . . Do you see it?"

"Lots of times."

"What?" Purple asked, scowling.

"Cows and bulls doing, you know . . . the fornication."

Purple dropped his head a notch and looked disgusted. "No, you blamed idiot! The cow." He pointed to a longhorn about ten yards away, a wicked-looking yellow-hided thing with horns like bayonets. She had her eyes on us, smoky and guarded. "Calf is there," Purple said, and he pointed out the calf in the shadow of a mesquite bush. It was a wobbly, dark-colored, newborn thing with its hind legs straight and its head on the ground. It was contemplating the mechanism of its forelegs, wondering if they'd work. Its eyes were glazed with dreamy concentration as it thrust and shuddered, trying to stand. My first thought was to go over and help the calf get up. "Well?" Purple said.

I looked at Purple. I felt blank inside and kind of weak.

"You goin' to shoot, or wait for Sunday?" Purple asked.

I patted Ruddy Bob to let him know, then I raised the Sharps and sighted on the calf.

It was a shot I wouldn't ordinarily have missed. I'd shot enough not to miss an easy shot like that. The calf's head was big in the sights, and I had it spotted right above the eyes on the tender flat of its head where the still-damp hair swirled in a patch of white.

"Not the head!" Purple hissed. "Chauncey wants the brains."

"Oh," I said. I lowered my sights to the neck to sever the spine. It was an easy shot. Nobody could miss a shot like that.

I didn't.

The Sharps bucked and belched black smoke, but Ruddy Bob was steady as a gravestone under me. The calf had just about pushed up when the bullet struck. The impact threw the calf's head back, and its hind legs flopped up, kicking feebly as a gout of blood stained the earth.

I sat there feeling accomplished and miserable when Purple yelled, "Ride, Wylie! Ride!"

I saw that longhorn cow cleaving through the brush at me like a locomotive. I kicked Ruddy Bob, and he set out ahead of those slashing horns, twisting and dodging through the brush that snatched at my chaps, threatening to pull me from the saddle and leave me skewered on those bayonet horns like chicken on a spit. And by the lights of that cow I deserved it. I was a calf blaster, convicted in any court.

At last the cow wore down and went back to examine her calf. She stood over it lowing as though to call it back to life, and had I the power to do so, I would have granted her prayer.

Purple rode up and looked at me. "Good shot, but you forgot to skedaddle," he said.

"I'll remember next time," I said.

As we waited for the cow to recognize her loss, I saw what Purple meant about the look in their eyes. She raised her head to the sun as though she'd been played a dirty trick and something burned out in her, after which she went along back to the herd, docile as an old milch cow.

We put the calf corpse in the sack for Potter and didn't say much on the way back, but after we'd turned the cow into the herd Purple took off his hat and brushed it with his gloved hand. "None of us likes it, Jackson," he said.

"Got to be done," I replied, feeling grown-up and sick at the same time.

I gave Potter the sack and expected he'd have something to say, but he didn't.

After I'd curried Ruddy Bob I went back to the crowd and slung my saddle into the wagon. I wasn't hungry so I laid my bedroll out and sat down with my back against the wheel.

The night guard finished their grub and went out to settle the herd. Mr. Boardman and ZeeZee walked to the remuda, talking softly. I supposed, being family, they had things to say, but if I was John Boardman I'd sure unadopt ZeeZee first chance I got.

Fifteen hundred head of cattle belching up and chewing their cud is a contenting sound. They lowed

61

and grated grass mash in their teeth with their bodies heavy against the ground. They were reported to be dumb, but I wondered if maybe they didn't have an appreciation of life. I didn't see why not. Maybe they didn't know fractions, or history, or *The Charge of the Light Brigade,* but they knew the scent of the earth and the freshness of water. Surely they too could see the stars and wonder.

I was feeling morose at having become a calf blaster, but what the hell, the whole herd was going to be turned into hide, tallow, meat, and bone, so what was the difference when they died, now or later? That dead calf was better out of it, I argued, but I was not convinced. I'd seen the look in its eyes before my bullet snuffed them. It had just begun to wonder what, and who, and where it was, when suddenly it was not. It had a glimpse of existence, a sliver of life; then there was an explosion, and it was over.

The stars filled out overhead, way off, way out there on the edge of things, suspended by gravity or something, and I sat there, unhungry, wondering if the cattle knew they were going to Wichita. I saw by the cows' protective reaction to any threat against their calves that they knew about danger and death. These were not things they welcomed. These were things they would fight against, given a chance. But that calf hadn't a chance in the world when I drew a bead on it. Not one, and I felt bad. I'd killed other things, spiders and birds, chickens and snakes, but nothing so new and helpless, nothing that hadn't lived long enough to at least know what it was.

Someone hunkered down beside me. It was Potter

with a plate and a cup of coffee in his hands. "I'll just put this down beside you," he said. "It's beans, canned tomatoes, bread, and coffee."

"Thank you, Mr. Potter," I said, then I got his drift. "I'm not afraid of meat, if that's what you're saying."

"Just recitin' the menu, Wylie. Sometimes things taste different in the dark, so I wanted you to know what it was. We'll have meat in the morning for them as like it."

"I'll have my share," I said.

"Fine enough."

Potter made to push himself up, but settled again when I asked him a question. "Mr. Potter, do you suppose these cattle know they're going to Wichita?"

"Not likely."

"Someone ought to tell them, just to be fair about it."

"Well, Jackson, if you see a way to let these cows know where they're going, you let me in on it."

"But you know you're going to Wichita, Mr. Potter," I said.

Potter looked thoughtful for a time, then he nodded. "That's so," he said, just as dumb and wondering as if he hadn't known where he was going all along. "We're all goin' to Wichita for certain," he said.

SCRAMBLED BRAINS AND EGGS.

CHAUNCEY POTTER.

❖Being careful not to shatter the contents, cleave open the skulls of three calves. Remove the brains, severing the connective cords to the eyes and spine. Place the brains in a large pan and remove membrane. Soak brains in cold water with a gill of vinegar to release the blood.

❖When ready, steep the brains in hot water for about twenty minutes, then dust with cornmeal and cool. Heat a large iron skillet to receive brains and eggs. Grease skillet, adding garlic or onion. Whip a dozen eggs, dice brains, and fold them into the eggs. Add salt and pepper and fry until firm.

❖Serves fifteen men.

Chapter Six

❖　❖　❖

The next morning Potter and I were up first, as usual, to make breakfast. I stirred and fed the fire and put the water on to boil while Potter thrashed up a pot of eggs and something. I excused myself as having a call of nature and headed for the herd to check on Roselle, since I hadn't seen her the day before. The other cattle sensed the difference in Roselle and would fend her away with their horns if she got too cozy with them.

I found her snoozing at the edge of the herd. "You Roselle!" I called.

Roselle clambered to her feet and strolled away from me. "Say, don't you remember me?" I asked.

Not only did she not remember me, she seemed disinclined to renew the acquaintance. She increased her pace, so I had to jog along beside her to keep up. "I'm taking you to Enid," I said.

She was not impressed.

The other cattle were getting up, and I guessed I'd better make scarce or I'd have them on the move before the drovers ate breakfast. I turned my back on Roselle and headed for the chuck wagon. Roselle then took it in mind to give me a butt from behind. It propelled me forward a few steps before I got stopped. I turned and gave her a swat on the snoot. "One more of those," I said, "and you're going to be a side dish for French fries."

Roselle tossed her head and pranced off.

67

I came to the yellow longhorn whose calf I'd shot the previous afternoon. She was standing at the edge of the herd in an attitude of puzzled submission, and I was sad for her. I put my hand on her warm, dusty neck. "Sooo, sooo," I soothed. She looked at me with no recognition, her deep eyes noncommittal, but her horns looked as though they could have pried open and sunk the *Merrimac.* "I got something to say," I whispered.

She appeared willing to listen.

"The thing about it is they're driving you to Wichita," I said. I felt the muscles in her neck shudder and took this for an acknowledgment. I knew it was unlikely she'd know about Wichita, so I explained it was a place from which they shipped cattle to Chicago, where they had slaughterhouses. "That's where they kill cattle . . . your people, you see. They put you in a chute, hit you on the head with a sledgehammer, strip off your hide, and butcher you for meat while you're still warm! You tell the others now, you hear?"

She seemed undismayed.

"They're going to kill and eat this whole herd," I declared. "If you're smart you'll skin out. You'll slide away from this crowd and head south. Tell the rest."

At this she backed away from me, nodding agreeably; then she humped up and charged, hooking her horns for murder.

I ran with my rump tucked in, expecting any second to feel a rip no darning needle could mend. I ducked aside and she cut past me, turned, and came on again. The one thing cowboy boots are bad for is running. The heels pitch you forward. The toes don't give much purchase on the ground, so you pitch and stagger. I fell and rolled away from the cow's hooves and jumped up as she began lifting earth on her horns to plant me like a sapling. Then Al Peach, one of the drovers, galloped up and snatched me around the shoulders. He jerked me over his saddle just as those savage horns slashed by.

When we cleared the herd Peach dropped me like a sack of meal. "You tryin' to get yerself killed, or what?" he demanded. "What you mean by chousing up them cattle?"

"She musta recognized me," I said.

"You never go afoot among cattle! God damn, boy, you coulda set them off, and Boardman would have turned you inside out!"

"Yes, sir. I'm sorry."

"Sorry is too late, girlie. Grow some brains!" Peach rolled his eyes upward as though appealing to heaven for strength; then he rode out to relieve the night guard.

As I walked back to camp I realized the fault was in my poor grasp of cattle lingo. To tell those beasts what was in store I had to find how to communicate with them. I was surprised I hadn't thought of this before.

When I came up to the chuck wagon the other hands were seated around the fire, gulping and swilling. Potter met me with a comment on my prolonged absence. "Sticky beans?" he asked.

"I never ate 'em," I said.

"Them's the worst kind to pass," he said, and he thrust a tin plate of addled something into my hand. "This'll help," he said.

"What is this in the daylight?" I asked him.

"Calf's brains and eggs," Potter said.

I sat down near the fire and studied the mess on my plate. I could see the other hands were waiting, looking at me from the corners of their eyes while pretending to mind their own business. Mr. Boardman came up, throwing a black shadow over the fire, and the sun wasn't yet over the horizon. He stood there with his thumbs notched in his belt, whistling soundlessly through his stitched-up lips and spiking the coffeepot with his rusty eyes.

ZeeZee had an especially nasty grin on his face, which put me out a lot. I never disliked a person faster in my life than ZeeZee.

I knew they were all waiting for me to swallow and puke so they could have a big laugh, and I was determined to rob them of the pleasure. I took my fork and stirred a bit, thinking all the thoughts they knew I'd think, about how I'd killed the calf to which these brains belonged. But I thought of something else too. I remembered how Indians ate the hearts of bears to get their strength, and Indians aren't so dumb as politicians make them out to be. If the Indians were right, then maybe the way to learn the thoughts of cattle was to eat their brains.

I took a forkful and shoveled her in and it wasn't so bad—a bit slippery on the teeth, but I swallowed and it went down easy. The men near me pulled their boots back, expecting those brains to come right up again, but I had a purpose, and I was mad at them galoots waiting for me to puke like that. Those calf's brains were going to help me talk to cows and tell them about Wichita; then we'd see how big the herd would be fifty miles down the trail. The drovers would have nothing left but the stupidest, most suicide-bent cattle ever born. I could see the looks on them drovers' faces when they had to rope and tow every cow to get it faced toward Wichita. They wouldn't walk there. No, sir! They'd just lie down. I'd see some looks then, when the drovers saw their pay and profit get up and walk off south, shaking their horns and saying, "Oh, no, we ain't going to Wichita. Send out a call for volunteers. We aren't the ones. Wylie Jackson put us wise!"

Thinking this, I cleaned the plate and had begun to feel sorry for everyone because this drive was going to be such a bust. When I looked up they were all goggling at me except for Mr. Boardman, who walked over his shadow to his horse. Burt Purple had a particularly odd expression on his face, which annoyed me, so I stood up and called, "Hey, Mr. Potter, you got any more brains?"

"Not me," Potter said.

There was a moment like all the air had been sucked out of the sky. Then V. A. Eberhart whooped and slapped his leg, and the air came back full of noise and laughter and yells, and Warren Steele was hammering my shoulders and hollering, "Hey, Chauncey, you got any brains?"

I saw Mr. Boardman on his big trail horse grinning so his teeth showed, like he'd busted all the stitches in his lips. Then he did a thing I never expected, kind of bobbed his head and winked at me, before he can-nonballed those drovers to their horses and they all rode off to start the day.

For the next few days there were no calves flagged, so I didn't get to ride with Burt Purple. I missed being up on a horse, but I was glad to avoid the killing. The more I thought about all those doomed cattle the less I liked the prospect of it. Maybe three hundred times as many men as all these cattle had been killed in the Civil War, I thought. But that didn't make it right.

Seated beside Mr. Potter on the chuck wagon, I looked at the herd. That they should all be killed was awful and I felt sick about it. Potter must have guessed my train of thought because he spat noisily to clear his talking tools. "I'm sorry I sent you back with Purple," he said.

"I'll get used to it," I said.

Potter looked at me fish-eyed. "You will, will you."

"Somebody has to do it. When Mr. Boardman sees what a good hand I make, he'll put me on regular before the drive is over or when one of the hands gets hurt or something like that."

"Why, by that time you'll be such a calf blaster you'll be able to shoot one of the boys just to make yourself a place," Potter said, and he gave the mules a nasty slap with the reins.

After my experience with the calf's brains the drov-ers had got in the habit of calling, "Hey, Chauncey, you got any brains?" when they passed the chuck wagon. Then they'd whoop and holler like it was the biggest chunk of wit in the world. Whenever one of them did something stupid, like scalding himself with the coffeepot, that was a "Hey, Chauncey." Any mistake got to be a "Hey, Chauncey," and Potter laid all this at my doorstep because I'd started it.

I watched the cattle pretty close to see if there was any sign of rebellion, but they seemed content to be marching to their slaughter. The brains I'd consumed had not improved my ability to communicate with the cattle as far as I could see. This shook my faith in Indian lore, but I saw the logic of it. Perhaps the fault was in eating the brains of a critter that hadn't had time to learn anything for itself. Maybe if I ate the brains of an experienced, full-grown longhorn I'd find the knowledge I was after. Or maybe I just didn't get it, like fractions.

Potter was driving, slumped down as usual. Now and again he'd look at the wagon wheel. One spoke was painted red and by watching it rotate he could estimate how far we'd traveled. He'd count the turns, tote it up someway, and announce we'd come seven miles, or ten, or whatever. How he did this I did not care to learn. Mathematics gave me hives, but I grew out of it. "Right about here," Potter said.

"What?" I asked.

"I lost my hair."

I waited, hoping he'd go on, but he seemed disposed to silent contemplation of that event. My curiosity got pretty heavy. "Lost your hair," I prompted.

"Scalped," Potter said, as though I hadn't known this. He doffed his hat, revealing his skullcap. It was blue for Tuesday.

"I know that," I said. "But how?"

"With a knife."

He was making me squirm for it. "Who did it?"

"Comanche."

I decided to reverse course. "Don't tell me, Mr. Potter," I said. "It's too horrible to contemplate. I'd be awake all night if you told me. Let's change the subject."

"Fine," Potter said.

The wheel spoke turned a hundred times, and I was getting tighter and tighter. I imagined the red devils howling and dancing around Chauncey Potter's recumbent form, their scalping knives glinting in the firelight. I saw the Comanche warrior kneel, deftly slice a circle around Potter's head, and jerk the scalp free with a hideous yell, holding it aloft and shaking the gory locks. "Tell me!" I exclaimed.

"Why, it's not much to tell," Potter said.

"They scalped you!"

"It was only one of them."

"One Comanche?"

"I was drunk, which is why I swore off liquor from that day to this."

"It wasn't a war party? Just one?"

"And his wife. I was dashing through this place being chased by a swarm of irate cavalrymen out of Fort Elliot because I'd watered their liquor ration by half—"

"You what?"

"You listening or talking? I delivered two kegs of rye whiskey they'd ordered at the fort, but in a fifty-mile trek I'd drunk half and replaced it with creek water. They detected this right off and were determined to wring the stolen whiskey out of my carcass.

74

Running ahead of them, I hit a streambed full tilt and my horse went down with a broken leg, so I had to shoot him. It was dark as sin but I pushed on with my saddle on my shoulder. I could hear those cavalry boys yelling. They'd found my shot horse and were casting around to pick up my trail. Then out of the dark there came a Comanche leading his squaw on a horse pulling a travois laden with their camp goods. I appealed to them the best I could in my still-soused condition. 'I'd give my hair for a horse,' I said."

The red wheel spoke turned a dozen or so more times. Evidently Potter thought he'd concluded his tale. "Well?" I said at last.

He looked at me, startled. "Well what?"

"What happened?" I cried.

"Why, the Comanche took my hair, gave me the horse, and his squaw had to tow the travois."

After this I never credited anything Potter told me. If he didn't want to say how he'd lost his hair, that was fine with me, but I wasn't going to swallow such a story as that. It was too disappointing and stupid, and I thought he was grinning in his whiskers.

That evening I missed Roselle. I usually spotted her tagging up to the bed ground after the main herd had begun to settle. Now she was overdue, and I borrowed a horse from Kaufer when he came in from the swing and rode out to find her. I saw Purple ahead of me, going back along the trail calf blasting, and wondered what I'd done to be demoted from that task.

I went on searching the brush for Roselle and was relieved when I saw her not too far ahead. She was standing stone still, facing away from me. As I approached I saw Purple again, rifle ready, as he stalked in, looking for a calf. I saw the marker. I saw the longhorn cow.

As I reached Roselle, Purple fired. Roselle jumped and I thought she'd been hit. The calf was already on its feet when the bullet struck. It staggered toward Roselle, and Purple fired again, dropping the calf in a flurry of legs and tail and neck. Roselle turned and ran in my direction as the mother cow charged Purple's horse. I went with Roselle and saw the terror in her eyes and knew she'd made the association between guns and death. It was so clear I'd had to have been blind not to see it.

When we reached the herd I dismounted and tried to soothe Roselle, but she kept circling and shaking her head as though trying to dislodge the picture of death and the sound of gunfire from her brain. When she calmed down I rubbed her head for a time, saying I'd see to it she was never shot, making the promises grown-ups offer children but which they can't be sure of keeping. When Roselle settled, I rode back to the chuck wagon and gave Kaufer his horse.

Later Purple came in driving a cow and lugging a dead calf in a sack. He turned the cow into the herd, then rode over and flopped the calf on the drop table of the chuck wagon.

"Here's a fresh one, Mr. Potter," I said.

Potter looked at me like I'd spit in his coffee.

"More veal," I explained.

Potter slung his ladle into a pot of stew he was working up. "You got it," he said. "You butcher it. You dress it. You cook it, and you eat it. I'll be

76

damned if this outfit gets another 'Hey, Chauncey' on me!" With that he stalked off to the wagon and commenced reading Bible tracts about two pages a minute.

Well, dang if I was going to flunk any more tests. "Fine, I will," I said.

"Do as you please, blaster," Chauncey growled.

I'd never cut meat bigger than a chicken before, but I wouldn't let Potter get a hand up on me, so I honed the knives and went to it. I had no more idea how to dress a calf than a dog has how to open a tin can. I'd seen the carcasses of beeves and lambs hanging in butcher shops back home and cuts of meat on my plate, steaks and chops and such, but that doesn't tell much when you're faced with a whole body, even a little one.

I slit the hide down the belly, down the legs, and under the neck. I peeled it back from the head, then gave it a yank and was satisfied to see it come away in one piece, even the tail. I saw where the bullet had entered the chest between two ribs and where it busted three coming out. I stared at that skinned calf for some time, then began to work the legs to see how the muscles moved. I wanted to know how it was connected up and took a knife to get in deeper. I separated the muscles from the legs and laid them out to see how the tendons and joints hooked up, then I went inside to examine the layout of its guts.

I didn't notice the men come up or hear the clank of their dinnerware as they spooned stew and swallowed coffee. I was so intent on my work I didn't notice the sun go down.

Burt Purple came up beside me with a kerosene lantern. "Jackson," he whispered. "What the hell you doin'?"

"Butchering this calf."

Purple set the lantern down and looked at the muscles, tendons, guts, and bones spread over the table. "That's not butchering," he said. "The boys are wondering."

I glanced over my shoulder and saw the drovers hunkered around the fire staring at me. I took the big cleaver and split that calf's skull in two parts, so neat it might have been a picture.

Purple gulped and backed away, but I didn't give a dang what he thought, or they thought. I wanted to know how that calf's head worked, so I pulled the lantern closer and began to take it apart. I saw how the brain lay in the bone, and it was a pretty good size, too. I followed out how it was attached to the eyes, then took one from the socket and pared it apart.

I worked on by lantern light, and I got to know the insides of that calf's head and heart and belly until I thought I could have put one together given the parts. But when I'd finished and stood there looking at those scraps I knew I'd missed the point somehow.

I saw Mr. Boardman standing on the other side of the fire. He was scowling at me. He dashed the remains of his coffee into the embers and came to my side. He set his cup on the drop table. "Bury it, boy," he said.

"Yes, sir."

I scraped the parts into the hide and was surprised

what a little bundle it made for such a complicated thing. I scrubbed the table, took the shovel, and walked out under the night to put the creature down. I dug the hole and found stones to keep scavengers from rooting it out. Then I stood beside the grave, head bowed, and it came to me that if I could not save all these cattle from perdition, the least I could do was to cease being counted among those who devoured them. What other men did I could not govern. For my part I vowed never to clamp my teeth into meat howsoever long I lived. This was my prayer and my conversion over the body of that ever nameless calf. It, at least, had not died in vain, for it had stricken one human being from the rolls of the beef eaters and made of him a vegetarian.

When I raised my head Mr. Boardman was standing nearby. "Oh," I said, startled.

"I'd like you to ride drag with Eberhart," he said.

I opened my mouth to reply, but all I managed to do was nod my head.

"Take Ruddy Bob," he said, and he strode off.

It took me a time to recover the use of my legs. I'd been promoted from *coosie segundo* to drover! I'd be up on horseback among the men! If ever an unspoken prayer had been answered, this was it.

On to Wichita!

PEACH PIE.

WYLIE JACKSON.

❖My piecrust is simple and made in the skillet.

❖To a cup of lard add a quarter cup boiling water and thrash until cold and creamy. Add two cups flour, a half teaspoon baking powder, and a pinch of salt. Mix and let cool. Pat into pan and cook ten minutes until browned.

❖For filling blend four egg yolks with four pinches of flour, one cup of sugar, a dash of vanilla, and some butter. Pour this over canned peaches cut side up in the pie shell. Put in hot Dutch oven for thirty minutes.

❖For the meringue whip four egg whites with a spoonful of vanilla and a dash of cream of tartar into one cup of powdered sugar. When frothy and firm open the oven and lay meringue over the pie. Cook another twenty minutes until the meringue is firm and slightly browned.

CHAPTER SEVEN

❖ ❖ ❖

Next morning I was up before Potter. I made coffee and was working on the biscuit dough when he rolled from under the wagon, popped his hat on his head, and shrugged out of his bedding. He was pulling on his boots and grunting with the strain when I spoke up. "Mr. Boardman said I was—"

"I know," Potter said. "You're riding drag."

I never knew how word of things got around. Everyone seemed to know what was on the tapis without the necessity of speech, and I wished the cattle were similarly endowed. "I'll still help you, Mr. Potter," I said. "I'll help with breakfast in the morning and clean up at night."

"I managed without you for fifty years. I guess I can struggle along a few more."

Breakfast done, I put my chaps on and followed the drovers to mount up. After my display of calf dissection the men stood away from me as the longhorns stood away from Roselle. They didn't say anything, but I could see I'd fallen into disfavor. Well, I knew more about the insides of a beef than all of them put together, and I was determined to show them what a good drover I could be.

V. A. Eberhart was a long-faced poke built in a triangulated way, narrow in the hips but broad in the shoulders, narrow at the chin and wide in the eyes. His voice was leathery and creaked like an overladen saddle with the strain of stringing words together. When I mounted Ruddy Bob, Mr. Boardman trotted up and paused nearby.

"I sure want to thank you, sir," I said to him.

"Stay out of the sunshine," he said to me; then he clipped off to the point.

From this I knew Purple had told Mr. Boardman about my being a sunshine rider and wondered if everything I did or thought was general knowledge in this bunch. It didn't seem right, them knowing everything about me and me only pecking up crumbs about them.

I saw ZeeZee scowling at me and wondered what his bellyache was now. I suppose he'd expected Mr. Boardman to crucify me for riding Ruddy Bob and that when it turned out different he was galled. I met his eyes without flinching, but it took all I had. ZeeZee snorted and rode away.

V. A. Eberhart beckoned, and we headed for the tail end of the herd, which was up and on the move, bawling and complaining as they worked the stiffness out of their muscles. Eberhart and I rode down the flank to the drag, where it would be our duty to drive the laggard stock back to the herd, flag any birthing cows, and generally keep the cattle together as they grazed along.

So far we'd been lucky as to grass and water, which were plentiful along the trail. We were following a ladder of rivers and streams as we headed north, leaving one and bedding near another. Though it was late in the season, other herds, many of them larger than ours, had not used up the trail.

This morning the sky was lower than usual, threatening weather. Dark clouds loomed over the range, and the mournful ghost of a wind raised dust devils along the trail. I judged I wasn't likely to make a fool of myself in the sun on such a gloomy day and was riding along trying not to look too grand when that fool cattalo, Roselle, dashed up and began nuzzling my saddlebag. Alarmed by this display, Ruddy Bob reared back, nearly unseating me, then struck off at a brisk canter trying to get away from Roselle. But the danged cattalo came right along, prancing and baaing like she wanted to get on board Ruddy Bob with me.

At first I thought she was loco; then I remembered Alice Beck's drawers were in my saddlebag. Roselle had caught their scent and thought I was Alice, or that Alice was nearby. Who knows what cattalo think?

Ruddy Bob broke into a lope, and Roselle pranced right along beside him. "Get away, you dang fool!" I yelled at her.

By now Ruddy Bob was spooked and had commenced to turn in tight circles, backing away from Roselle, whose nose was aimed at my saddlebag.

V. A. Eberhart was gazing at me with a question mark on his face.

"Haul off, you crossbred she-buffalo!" I yelled. But Roselle thought it was a game. She pawed the ground, counting like Alice had taught her. She flopped down and rolled over. She jumped up and rose on her rear legs, hoofing the air.

Ruddy Bob shied and trembled and danced away on his rear legs, whinnying and striking out with his fore hooves. I was nearly unseated again. Then I heard a deep sound and saw V. A. Eberhart kick to a gallop, his elbows flapping like wings, the neck of his horse stretched a mile.

I looked around. The cattle had vanished as though they'd been sopped up by the blotter of God. One minute they had been moving along peacefully, then they were gone, and I heard the thunder of their hooves.

"Stompeede!" Eberhart yelled. "Stompeede!"

Then I saw the cattle, merged with the landscape, moving fast like a buffalo robe being snatched from a trader's counter.

I put Ruddy Bob in motion and left Roselle behind.

Lightning flashed, blinding and close enough to smell. Ruddy Bob skipped two strokes sideways, then righted himself. I was downhill over his neck with my heart beating just behind my clenched teeth. Rain spilled from the sky, a lavender downpour, filling my eyes. Thunder struck, flattening the hills, and the earth was hock deep in mud.

I heard Mr. Boardman yelling, "All hands and the cook!"

I glanced back to see where Roselle had got to, but she was screened by the rain. Chauncey Potter loomed out of the wet, riding bareback on a wagon mule. He was beating on a frying pan with a ladle. "Turn them!" he hollered. "Turn them! Turn them!"

Ruddy Bob knew better what to do than I did. I clung to him with my knees as he lunged for the point of the herd. We came to Steele, Peach, and Doug

Kaufer with their horses leaning into the leaders of the run, trying to turn them. The men fired their pistols and yelled their lungs dry. Lightning seared and thunder boomed.

Mr. Boardman was out in front of the leaders with a yellow slicker in his hand, flashing it in their faces and cursing them loud enough to drive thunder back into its cave. Chauncey Potter larruped up, bouncing on the bareback mule, beating on the frying pan and howling as though his scalp was being lifted for a second time. ZeeZee cut in with me. "Turn 'em!" he yelled. "Turn 'em! Turn 'em!"

V. A. Eberhart's horse caught a gopher hole, and I saw him catapult over its head and bounce off a rampaging longhorn. He fell in a heap and tried to roll away from the hooves. Ruddy Bob dashed in, and I caught Eberhart's hand and swung him up behind me, wondering even as I did it how I did it. Eberhart clung to me as we breasted the cattle and reached the edge of the herd. "I owe you, Jackson," Eberhart said as he dropped to the ground and looked for a horse.

The herd split around Boardman. Blue foxfire was playing around the brim of his hat and on the ears of his horse. He twirled his mount, firing his pistol, roaring, and swirling that yellow slicker, and the cattle faked away from him, their eyes rolling white with panic. Beyond Boardman they joined up again, but the pressure had been taken out of them, and they began to mill.

I saw Ed Pillow's horse riding empty and went to it. Eberhart caught Pillow's horse and began yelling for him. A man down in a stampede was the worst that could happen, and everyone was calling for him. "Pillow! Hey, Pillow! Pillow!"

Eberhart and I found him in the cattle-trod mud with two arms broken. We dug him out and dragged him aside. The rain washed Pillow whiter than any man ever had been. He was a skinny drover with sandy hair and freckles that were lost in his pain. His broken arms hung down, and I hurt all over just looking at him, but he said not a word. "Stay put, Ed," Eberhart said. "We'll come for you."

I goggled at Eberhart. "We goin' to leave him?" I gasped.

"Herd's first," Eberhart twanged. "Come on."

It took us another hour to bunch the herd and get them calmed down. The thunder and lightning let up, but the rain continued, and the sky was dark. Boardman, with his lips stitched as taut as I'd ever seen them, nodded "suggestions" this way and that as he surveyed the ruin. I heard him say we'd lost fifty head and wondered how he knew. ZeeZee went to locate the horses that were scattered. The rest went seeking the lost cattle.

"Bring the wagon up for Pillow," Potter said to me.

I rode to the wagon, got one mule in the traces, and was about to head back when I remembered that Alice's drawers were still in my saddlebag. If it was ever known what had caused this stampede they'd likely hang me, not by the neck, but by the ankles from a pecan tree and let me starve to death.

I took the white packet into which Alice had sewn her drawers and looked for a place to ditch it. If I threw it away, some drover was sure to find it and trace it to me. None of the other hands was likely to have had ladies' drawers in his kit, and they'd put them to my account by deduction, or however they all knew what was going on. There was no time to be fooling around with Pillow out there in the rain, so I wedged the drawers way down in the forward corner of the wagon, planning to bury them when peace descended.

Potter and Eberhart had set Pillow's arms by the time I got back. They were simple fractures, but Pillow was limp as a washrag as we made room for him in the wagon and laid him on the floor. Potter got to rustling around for something to make splints, but in the coonie I found some box slats I'd been saving for kindling. "Go help the others," Potter said to me when we'd made Pillow comfortable.

We recovered twenty-two strayed cattle, but there were others missing. I found Roselle covered with mud from hooves to hornbuttons. When I rode by she made no sign, and I vowed to put Alice Beck's drawers in an Arbuckle coffee can and bury it three feet deep so Roselle could never catch the scent of them again and spook cattle into a stampede.

We lost the day and would lose the next since the cattle were too nervous and exhausted to be moved. The rain brought our spirits down. We raised the Sibley tent, then sat around the chuck wagon under a tarp gazing at the fire. Mr. Boardman, hewn by the firelight, was drawing lines in the damp earth around his boots. The closest town where a doctor might be found was Tascosa, forty miles northeast. Steele volunteered to ride there with Pillow the next day, and Mr. Boardman agreed.

"Looked to me she started in the drag," Peach said.

Boardman nodded, waiting.

I looked at Eberhart, knowing he was going to have to speak for us and dreading what he would say. "That's so," he said.

"They just got humping up from the rear, like a wave run through them; then the leaders broke," Kaufer said.

"Lightning," Eberhart said.

"The front of the herd was shoved into it," Purple said.

"Lightning," Eberhart said again.

"That'll do it," Boardman said, and I felt I'd been reprieved while standing on the gallows trap with a noose around my neck. I kept my eyes dead and studied the ground, and it came to me that Eberhart knew what he was talking about, that perhaps it had been lightning and not Roselle's cavorting after Alice Beck's drawers that set the cattle off. This eased me some, but when I looked at Eberhart he refused to meet my eyes, leaving me in no doubt that he had other thoughts on the matter but had kept them to himself, and also that he no longer owed me. "Yeah, it started in the drag," ZeeZee said.

The next day the rain let up some, but the sky was low and overcast. Steele tied Ed Pillow to the saddle of a gentle horse and wrapped him in a slicker. They set out for Tascosa with Steele leading Pillow's horse by the halter.

We examined the cattle for injuries and soothed them down. By midmorning some of them were grazing. I helped Mr. Potter with the cooking and decided to make a peach pie.

"It might cheer things up," I said.

"You don't cook a little bit, do you," Potter growled.

I made a big pie, hoping I might earn my way back into the good graces of the bunch. Potter didn't lift a finger, but when the pie came out of the Dutch oven full of canned peaches in vanilla sauce and topped with meringue as high as a mountain, he set it out for everyone to ogle and credited me for it. When the pie was distributed after supper it eased the general misery some.

We kept our horses saddled in case the cattle took fright and bolted again. Purple and Eberhart had first shift of the night guard and the rest of us—except Potter, who chose to sleep in the chuck wagon—turned in under the Sibley tent, exhausted.

About two in the morning we all woke up with Potter yelling blue murder. "Catamount!" he hollered. "It's climbing in to get me!"

We heard a scrabbling sound at the wagon and dashed out of the tent. "Can't find my Sharps!" Potter yelled.

We saw a beast trying to get into the wagon. Potter was raving and calling for help. No one dared fire a shot, which was sure to spook the cattle, so we ran around the wagon and there was Roselle with her forelegs on the wagon seat and one rear hoof on a wagon spoke, trying to jump inside the wagon. It was a comical sight to everyone but me.

Eberhart, Steele, and the others broke into fits of laughter as Potter leaped from the wagon, convinced it was besieged by a bear.

"Hey, Chauncey!" the drovers howled. "Hey, Chauncey, you been spooked by a heifer. She loves you, girlie!"

"A catamount cow!" Kaufer cried. "Hey, Chauncey!"

Mr. Boardman came up, fully clothed, as though he never was any other way. "I think we've had enough of that, boys," he said. "That heifer is trouble to us."

It was a death sentence as sure as stones fall down. I hadn't yet told Mr. Boardman my deal to deliver Roselle to Enid, but that no longer mattered. She was a goner. What they didn't eat they'd pickle and jerk.

Potter glared at the cattalo. "We'll find what she tastes like," he said dourly.

I grabbed Roselle by the ear and tried to pull her away, but she was convinced Alice Beck was in the wagon and wouldn't come.

ZeeZee was there with a blanket draped around his shoulders. "There's somethin' inside that wagon she wants," he said. "Let's have a look."

I jumped into the wagon ahead of ZeeZee, rummaged in the corner for Alice Beck's accursed drawers, and tucked the packet into my shirt as ZeeZee came in. It was dark, but he caught my motion. "What's that you got?" he asked.

"What?"

"In your shirt there," he said, reaching for me.

"Nothing!" I declared.

"You hid something in your shirt!"

I knocked his hand away and rolled behind a sack of rice. I knew if what I had was found I'd never live it down, not in a thousand years, not if I lost myself in the Amazon, or Africa. The tale of Alice Beck's drawers would be told at drovers' campfires as long as men could laugh.

ZeeZee caught me around the neck, and I fought and kicked and banged him with my head. My desperation surprised him, and I broke away.

I threw myself out of the wagon, hit the front seat, and fell to the ground in a heap. Kaufer pulled me up, but I twisted out of his grip and ran to the remuda. There I unhitched Ruddy Bob, rolled up into the saddle, and galloped away. I was crazed with fear of discovery, and that fool Roselle came with me. She couldn't keep up, of course, but she tried.

I heard ZeeZee yelling and other men mounting their horses, and I heard Mr. Boardman call, "Wylie, you come back here!"

The rain had increased again, so heavy I couldn't see beyond my hat brim. I rode fast and heedless as the men spread out behind, calling me now and again. "Jackson! You Jackson!"

I didn't slow until I no longer heard their voices and then only to a quick trot as I took stock of my situation. I put Alice Beck's drawers in my saddlebag determined to bury them where they would never be found or until I was safe in my own grave. The Sharps was in the saddle scabbard, which was why Potter hadn't been able to locate it.

I'd stolen Mr. Boardman's horse. I was a bunch quitter and a thief. My reputation was a shambles forever . . . and not all the wet on my face was from the rain.

BUFFALO GOURD MUSH.

WYLIE JACKSON.

❖Green-and-yellow-striped buffalo gourds are common on the high plains and can prevent starvation. Split gourd and remove seeds. Dry these in the sun or roast them on a rock beside your fire. When dry these seeds can be eaten like sunflower seeds or pinyon nuts. Or grind the seeds, add water, and cook into a paste.

❖Miserable without salt but can be swallowed.

Devil's Claw or Unicorn Seeds.

WYLIE JACKSON.

❖The devil's claw can be eaten fresh when very young. Gather pods, wash to remove hair, and chew. The fresh seeds of larger devil's claw pods can be chewed for their juice. It gives a slight kick.

CHAPTER EIGHT

❖ ❖ ❖

Two hours later I dismounted and listened for the sound of the Circle Six drovers. I heard nothing but the rain falling and the mournful sigh of the wind. I felt low and hunkered down, staring at my boots as they sank slowly into the muddy earth. The way I felt, I'd just as soon have been swallowed up by it.

I supposed Mr. Boardman would inform the law the first chance he got and tell Aunt Clara how I'd turned out. Well, the die was cast, as someone said, and I'd crossed the Rubicon, as Eldon Larkin said Caesar said, though I never understood why that river was commemorated above so many others such as the Pecos or the Washita. History, I guessed, was a first-come-first-served affair in terms of notoriety. I'd never thought my glorious fate would turn on Alice Beck's drawers, but it had, and I would never rival Caesar in the history books except as an object of ridicule. Those drawers were a secret I'd have to carry to the grave, gnawing at my vitals, or risk being laughed off the continent.

I was musing in this fashion as the sky lightened, and I guessed I'd better find a place to lie low until I was out of range of Mr. Boardman and the drovers. I mounted Ruddy Bob and we were about to push off when lo! there came that fool cattalo, Roselle. She was plodding along following her nose sure as compass needles point north. I knew cattle could scent water forty miles away and would sometimes get running for it if they weren't held in check, but I wondered what perfume Alice had soaked her drawers with to pull that heifer to them. I sure couldn't smell it, but Roselle was drawn to it like bees to blossoms. I confess my spirit lifted some to see her.

"Ho, Roselle," I called.

"Baw!" she replied, and she pranced up to me convinced she'd located Alice Beck.

"Sit," I commanded.

Roselle sat and looked so comical I had to laugh. "All right," I said, "come along."

I pointed Ruddy Bob northeast in the general direction of Enid, and Roselle trotted along. I had only ten cartridges for the Sharps and figured I'd better save one for myself in case I came upon some Comanches such as those who'd lifted Potter's hair.

We had no food, so we'd be living off the land. One consoling feature was that we were all vegetarian, me and Ruddy Bob and Roselle, so we were not, in desperate times, likely to eat each other. I wasn't the grass variety, as they were, and I hadn't paused to collect a cooking pot or skillet, so I was going to be subsisting on nuts and berries for a time.

We plodded on to put as much distance between us and the carnivorous cowhands as we could. Having all that doomed cattle to move, they couldn't search for us very long without risking the welfare of the herd or missing their delivery date for the slaughterhouses of Chicago.

We came to a shallow creek bed and traveled down the rocks of it for a mile or so, then up over some shale and down an arroyo. When first light appeared I judged we were lost. I dismounted and set a bit to consider our case. I concluded being lost was about the best hand I could hold if anyone was looking for us, since lost things are harder to find than others. While Ruddy Bob and Roselle grazed I found some wood sorrel and made my breakfast of the violet flowers and leaves, which had a sharp salty flavor. I also found some prickly pears, which I trimmed of their spines with my barlow knife. Some I ate, and some I stored in my saddlebag for dinner.

Roselle and Ruddy Bob got on well in spite of their first meeting, which had caused the stampede. The horse probably mistook Roselle's fondness for the drawers as affection for himself. I got to thinking what a comfort it would be to know as little as these beasts did and live from heartbeat to heartbeat, without lugging a war bag of regrets such as mine because of all the people I had betrayed and let down—my aunt Clara, Mr. Boardman, and Chauncey Potter, among others.

There was a kind of easy acceptance in Roselle's eyes that I've heard called dumb, but I supposed it would be reclassified if we carnivores had taken a liking to horse steak and drove herds of horses to Wichita, riding steers maybe. Then it would be thought that cattle were smarter than horses because I saw how needful it was to downgrade the intelligence of those beasts you were planning to kill and eat.

Until I got to contemplating Roselle, I'd had that prejudice myself. One sort of intelligence may differ from another, but human intelligence, whatever other virtue it may possess, just naturally gravitates to slaughter no matter how you cut it. I never heard of a horse or cow convicted of cold-blooded murder or declaring a civil war that laid waste to half its nation and left thousands of orphans, such as myself, in its wake. Civil war was a concept that had not yet entered the minds of cattle and horses, which I took to be a good thing, as they had no slaves to free.

It stopped raining, and that day we stayed put. The next two days we moved easterly, and I loaded up on pecans, ground cherries, and sunflower seeds with a variety of greens washed down with creek water. I was beginning to wish pretty bad for a pot to cook in, for unlike Ruddy Bob and Roselle, who were geared for raw grub, my belly had to work overtime to digest this stuff.

Coming as we had from the Bozeman Trail, I figured we'd intersect the Western Trail somewhere above Washita and take advantage of what cattle traffic might be there.

On the morning of the third day we came on a herd of OHO-branded stock. I judged they could not yet have been informed of my miscreant nature and decided to risk joining their party.

The outfit had just been roused by the cook beating on a pot lid. I rode up to the chuck wagon and asked to speak to the boss. He was pointed out and his name given as Lemmon, which was about right since he had a squeezed look with eyes like two pips. Etiquette required him to ask me to breakfast, which invitation I promptly accepted.

I kept my fork moving pretty fast on the biscuits

and gravy and had my nose in a tin mug of coffee, which tasted about the next thing to heaven after being without it for so long. Lemmon and the drovers asked about Roselle, who was hanging about like she belonged, and I said she was a cattalo, the offspring of a buffalo and a longhorn. This amused them some. One drover allowed if such got to be a habit they was like to come out with sheepalo and pigalo.

While they were hooting about this, I was trying to think myself up a name. I hadn't thought this would be a problem. There are names all over the place, except when you want one. Also, there is something about the name you're born with that gets branded in your mind. I kept rolling through the alphabet trying for a name that would do me as well as my own, but nothing shone as good to me as Wylie. Walter and William didn't compare to it, and I went through the alphabet again hoping to strike something suitable. I was in the *P*'s and there wasn't much in the way of good names there, and I'd put Philip among the *F*'s anyway. I was up to Percy, which I'd sooner die than be called, and was roving through Penrod, Peter, Preston, and Perry when Lemmon popped the question. "What do you go by, boy?" he asked.

I had a mouthful, which gave me one swallow before I grabbed a handle that would serve me the rest of my natural life. My brain cut loose and bang, out she came. "Axel," I said.

Now there was no reason for me to have skipped clear back from *P* to *A* except that I was looking at the chuck wagon axle at the time. But to jump from Perry to Axel didn't make a lot of sense. There was a grease bucket hanging on the axle, and I might as easy have said "grease," and having thought of this I wasn't sure that wouldn't be the next word out of my mouth. Axel Grease. There's a name certain to arouse suspicion. To save myself I said, "Bean. Axel Bean."

Mr. Lemmon seemed satisfied, which shows how quick people will accept counterfeit money and also how the human brain doesn't have much candlepower over that of a cow when it comes to logic, at least not mine. At any rate Axel Bean went down fine. It felt strange on me, like a new skin, but I figured if I rehearsed it long enough I'd grow used to it in a few years' time. I told Mr. Lemmon I was headed for Enid and asked if I could ride along, volunteering to help the cook, whose name was Archie Stone. I guessed he'd been standing near a bridge when his name was asked. Mr. Lemmon was agreeable. "Fine, Axel," he said.

I jumped some since this was the first time I'd been addressed by my wrong name, but I absorbed the damage and we adjourned to the trail.

Ruddy Bob was in good spirits and made a fine show of himself with Roselle frolicking along at our side.

The four men on the swing and the drag were known as the Gospelers, Matthew, Mark, Luke, and John. I wasn't sure which was which. I think they switched around some. I decided to call Ruddy Bob Pete, just in case, and worried about how to spell my name. Bean? Beene? Beane? Axle? Axel? Spelling wasn't my long suit, but I figured I'd better know how to spell my own name and settled on Beane, with the *e* added to keep it out of the can.

There were about a thousand head in the OHO herd, but they were trail-broke and not much trouble. Luke or John told me they were going to the Niobrara reservation to deliver the herd for Indian beef rations since most of the buffalo had been shot off the range for hides and tallow.

Alas, poor buffalo! I knew him, Horatio; he hath borne me on his back a thousand times!

That Eldon Larkin! The trouble with education is that it sneaks up on you when least expected. I thought of Eldon hauling stovewood for Aunt Clara and had a sudden fit of homesickness for the chores of yore and my bedroom under the eaves with a clear slingshot from my window at any buggy passing on the road, especially the one belonging to Eldon Larkin, who deserved all he got for loading us with all that Shakespeare.

Presently Mark or Matthew rode up beside me and began to admire Ruddy Bob. "Say, that is the finest cutting horse I ever saw. What did you give for him?" He looked at the neat Box Z brand on Ruddy Bob's rump, and I wished it weren't so prominent. "That's John Boardman's brand," Matthew or Mark said.

"He's my uncle," I lied straight off. I didn't recall ever having told a lie with such conviction. It made me feel that I was lapsing into adulthood.

"Your uncle! Is that so?" Mark or Matthew said.

"On the Beane side," I said.

"I thought his wife was Zenobia Zeff."

"Once removed," I appended.

"I worked for Boardman one season," Mark or Matthew said. "I know that family. I know that horse."

"Yes, well, his sister, Agatha, of Minneola, Minnesota, was my mother, but I came south with my father after the war."

"Union man?"

"Confederate."

"From Minneola, Minnesota?"

"No, she was from there. He was a Texan."

"You mean Beane?"

I nodded. "My mother, Agatha."

"Agatha Beane? I thought she was Boardman's sister."

"Why, sure! She's his half sister only, which is what makes us once removed, you see. She was half Boardman, half Beane."

"And she married a Beane."

"What?"

"Your father."

"Sure, but he was a whole Beane, from a different patch than the Boardman Beanes."

We rode along in silence for a time while I let my perspiration dry. Matthew or Mark was grinning at me. There are times when obfuscation works, and there are other times when it does not. This was one of those. That Gospeler was onto me like barnacles. "What'll you take in trade for that horse?" he asked me.

"I got to take it back to Mr. Boardman," I said.

"Is it missing?"

104

"I have the loan of it, being Mr. Boardman's nephew once removed, you see."

The Gospeler laughed. "The trouble with you, Beane, or whatever vegetable you're passing as, is that you're not a born liar. You may prove up with practice. I expect you will, but right now you're a wreck. I'm going to Dakota. A horse like yours won't be missed up that way, so you just fix what you'll take for him, sling your saddle on that cattalo, and powder out of here. I'll give you until we reach the river." With that he kicked off, leaving me to contemplate my fate as a horse extortionist. I supposed he was talking about the Red River, which was about two days ahead.

The sun was up, and the trail had hardened after the recent rains. There was even some dust beginning to tease my nose, and I put my bandanna up to filter it.

We were going along fine with a nice set of white clouds off to the east when I saw a steer pull out of line and went to shoo it back. Instead of lumping along, as most do when they're waved and yelled at, this steer just stood there looking abused, then it let go a stream of water that was bloodred and foamy, something I had never seen.

The steer was a black box-headed beast and a bushel basket wouldn't have held the sorrow in its eyes. Two of the Gospelers rode up and had a look, then they galloped to the point to have a talk with Mr. Lemmon.

What happened next anchored forever in me a sense of my own frail mortality. That herd began to die in large numbers and there was nothing we could do to stop it.

Mr. Lemmon diagnosed the problem as anthrax, or the red water disease. The first thing he did was to send the Gospelers galloping four ways of the compass hoping to strike a vet or a doctor and to round up whatever men they could find who'd be willing to help us.

We drove the cattle off the trail and bunched them. Mr. Lemmon tried to sort the cattle he judged were not infected, and we split the herd in two groups, one for well, one for sick, but by nightfall the distinction broke down.

We chose a dying ground close by and tried to get the steers to it before they dropped. We built fires to light the work and kept them burning all night.

Archie Stone gave me a warning that alarmed me. "That cattalo of yours has a better chance than most, because the disease goes for mature stock, but you'd do well to keep her clear of this place."

I took Alice Beck's drawers from my saddlebag, led Roselle away, and parked the drawers in the branch of a tree half a mile from the herd to hold Roselle. She sure enough stayed there, and Ruddy Bob and I returned to the dying herd.

We worked all night, sorting, roping, dragging, and shooting steers too far gone to survive. I was warned again, this time by Mr. Lemmon, not to work the cattle if I had any open cuts or wounds. "Anthrax will take a man or a horse too, if it gets in the blood."

This made me feel temporary, and I was extra careful not to take a scratch or nick on me or Ruddy Bob.

The herd was fevered so high that heat rolled off it in waves. The cattle breathed like a bellows, so it made me afraid of the air for fear I'd catch what was killing them so cruelly fast.

By morning more than half the herd was down in the red anthrax-infested mud, and Mr. Lemmon's face had taken on a look of bewildered rage such as I had never seen in a man. I thought he would break into tears and that it would do him good if he did, but he just sat there on his exhausted horse staring at those dead and dying cattle. The unseen disease made my flesh crawl, and I wanted to take a bath in turpentine. I kept my bandanna pulled up, but the stench was strong. When the cattle died, they stiffened and bloated, and their legs stood out like branches on stunted trees. Mr. Lemmon sighed so hard it seemed to me he'd never laugh again. "Well," he said at last, "from here on, it's kerosene and shovels."

If you've never seen six hundred dead cattle in one spot, there's no way to say what it does to your mind. I sat there on Ruddy Bob looking at all those fatalities of a war that had never been declared, where no shot was fired and there was no chance of victory. It was more cruel even than Wichita, which at least had the purpose of feeding and shoeing the carnivores, which tribe I had forsaken before this. Had I not, I would have sworn off flesh from this experience alone. If I had found the gift of talking to cattle, what would I have said to them about this? Easy enough to tell them about Wichita, Dodge City, Abilene, or any of those gates to death along the Atcheson, Topeka, and Santa Fe, but what had I to say to them about diseases that could strike from nowhere and make them pant and burn and suffer to death?

Nothing.

I knew nothing about it, except that I was bone scared and praying the sickness would not get me or Ruddy Bob or Roselle. One centers on himself and those dearest to him when the chips are down.

I rode to the chuck wagon, where Archie Stone had taken a five-gallon can of kerosene from the stores. It was a piddling amount to do the job, and we knew it. It would take a ring of fire to contain the disease and consume so many cattle. Stone looked hopeless and miserable. "I've never seen this," he said.

"No," I said.

He looked off, and his expression eased. "Here comes help," he said.

I looked around and saw a group of men riding toward us. The one I recognized first was Mr. Boardman, riding as usual with all four of his horse's feet off the ground. I judged I had two minutes to skedaddle. "I got to git," I said to Archie.

He read my face. "Take what you need," he said.

"A pot would come in handy," I said. "And I'd like to swap this horse for another."

Archie gave me a pot, a wad of sourdough starter, some matches, and other things.

"This horse belongs to Mr. Boardman," I explained.

"We all knew that," Archie said. "You git. I been on the run myself and know the feeling."

I went to the remuda and transferred my saddle to a horse belonging to one of the Gospelers. Then I collected Roselle, put Alice Beck's drawers in my saddlebag, and we lit out. I hoped that if I let go of Mr. Boardman's horse he might not take so harshly to me. He'd know I'd been there, of course, but the drovers would have told him anyway.

I turned my newly stolen horse north and kicked off. By now men were arriving from other directions and pitching in. They cut brush, splashed it with kerosene, and dragged it flaming around the cattle and back along the trail, trying, I supposed, to kill whatever it was that got Lemmon's herd.

I spotted Purple, Eberhart, and Steele through the smoke. Other men were throwing quicklime on the dead cattle and covering them with earth.

I knew if Boardman spotted me I'd see a worse hell than this and made off at the fastest pace Roselle could sustain.

STEAK TARTARE.

ANON.

❖This dish was devised by a class of fugitives who dared not light fires for fear of being discovered. Having become addicted to raw flesh, they embellished the dish as follows.

❖Scrape or mince two pounds of lean steak with a bowie knife. Knead into this two egg yolks (quail or dove will do), chopped wild onions, three fresh snails, a fistful of squawberries, and chopped herbs such as dandelion or curly dock. Add Worcestershire sauce (which should be carried in a canteen at all times by raw-meat gourmets) and olive oil.

❖Heap this up and let set a spell. Best eaten with two forefingers or from the tip of a bowie knife.

CHAPTER NINE

❖　❖　❖

At a distance I stopped and looked back at the stain of greasy smoke rising from the corpses of the OHO cattle. It was a horrible picture, and I see it still in dreams, a senseless carnage of disease contaminating the plains and the sky.

We turned away and went on. Nobody chased us that day. I didn't suppose they would. A bunch quitter and horse thief doesn't compare much to that quantity of sudden death.

Toward nightfall I pulled up in a patch of trees and struck a small fire. I kept my newly stolen horse saddled in case I had to make a fast break. The tree leaves sighed like they knew how much death was in the air, and I got to thinking I was sick. I felt my head and took my pulse and listened to my breathing, and the more attention I paid myself the surer I was that I was dying of anthrax.

The firelight shimmered, and the horse I'd stolen chuffed and stamped, trying to understand why Roselle was so all-fired affectionate, nuzzling up to the saddlebag.

"I need a doctor," I said at last. "It's anthrax!" The sound of these words terrified me, and I wished I hadn't spoken them. An unvoiced illness is not nearly as deadly as one that has been spoken aloud. I knew at once I hadn't long to live and lay down to die. Roselle idled over and cocked her head, gazing into my eyes.

She seemed not a bit concerned and presently lay down close beside me, going straight to sleep as though nothing was wrong. Presently my fever vanished, my pulse and my heart stopped hammering, and I quit gulping air as though each breath was going to be my last.

I lay there thinking about this. Until Roselle looked at me so unconcernedly I'd been at death's door. Now I'd been cured by that heifer with a look and a sigh and by the reassurance of her sleeping so peacefully beside me.

And right there in that cottonwood grove below the North Fork of the Red River, at a place I can still find and show you, I decided to become a doctor. Why I hadn't thought of this before surprised me; it was so obvious once it came to mind. I reasoned it was easier to take money from sick folk than to rob trains or banks, and they thank you besides. If a heifer, like Roselle, could cure me of anthrax with a look and a snooze, I could sure do the same and charge for it. About all Doc Forbisher, back in Odessa, did was yell "Scott's Emulsion!" at any of his patients who tried to pry him from the bar. Sure, he delivered some babies and set broken bones, things like that, for which he charged extra, but mostly he did consultations in Dagget's poolroom and took the credit for any cures that happened in the four adjacent counties. Anyone could do that if they had the proper duds and a medical bag. I tried the profession on for size. "Dr. Axel Beane," I said aloud. Why, I felt perfectly healthy, and being a doctor was just the ticket!

I thought how proud Aunt Clara would be when I

drove up in my phaeton with two matched chestnuts. I'd be wearing a beaver hat, a frock coat, shiny boots, and a gold watch with all those honorary fobs displayed on my silk brocade vest. It would please her more than all get-out to see what I'd become after my poor start.

I slept that night with my head resting on Roselle, comforted by her deep and placid breathing. In the morning I decided to swap the Sharps for something more useful, like pills, a medical book, or some clothes more appropriate to the profession. I was willing to start at the bottom but anxious that a start be made, so I boarded the Gospeler's horse and we headed northeast. Roselle trailed along, and I tried to dredge up words that would be useful for the doctoring. In those days, a man was assumed to be what he said he was until this was disproven. Folks could tell a drover from a lawyer by how they talked, so the first thing I had to do was alter my vocabulary.

"Scalpel," I said. "Chloroform. Cadaver. Bone saw. Enema. Antiseptic."

I was amazed what came to mind when I put thought to it. I had no idea how versed I already was in terms of the healing arts. "Salve," I said. "Paregoric. Anesthetic. Anatomy. Castrate. Amputate. Cleaver."

I could see that none of these terms was readily useful in ordinary conversation and would have to be wedged in to establish my professional identity, but I figured I could yell "Scott's Emulsion!" "Peruna!" or "Honey Pectoral!" along with the best of the medical tribe.

"Pharmacopeia." There was a word that surprised even me. I even knew what it meant: drugs and such. "Pharmacopeia!" I yelled, and Roselle looked up at me with an expression of brooding annoyance in her brown eyes, as though I had no right to proclaim myself a medical man. "You're not the only sawbones in this outfit," I said to her. "All I have to do now is cure something. Most anything will do." So I set about thinking what I could cure and how much to charge, particularly the latter, and I came up with the figure of five dollars as the bottom rung in my ladder of professional fees. Ten patients a day was fifty dollars right there. Ten days was five hundred, and, let's see, three hundred and sixty-five days a year, but make it three hundred with sixty-five off for good behavior and attending honorary banquets and such. Why, that was, let's see, fifty times three hundred . . . and all for the sake of suffering humanity too . . . was, let's see, three oughts, was it? Three oughts! Why, hell, there was fifteen thousand dollars in just one year! Why, doctoring was a gold mine! And after a little success I could raise my fees. Let's see, ten cures at ten dollars would be . . .

But my analysis of the medical profession was interrupted at this point by a posse of sodbusters bristling with arms and whiskey bottles. "There's one of them!" their chief bellowed. "Come on, boys!"

Before I could say *suture,* I was surrounded by as mean and riled-up a bunch of men as had ever been my discomfort to diagnose. Clearly they had mistaken me for a horse thief or a rustler instead of a doctor.

116

"Gentlemen," I croaked in my best bedside manner, "to what do I owe this sudden call upon my services?"

"Get a shovel, Hagstrom, we'll bury him right here!"

Hagstrom, thus addressed, dropped from his horse, unlimbered a shovel, and commenced to dig.

"Where you from, boy?" the chief of this band asked, showing no interest in my probable answer. He instead eyed Roselle with his ugly lips and nostrils curled back, like he was going to eat her raw.

"He's one of them, Amos," another of the band put in over the mouth of a whiskey bottle. "Kill and be done with it, and let's get on to the rest of 'em."

My interrogator, Amos, was a lean man with a lump of tobacco in his jaw who spat frequently into the hole being dug to receive my body. To be shot dead for theft of a horse was not unusual in those days. To take a man's horse and leave him afoot on the plains at the mercy of Indians and the elements was a capital offense. How they knew I had no proof of ownership for my present mount was a question I thought better not to ask since I had no answer for it. I was too proud to beg and too frightened to pray. I tried to recall the medical words I'd been rehearsing, but they had fled. "Hypolarium," I said at last, having no idea where this came from or what it meant, but my interrogator, Amos, shied back a bit.

"What's that?" he demanded.

"You do not look entirely well, sir," I replied, clinging to my soon-to-be-terminated medical ambitions.

"I trust you are under the care of a good physician, for I judge you have the hypolarium, a porous condition of the spleen and the bias."

The man with the shovel stopped digging, and the other men in the posse drew off a bit, looking at their leader in a wary fashion.

"Hypolarium," the chief said, and I saw the light of anxiety flicker in his eyes. "Is that like anthrax?"

"A close cousin, sir," I said. "It's a disease of the abscess which endangers the brain, an ailment of the bowels and larynx. Hypolarium, sir. Allow me to introduce myself: Dr. Axel Beane, diagnostician. Surely you must have noticed you've been feeling poorly lately, sir."

"You were complainin' of your gut this morning, Amos," the whiskey soaker said.

"Gone that far, has it?" I said with a woeful sigh.

"You're no damned doctor," Amos declared, but I saw his resolve to kill me straightaway had been undermined by doubts about his health. "You're too young!"

"My youthful appearance is due to regular dosages of Epsom salts and tea made from fried chicken-gizzard lining steeped in sulfur water. I am in fact twenty-four years old and a recent graduate of the Arkansas Academy of Physical Sciences. My present unprofessional appearance is due to being robbed last night by a pack of scalawags who took my proper vestments and medical bag, leaving me in the poor condition in which you now find me. Had I not cured one of their number of a sad condition of bearitonitis,

118

they might have left me dead on the trail. As it was, their limited gratitude is expressed in these shabby habiliments, this horse, and that young cattalo of mine."

"Talks like a doctor," Hagstrom, the digger, said, and the space around their chief widened.

"Here now, damn you!" Amos protested. "We got business! Those Texians ain't goin' to cross into Oklahoma with anthraxed cattle. Kill this ugly thing and let's get on with it."

I saw then it wasn't me they intended to kill. It was Roselle. The whiskey soaker drew a Navy Colt, and I jerked the Sharps from the saddle scabbard and aimed it in his direction. This stupidity surprised me some, but having done it there was no going back.

"Here, Doc," Amos declared, "there was a whole herd of Texas steers went down with anthrax yesterday, and they aim to drive the survivors across our line, but we ain't having any of that anthrax getting among our stock."

The whiskey soaker now had his pistol aimed at my umbilicus, and he seemed perfectly calm. I was trembling since the Sharps was not loaded, among other things.

I knew there'd been a lot of border fights over diseased cattle, and I could see these settlers meant business. If I was to say I wasn't tempted to let them have Roselle I'd be lying, but she'd cured me the night before, and by now the danged cattalo had gotten to be like kin to me, so I couldn't let her be killed. Not even a little bit.

"Why, sir," I said to Amos, "this young beast is not, as you think, merely a heifer. It is a miracle of medical science, a hybrid of the buffalo and longhorn breeds which carries in its precious blood intoxicants against such foul diseases as smallpox and ringworm. It has come with me clear from Arkansas as a walking pharmacy against illnesses that may assail your wives and children. However, if your territory is closed to the benefits of medical science, I shall turn my back to it and head south. Murder us if such is your kind, but I will not give over this heifer!" Thereupon I pulled my stolen horse around and headed toward the Indian nations with Roselle trotting beside me.

I felt the eyes of that crowd on my back like the sting of hornets and wondered if I'd hear the shot before the bullet struck me, or if I'd be dead before the sound reached my ears. I kicked my horse to a jog and tried to concentrate my vital parts into the smallest possible target. Then I heard a horse galloping down on me, and when I looked around there was the posse chief. He was perspiring, and he looked green. "Say, Doc," he said, "would the blood of that heifer do anything for the hypolarium?"

"Unfortunately not," I replied. "Camomile tea and bed rest is your best chance."

He nodded worriedly and rode along at my side. "I been carrying this onion in my pocket," he said, "and I got a bag of asafetida around my neck." He whipped this article out of his shirt and showed it to me. "But it don't seem to take. Must be because I didn't know what I had."

"That's it, surely," I said.

"I take my tonic regular, which cures most everything, but this hypolarium has got me beat."

"What's your tonic, sir?"

"Half a bucket of rusty nails soaked in vinegar."

"You strain out the nails, I trust."

"Oh, sure. Oughtn't I?"

"Yes, sir. Horseshoe nails in particular. For a quick cure, sir, brandy and red pepper is to be advised."

"Abe Gelsen used that to good effect for the cholera last year."

"Yes, that is good medicine."

"He also cured Vic Ellis of canker, with hog jaw marrow and gunpowder paste, but he died a week later of the dropsy. Gelsen is about the best curin' man we have up our way. He tried me on beef gall and whiskey last month, but it didn't touch this hypolarium. If the boys weren't so dead set against anthrax I'd talk them around to letting you cross, Doc, but you let one get through, and you know how it is."

"I understand, sir."

"It's a big help knowin' what I got, Doc. And I'm sure goin' to try some of that Epsom salts and fried chicken-gizzard lining and sulfur-water tea. No use a man aging faster'n he ought to."

"That's so, sir. The ladies like it, too."

"One thing though, Doc—you should let yourself get to looking some older. It inspires trust, you know what I mean? If you had a mustache it might help."

"I take your point, sir."

"What you do for that is lay a little fresh cream on your top lip and let a black cat lick it off at midnight. It works every time."

"I'll do that at once, sir, and I thank you."

The chief said farewell and fell back to his gang. The last time I saw him, he waved his hat and called his thanks again for my prescription against the hypolarium.

WILD ONION SOUP.

TIM-OO-LEH.

❖This was my first dish under Tim-oo-leh's roof.

❖Two cups sliced wild onions. Four cups condensed milk, diluted. Goat cheese, four spoons. Two spoons of flour. Three egg yolks, whipped. Salt.

❖Fry onions until limp, add flour, milk, goat cheese, and simmer. Add egg yolks slowly and simmer, do not boil. Good!

Squash Blossom Pudding.

TIM-OO-LEH.

❖Remove kernels from three ears of green corn and cook for half an hour. Also boil three cups of squash blossoms and when tender mash to pulp. Mix blossoms into green corn and cook until firm. Salt and devour.

CHAPTER TEN

❖ ❖ ❖

Having propelled myself into the medical profession first crack out of the box, I rode along right proud, but two days later, alone and hungry, I felt a good deal less confident of my medical prowess and would have swapped it for a mess of sweet potatoes. I had made some gooseberry tea and roasted up some bread-root, but I had no condiments, and it was pretty taste-less fodder.

I was figuring how to skirt around and head back toward Enid, but I wasn't sure where the Boardman outfit might be. I decided to stay put a couple of days to let the Circle Six bunch clear north if they could; then I'd pick my way east.

At nightfall I put my campfire out, figuring that if there was trouble along the border the Indians would take advantage of it. One advantage they liked to take, according to everything I'd heard, was to find some stray drover and treat him to some examples of primi-tive surgery while roasting up any stock he had in his possession and stealing his horse.

I had no desire to be scalped and left alive for a joke, as Potter had been. Hence I felt safer without a fire and lay down to sleep with my blanket snugged up close to Roselle and my saddle for a pillow.

Eldon Larkin's Indian-loving tales of how the red man had been plundered and defiled were all right down in Texas, but here among the Indian nations it did me no good to contemplate those injustices that had been wrought on our red brothers. I figured they had some right to be annoyed but not with me. They'd all been shoved onto reservations before my time, and I was not as yet of voting age or I'd have elected to get them out. As it was, I knew there were Poncas, Kickapoos, Cherokees, Creeks, Choctaws, Chickasaws, Kiowas, Comanches, Cheyennes, Sacs, Arapahoes, Seminoles, and others I couldn't remember all roaming around in various states of disharmony, looking for loose cowpokes and cattle to carve up. Me and Roselle fit both categories.

Roselle, of course, wasn't cursed with all this anxiety and slept without care. I wished I was as dumb as she was, but concluded maybe she wasn't so dumb since I was worried about something that had not yet happened. I decided to copy a leaf from Roselle's book. *Tomorrow is soon enough to worry,* I thought.

And I was right, because in the morning it happened . . . that thing about which I was not to worry.

When I woke up an Indian was standing up to his waist in ground fog, floating there like he was packed in cotton. He was staring straight at me, and right then I took a lesson in the art of instant hypnosis and the anesthesia of fear. If someone had stuck a hot poker in my ear, I don't think I would have winced. He was the essence of Indian. The final painkiller. Death.

He didn't move.

I couldn't.

The fog drew off slowly, revealing more of him.

His legs were attached to his feet, which were planted firmly on the ground. Roselle was gazing at him also with no sign of alarm, but what did she know?

I saw first off that this Indian was old and had done a good deal to disguise this fact by decorating his face. His nose was painted carnelian and looked like the bloody beak of a condor. There was a black check mark over his left eye and a yellow half-moon on his right cheek. He had a red, white, and blue turban on his head, which I supposed he'd snatched from General Custer during the Last Stand, and there was a foxtail hanging out behind this. He carried a staff with some crafty devices carved on it and was otherwise dressed in buckskins that had seen better days. One surprise feature was he had a stethoscope around his neck such as Doc Forbisher sported, and I at once wondered about Forbisher's current state of health. This concern for the well-being of others vanished when the heathen took a step in my direction.

Roselle lurched to her feet.

Painful constrictions occasioned by a mixture of terror, poorly digested breadroot, and gooseberry tea ran through my interior. I wanted to rid myself of the whole mess, but all my ports were shut tight.

The heathen hunkered down and gazed intently at me. "Are you ill?" he asked in surprisingly soft-toned English, which made me think he might be judging my edibility.

Having such a question asked in my native tongue shocked me more than a little. I closed my eyes, feigning death as I rambled through my scant stock of Indian lore to see if there was anything in it about white men not being killed by Indians if they were ill. I could not recall such a ruling. On the other hand, I had heard of several whites being killed while in a state of perfect health, so I elected to be ill and take my chances. "Yes," I said. "I am ill."

"Where does it hurt?" he asked.

"All over," I replied, hoping thereby to frighten the superstitious Indian off, as I had done with the sodbuster posse. "It's the bubonic smallpox," I said.

This failed to alarm him. He placed his hand on my forehead, and I shot off two farewell prayers, one for my aunt Clara, the other for Alice Beck—with a codicil for Eldon Larkin, that he croak on James Fenimore Cooper—and commended my portions to God, hoping He could reconstruct me in the hereafter.

After a moment, death having not delivered, I opened one eye and found the red devil testing my heart with his stethoscope. "Say ah," he said.

I did as instructed.

"When did you eat last?"

"Yesterday."

"Breadroot," he said. "You've got sour stomach."

Now I don't know why the mention of sour stomach eliminates apprehensions of imminent death, but I know it does. Tell a murderer on his way to the gallows that he has sour stomach, and he wants something for it right off. Give him a bit of peppermint, put the noose around his neck, and he'll suck his way to glory, believing to the instant of death that he's curing his stomach as though it was apart from him-

128

self. So it was with me. I looked at that painted assassin and said, "I knew something was wrong."

He stood up and beckoned me to rise. I did so feeling much the same as Lazarus must have when Jesus plucked him from the grave.

"My name is Tim-oo-leh," the ancient red man said.

"Dr. Axel Beane," I replied.

He looked at me with a little catch in his eyes as though he'd seen the lie in flight.

I decided to reduce the citation, just in case he was on the local licensing board. "Veterinarian," I amended. "I'm an animal doctor. This here young heifer is my patient. Two days ago she was on her way to extinction, but I pulled her through with sarsaparilla and ipecac."

Tim-oo-leh gazed at me as though there was something missing. He waited for me to supply it, but when I remained silent he set off. "Follow me," he said.

I have never understood the saying "It is as well to be cooked for a goose as for a gander," but it was with this feeling that I hoisted my saddle, took my stolen horse by the bridle, and followed Tim-oo-leh along a creek trail half a mile to a stone-and-log structure set against a hillside and surrounded by brush and trees.

There was a pen with goats and sheep, a chicken coop, a couple of horses in a corral, and a root cellar or steam house, all well concealed from passing tourists. Tim-oo-leh told me to turn Roselle and the horse into the corral and come on in. When I did so, I found the miserable front of the soddy bore no resemblance to the interior, which was a large cave done up fine and dry, with rugs and furs and a variety of furniture no doubt taken in raids from the luckless pioneers. Tim-oo-leh was smashing something in a mortar with a pestle as I entered, and all over the roof of the place were swatches of brush and leaves hung up to dry for kindling, I supposed, but I saw they were labeled by tags with writing on them which I could not make out.

Tim-oo-leh came to me with a mug of some concoction and told me to drink it.

I saw I had come into the den of a poisoner and measured the distance to the door. "What is it?" I countered.

"Gentian," he said. "For your stomach."

Like hemlock was for Socrates, I thought, but he had the heavy pestle in his hand, and given the choice of being pestled or poisoned I chose the mug and drank it off.

If bitterness was a cure, I'd had mine for life. The gentian went into my mouth and came straight out my eyes in two pints of tears. I lowered myself to a bench and waited for the shades of life to pass.

"Hold it down while I get some food and we'll parley," Tim-oo-leh said.

I sat there with my eyes clenched, and after a bit I felt better than I had before, when I didn't know I was sick. And right then I understood how easy it was to go along being unwell and not know it. People tend to forget how good they feel when they're healthy and take illness for a natural condition. I got to feeling so good I judged I must have been sick for several days and not known it.

I opened my eyes and looked at Tim-oo-leh with new respect. He hadn't yet threatened to parboil me, scalp me, shoot me, or do me a single depredation. All he'd done so far was to invite me home and make me well, and now he was setting out a spread of goat's milk, cheese, and corn cake, which when soaked up with blackberry juice made me feel better yet.

"Tim-oo-leh," I said expansively, "you're all right by me."

"Thank you, Dr. Beane," he replied.

What I didn't know then, but found out later, was that I had fallen in with the chief medicine man of the Indian nations. Tim-oo-leh was top of the totem pole, and medicine men from all over came to him for review courses and the latest improvements in the healing arts. His location was kept a secret to avoid interference by Indian agents, soldiers, and other meddlers who wouldn't balk at gulping Hostetter's Bitters (forty-four percent alcohol) or curing the earache with the blood of the bessie bug but who thought Indian medicine was a joke and ought to be stamped out, since it threatened to preserve the red race when the common thesis among whites was that the only good Indian was a dead Indian.

Since I was in no hurry to expose myself to white society I accepted Tim-oo-leh's offer of hospitality as a courtesy of our mutual profession. In exchange I offered to teach him what I could of the white man's medicine, such as the cure for warts, which I got from Buck Hodfelt, who was afflicted on the nose, to wit:

Take a limb from a peach tree and cut a notch in it for each wart that afflicts you. Touch each wart with each notch, then bury the limb under the peach tree. When it rots the warts will disappear.

"When which rots?" Tim-oo-leh asked me. "The tree or the branch?"

I hadn't a clue. "The branch," I said.

"Does it work?" Tim-oo-leh asked me.

"I don't know. The branch hasn't rotted yet."

Of such cures as these Tim-oo-leh's opinions ranked from indulgent amusement to scorn. I gave him the cure for nosebleed, which I got from Sally Carter, who also had freckles: Stand with your back to a mulberry tree and measure your height against the trunk. Bore a hole in the tree where your head touches. Cut off a lock of hair and put it in the hole, then drive a rusty nail into it.

I never saw Sally Carter have a nosebleed, so I was confident this worked, but she was always scrubbing her face with buttermilk and cucumbers to get rid of her freckles. She'd still had them when I left Odessa, so I didn't put much stock in that cure and didn't waste Tim-oo-leh's time with it.

To understand the labels on all the brush Tim-oo-leh had hanging around the place I had to learn the Cherokee alphabet, which, if you've never seen it, is an odd set of crooky-looking letters that makes you think of witches and devils right off. But it works as well as our alphabet, which also gives the wim-wams to some, now that I think of it—to beginning readers, for instance. The Cherokee alphabet was invented by

Sequoia, a Cherokee who left the reservation and died in Mexico out of spite.

Tim-oo-leh explained to me how the tribes of the Indian nations had originally come from different places, from Florida, Georgia, Alabama, Mississippi, and so forth, which made a medical problem for them inasmuch as the shrubs and stuff they'd used to cure themselves in those places often did not grow here.

Tim-oo-leh had spent his whole life gathering, testing, and labeling as to their curative functions all the twigs and leaves I saw hanging from the rafters. Some of the stuff, he confessed, was imported from other parts of the country. Virginia snakeroot, for instance, comes from Virginia. With Texas snakeroot not having, in Tim-oo-leh's opinion, the curative potency of the eastern variety, he preferred not to use the local stuff except in emergencies. Both are good as a mild stomachic, to raise the pulse, to cure putrid dispositions of the humors, and, as the name clearly indicates even in Cherokee, for snakebite.

One of the first things I learned about plants was that if you know their names you have a pretty fair idea what they're useful for. Snakeroot, as I've said, is for snakebite. Lungwort is good for the lungs, and bloodroot is good for bleeding, just as we in the white world know liverwurst is good for the liver. Of course, in the wild these plants don't go around with their names tacked up on a placard, but since I eventually made trips all over the countryside with Tim-oo-leh collecting leaves and brush and bark and seeds, I got to know the names of most of them pretty good.

133

Each plant has its signature and its sign, Tim-oo-leh told me. "By shape, or by color, like cures like. Red plants are good for the blood. Yellow for the jaundice. Look and you will see."

Well, that peeled my eyes! After that, when I got off into the hills collecting I'd see cures for diseases I didn't even know existed. There was fungus for canker and the scabies, lobelia for the lobes, prickly ash for the pricklies, hops for the nerves, pokeweed for the pokes, and so forth. Walking through the woods was like walking through a hospital ward full of terminal patients. There was death and blood and disease on every side, but I steeled myself to it, as you must do if you're going to be a doctor.

As I got deeper into it, of course, I found there were exceptions to the laws of common sense. You would think dogwood was for the dogs, but in this you would be mistaken. Dogwood bark is good for worms, malaria, and pains in the legs. If you thought boneset was for setting bones you would be wrong; it is made into tea for fits and the ague. Bearberry isn't for bears, just as elderberry isn't for the elders and butterfly weed isn't for curing butterflies. But these exceptions are what you hire a doctor for. He knows, so put your trust in him.

There is also, after gathering all this bark and foliage, the process of preparing it for use. You can't just run off into the woods and snap your teeth into the first thing that looks suitable for what ails you. Don't do it! You go out and eat a patch of fleabane to rid yourself of fleas, and it's like to kill you. That's not the way it's used for fleas. You dry it and burn it and the smoke gets the fleas, or you make it into tea for the gout. That again is what the doctor is for, to prepare all this flora into its proper form and dosage. Some of it is dried, some is pounded, and some is mixed with others, and Tim-oo-leh taught all this to me.

At night we'd sit before the fire talking and lacerating leaves and twigs and seeds and grass and mixing them with fat for salves, or steeping them in pots and putting the result in bottles for curing other complaints like whooping cough, sciatica, and tetters. To say my knowledge of medicine improved a hundredfold would be mild. Why, with all I'd learned, I could have given that posse of Oklahoma sodbusters diseases twice as bad as the hypolarium, and we hadn't yet even started on the drums, rattles, and chants!

Having discovered Tim-oo-leh revised my opinion of the professional red man. I was proud to count him among my medical colleagues and determined to teach him as much as his native intelligence could absorb.

GOLDEN GRIDDLE CAKES.

TIM-OO-LEH.

❖Heat the griddle. Combine dry ingredients, one cup ground lamb's-quarter seeds, one cup dark flour, three spoons sugar, pinch salt, spoon of baking powder. Mix. Add slowly two cups condensed milk, diluted, two eggs, bacon drippings.

❖Spit on griddle. If it spits back, it's ready.

Dandelion Root Coffee.

TIM-OO-LEH.

❖Skin and dry the dandelion roots until brittle. Grind them. Use one spoon dried ground root per cup water. Boil three minutes, strain, and drink with condensed milk and sugar.

CHAPTER ELEVEN

❖ ❖ ❖

About twice a week Tim-oo-leh would fire up the steam house, and we'd strip to the buff and sweat out our impurities, except for those we were born with. When we'd about stewed ourselves to extinction, Tim-oo-leh would bound up and make a dash for the creek. The first time this happened I followed him, thinking the place had caught fire. I plunged into the water and shrank a size and a half from the cold. My heart bucked up in my mouth like it wanted a new home, and I gave a whoop that nearly let it out to find one. Later I got better at it, but one day we had to break ice to reach the water, which alerted me to the passage of time. I'd been so intent on my studies I'd lost track of it, and Roselle had sprouted horns.

"Say," I said to Tim-oo-leh, "I think I've over-stayed my welcome."

"No," he said to me, "you stay now until the annual meeting."

"Of what?" I asked him.

"Of the Medicine Men's Society," he said. "You will be the honored speaker and tell us of the white man's cures."

I reminded him I was a simple veterinarian, not a medical doctor.

"I know this well," Tim-oo-leh said in his measured way, "but the Chickasaws have been troubled by coccidiosis and want to consult with you about its prevention."

Coccidiosis? I couldn't say the word, much less prevent it. It had to be worse than the hypolarium, but it was far beyond my ken. If the Chickasaws had it I didn't want any, but I couldn't confess my ignorance after all I'd taught Tim-oo-leh, who by now had grown reliant on me.

I tried to dredge up something to say about the prevention of the what's-its-name, but unless you're a politician it's hard to compose a speech when you don't know what the subject matter is. I came up with a short address for the Medicine Men's Society, so short I figured Tim-oo-leh would be justified in presenting me with a bill for grub and lodging and mortaring and pestling me besides.

By this time Roselle had got so sociable she came in some nights to enjoy the warmth of the fire. I rehearsed her in the tricks Alice Beck had taught her, and Tim-oo-leh was impressed. He came to regard Roselle as one of us and taught me how all living things are part of the whole of life and one form was no better than another and each had a purpose. I was inclined to agree with this as a general thesis but took it with a grain of pipsissewa insofar as snakes and spiders were concerned.

We worked some with chants, rattles, and drums, which Roselle cottoned to, prancing around and shaking her bearded head. Chanting, dancing, and drumming was mostly bunkum, Tim-oo-leh told me, but bunkum was often good medicine, and you had to do it right. The trick was to get a hold on the patient's

140

mind and make him think himself well. I knew what he meant, but I never got the hang of the drums and decided to call in a specialist for that sort of thing.

As the time rolled around for the annual meeting of medicine men I knew I had to leave to avoid making a big fool of myself and perhaps losing my hair to Indians less fond of me than Tim-oo-leh. I figured also that Mr. Boardman had delivered the herd to Wichita, and all that beef was decorating the plates of carnivores back east. By now my disappearance, or death, had been reported to Aunt Clara, who had probably married Eldon Larkin for consolation since he was always hanging around her with that intent in mind. Also I had to deliver Roselle to Enid, as I had contracted to do.

Having justified my plan to depart, I sought a chance to do so. We usually broke our fast with herbivorous omelettes both delicious and therapeutic, and one morning, seeking a chance to make my getaway, I mentioned we were short of jalap and yarrow and volunteered to go out and rustle some.

"They don't grow here," Tim-oo-leh said.

"Well, we could use some nightshade and mint."

"Wrong season," he said. "You get those in the spring."

I began to see skipping out was not going to be so easy to arrange. When we finished breakfast I began mortaring some jopi root for the typhoid. Then Tim-oo-leh announced he had to make a house call on the Kiowas and would be gone three days.

Here, I said to myself, *is an example of the thought fathering the cure.* We had been delving into some of

the deeper aspects of the profession the night before, and Tim-oo-leh had a theory that the faith of
the patient has as much to do with his recovery as the
medicine he consumes. To inspire this faith was the
medicine man's principal duty. One has to pray
the patient well, just as I had prayed for a way to
skedaddle, and Tim-oo-leh came up with the Kiowas.
I was amazed by how powerful even unspoken suggestion can be.

When he was ready to go, Tim-oo-leh, wearing his
fox-tailed turban and stethoscope, told me to make
free with the house and grub and that he'd be back in
three days. He turned his paint horse down the creek
trail and waved to me with his magic staff. When he'd
disappeared I shut the door and began to inventory
what I would steal.

Thievery was no longer second nature to me, it was
first. I'd stolen horses and a rifle and the trust of my
trailmates and come so far down the moral ladder that
my conscience didn't even twinge. Had it done so I'd
have chewed a couple of jimson weed seeds, which
have the effect of erasing scruples. I packed up a good
selection of curative herbs, salves, powders, and po-
tions, figuring since I'd helped make them I had a
right to a share. I outfitted myself in the best-looking
weasel-skin shirt I had ever seen and a set of deerskin
britches and moccasins. I boxed some grub and stole a
packsaddle for Roselle, who'd gotten so fat and affectionate I decided the time had come for her to start
earning her keep by hauling a load. I lashed a couple
of blankets and a buffalo robe to my stolen horse,

then sat down to write Tim-oo-leh a letter of resignation, to wit:

O great brother Tim-oo-leh,

As you have been robbed and cheated by every white man you ever knew, driven from your promised lands, bereft of your home and property, violated by treaty, captured or shot while bearing flags of truce, so now it will come as no surprise to find me gone with half your valuables. Since you did not kill me long ago when you found me defenseless on the ground, I know you have a forgiving heart. Had I been in your moccasins, knowing me as I do, I would have killed me. What stopped you then from killing me was your devotion to the healing arts, which is likewise what stops me now from killing myself and also because I am a coward. There are no herbs for that. Besides all this I am not even a veturinaryan, which I can't even spell in English, or Cherokee, and I don't know what it is that the Chickasaws got or how to cure it. I set out to be a doctor by assertion, and I will continue in that direction with little hope of success. Meantime I thank you for the grub and shelter and all the wood lore and such. May the Great Spirit increase your wampum.

Your treacherous friend,
Wylie Jackson alias

Dr. Axel Beane, (fake)
apprentice medicine man

*P.S. If I find out anything about what disease
the Chickasaws have I'll come back and let
you know. Please don't shoot.*

I put the note on the table, and when I was sure
Tim-oo-leh had cleared off far enough so I wouldn't
run into him, I boarded my stolen horse and set out
in the direction of Enid.

I cut southeast, intending to intersect the Chisholm
Trail and maybe pick up some company for the trip,
though the season was late for driving cattle, and my
Indian duds were likely to get me shot unless I could
raise a peace sign in quick order. There was frost on
the ground and the scent of snow in the air, but I
took this for a good sign since it would kill the anthrax and other dread diseases that thrive in warm
weather.

Roselle trotted along beside me on a lead rope,
which she didn't need since Alice Beck's drawers were
still her main directional guide. She had been spoiled
by our sojourn with Tim-oo-leh. She craved affection
and would sit down in the middle of the trail, packsaddle and all, and grumble if she didn't get it. She
was leggy now and a powerful spurt runner, but she
couldn't sustain the gallop of a horse, which annoyed
her some. She hated being outrun, and my telling her
it was the nature of the beast didn't satisfy her ad-
vanced opinion of herself. "You'll just have to make
do with what you've got," I said to her.

144

"Baaw!" she said.

"Baaw yourself."

She cast me a look of soulful irritation, which was her customary rejoinder in our conversations, and baawed again, since she always wanted the last word.

A day later we crossed the Chisholm Trail, but there was no traffic, just the frozen hoofprints of cattle that by now had gone to their doom. The sky was marbled with high clouds and the country was flat as far as I could see, but sometimes way off I'd spot smoke rising from some poor sodbuster's spread.

Along toward nightfall I saw the lights of a distant town, and it gave me a curious feeling to be approaching so-called civilization again. I'd been away too long, and life had been quiet and sensible with Tim-oo-leh. I missed him, and for two pins I'd have gone back and thrown myself on his mercy. I felt pretty low about how I'd treated him and was tempted to take a couple of jimson weed seeds.

Closer to the lights we struck a road, the first I'd seen in some time. It was rutted and potholed and littered with signs advertising such things as Gilbert and Parsons Hygienic Whiskey. I learned from a smaller sign that the town was Beaver City, now in Major County, Oklahoma. It was four miles off. I'd covered half the distance when I heard coming toward me what sounded like a wagonload of howling catamounts. Roselle was the first to take notice and abandon the road, which suit I followed on my stolen horse.

The sound came on, horribly. *Rattle! Bang!* Horses' hooves. Epithets. Cries of outrage and pain.

Boring into the gloom, I could see the source, a four-wheeled drummer's rig hauled by a galloping nag, pursued by an irate man on horseback flailing away with what I took to be a concho belt such as the Navajos wear.

"Money back!" I heard the drummer yelling. "You have my guarantee!"

"Money back be damned!" roared the flailer, and he hit the rig a lick with the belt that sent wood chips flying.

The rig veered and sideswiped a signboard for Bogle's Hyperion Fluid, then ricocheted across the road and struck a sign for Sparkies Nerve Food. It was being shaken to pieces in the potholes and ruts, and I saw a sign painted on the side of it: Dr. Majul Majul's Electric Belts.

"Mercy!" the drummer yelped as this paraphernalia passed me. He was immensely fat and swarthy, and his voice twanged with terror. He covered his head as the flailer continued battering him with the belt.

"I have returned your money!" the drummer wailed; then the front wheel of the rig let go and the vehicle did a somerset off the road. Dr. Majul was propelled outward over the mud bumper onto the pasture. His nag broke loose and ran off in terror, dragging the broken wagon shafts behind it. The customer reined back and danced his horse around Dr. Majul's prostrate body, continuing to lash at it with the belt. "Money back!" he screeched. "What about my generative organ?"

"Time will heal!" Dr. Majul cried, cowering and protecting his head from vicious cuts of the belt.

"It has about vanished!" the customer howled. "It is the laughingstock of six counties!"

With an expiring screech and an apoplectic shudder, the drummer threw his arms up and fell back, perfectly still.

The customer, a mean-looking individual with a red beard, continued striking at Dr. Majul with the belt. He tried to make his horse trample the corpse, but the beast wouldn't do it, so the man threw the belt down at the bloody head, aimed his horse for Beaver City, and galloped away.

When he was out of sight I rode over to see what medicine I could make of the drummer's remains. I knew that a rope taken from the neck of a hanged man was good for a sore throat, so I figured clothing stripped from this victim might be a specific against buggy wreck.

The drummer's head was bleeding profusely and was badly lacerated. His complexion was that of someone who had been washed in a spittoon. His nose was broken, and there wasn't enough hair on his head to tempt an Indian. I considered saving him for anatomical research but decided he was too fat to move.

I was loosening his collar when he opened one eye. "Is he gone?" he whispered anxiously.

"I thought you were," I said.

"Not yet," he said, and he sat up and commenced to test himself for broken bones. "Dr. Majul Majul at your service," he said to me while scrubbing blood from his nose and head with a dirty rag hauled from his hip pocket.

"Beane," I said.

"What tribe you with, lad?" he asked.

With my costume and in the dark, I didn't blame him for mistaking me for an aborigine, but I didn't want to slander my recent benefactor's race by pretending to be one of it. "I just borrowed these duds in the Indian nations," I explained.

"Welcome, Beane," Dr. Majul said. "We are brothers."

I let this go since I saw he was jarred out of his right mind. He rose and tested his nether extremities. Satisfied that these were whole, he suggested I locate his nag while he righted the wagon and tried to fit the wheel to the axle. I decided the Samaritan thing to do was to set the crazy fool on the road again, so I went in search of his horse. When I found it and returned, Majul had the wagon propped up and was fitting the wheel.

"You'll have to splint these shafts," I said.

"You'll find tools in the rear, lad," he said, looking anxiously in the direction of town. "I'll reward you for the trouble, but I'd like to move along before I'm found missing."

I took his point. If that customer returned with the undertaker and found Dr. Majul Majul gone, he'd likely come on to kill him again.

In the rear of the wagon, among a jumble of batteries and other electrical junk, I found a hammer, a saw, nails, and some boards. I set to work mending the shafts so they'd draw until he reached another town for proper repairs. When he was hooked up and ready to go, Dr. Majul begged me to accompany him. "I am in your debt, sir. You cannot leave me until I repay it."

This struck me as a peculiar form of enslavement, and I countered firmly. "My help is under the heading of Christian charity, sir," I replied. "You owe me nothing."

"But I am not a Christian, sir! You imperil my soul if you do not let me repay you. Please, sir. Ride along with me until I decide what must be done. Sit up beside me and let your animals trail along. Please, sir, I implore you."

I took pity on him and attached my stolen horse to his rig, remembering that town life held risks of apprehension for me also. On the theory that medical men must stand together against the ignorance of the world, I sat up next to Dr. Majul Majul, and we set out.

MASOOR DAL.

MAJUL MAJUL.

❖I got this dish by observation. I judged Majul Majul's pinches to be about a quarter tablespoon. I never saw a man eat so well out of sacks, a variety of tin boxes, and two cooking pots. It went something like this.

❖Boil a quart of water. Wash a cup of yellow split peas. Add salt and peas to water. Let water rise to boil, then cover pot and simmer until peas are soft. Add to this a pinch each of turmeric, cayenne, ground cumin, ground coriander, and chopped gingerroot. Mix well and remove from heat. Heat oil in the second pot. Add a pinch of mustard seeds and when they pop add one dried red chili pepper, seeded and chopped.

❖Into this now smoking cauldron pitch the peas; there will be a sound like a cow backfiring. This is to be expected. Cover the pot and let stand so the spices set in. Make rice in first pot, or if there is some left over, warm it up. Throw the dal over the rice and consume. It is a dandy surprise.

CHAPTER TWELVE

❖ ❖ ❖

As we put distance between ourselves and Beaver City the night grew cold and the stars crackled. Dr. Majul Majul pulled a robe around our knees, and his nag plodded along mindlessly in the direction chosen for it.

Dr. Majul Majul was telling me about a man in St. Louis who had sold him faulty batteries for his electric belts and how his business had been ruined as a result, but his accent was so peculiar I couldn't understand half of what he said. He spoke in a singsong whine, not exactly unpleasant, but hard for me to decipher, and at last I asked where he was from.

"I'm a Sikh Hindu from the Punjab," he replied.

"When we stop I'll dose you with pipsissewa and you'll sweat it right out," I said.

"Punjab is a place," he said.

"I'll make a poultice for it."

"In India," he said.

I was formulating how to pestle pipsissewa into a poultice for the Punjab when I remembered from geography that India was a country below China on the map. I put this to Dr. Majul Majul, who averred it was so.

"Then you're an India Indian," I said.

"Indelibly," Dr. Majul Majul confirmed.

"You're way off the reservation," I said. "How come?"

In response to this Dr. Majul Majul proceeded to tell me he was a missionary doctor sent to America to persuade Americans to forsake killing and eating cows.

"I incline that way myself," I said, "but you've got a long row to hoc."

"However that may be, I am a believer in ahimsa, the doctrine that all life is sacred and the cow in particular."

"How so?"

"Why, the cow voluntarily yields nourishment to man and aids him in his daily labor! For this should she be killed?"

"It is unjust," I agreed.

"She is furthermore sacred to Krishna, who rose to Go-loka, or the cow-world, as his heavenly abode!" Majul Majul exclaimed, and he pointed to the sky.

I looked upward, half expecting to see heavenly cows among the stars.

"She is the cow of plenty," Majul Majul continued, "the Kamadhenu; the earth cow, sacred to the sage Vasishtha. No good Hindu is allowed to shed the blood of an ox or to muzzle them while they are in the corn or to interfere in any way with their movements. Sikhs also are so inclined. Yet in your country what do we find? Heathen disregard for the rights of cattle!"

"True!" I affirmed.

"They are slaughtered without discrimination and devoured wholesale," Majul Majul cried, half rising from the seat in his agitation and bouncing down again. "They are herded out of their natural habitat and shunted to the canneries. Their flesh is displayed to public view in butcher-shop windows, carved and hewn within the tender gaze of babes. How can Americans grow up to be other than a bloodthirsty race when their childhood is flavored by sights of cows being chopped and sliced, broiled, boiled, roasted, fried, jerked, minced, flayed, and dee-voured! Is this not a stench in the nostrils of the world?"

"It is," I agreed.

"Can a race of men who conduct themselves in such a heathen manner prosper or matriculate?"

"They cannot," I said, for he was playing the keys of my philosophical disposition, and I was singing his tune. "Nay! Nay, they cannot!" I repeated heartily.

"We must stamp out this traffic! We must learn to venerate our benefactor the cow."

"Give them the vote, I say! Bulls too!"

"Baaw!" Roselle said.

"Nay," the Gospeler's horse objected.

Majul Majul warmed to his subject, and we shared the heat. "Hath not a cow eyes?" he asked. "Hath not a cow feet, organs, dimensions, senses, affections, passions?"

"True, oh, true!" I seconded. "They have all that."

"O Krishna! Visit thy enlightenment on America! Let thy message sweep the nation! Come to us, O Krishna, let us see thy visage!"

"Hold on, Majul," I cried, for he was in danger of falling into an ecstatic trance and driving us off the road. "I take your meaning and agree with your cause, and I am pleased to know there is a heaven in your tradition for Roselle. We will baptize into your sect at

155

the first opportunity; meantime we'd better hold our course before your recent killer comes back with a posse to bury your absent remains."

Majul Majul saw the wisdom of this and settled down. We jogged along at a good pace and M. Majul told me how he'd come to the present pass.

To support his religious endeavors on behalf of the cow, he had invented and hawked by mail the Majul Majul Electric Belt for three dollars and sixty-five cents, plus postage. Having sold several gross of these items in Oklahoma, he decided to visit his customers, hoping that additional sales of belts and replacement batteries would result when the curative powers of the Majul Majul Electric Belt were proclaimed to others by those in possession of them. The result of his first customer contact I had witnessed.

"It was leaky batteries!" M.M. moaned. "Corrosive acid seeped from the belts onto the purchasers' amative parts as they slept. I shudder to imagine the consequences."

"What was the belt supposed to cure?" I asked.

"Rheumatism, sciatica, catarrh, asthma, neuralgia, dyspepsia, constipation, heart trouble, paralysis, spinal disease, nervousness, varicocele—"

"What's that last?" I asked.

"Dilation of the spermatic veins."

"Oh, for a minute there I thought it was something the Chickasaws got. Go on."

"Torpid liver, throat trouble, kidney complaints, lost vigor, cold extremities, female complaints, sleeplessness, and all pains in the back and limbs."

"That's a healthy set of cures," I said.

"I wear one myself," Majul Majul said. He rapped his midriff with the butt of the buggy whip, and it sounded like someone had slammed the lid on a piano bench.

"And you've got none of those complaints," I said.

"Not a one."

Well, here was a big addition to my medical knowledge, but after seeing the first customer's attempt to murder Majul Majul, I thought I'd better have a demonstration of the belt before I put it to the tribes.

"Now I am ruined!" Majul M. groaned, and he slumped down like a gut-shot bison. "I had hoped to support myself in this way while proselytizing in the cause of the cow, but karma has decreed otherwise."

"Proselytizing is a disease with which I am not familiar," I said.

"You are a good candidate for such work, Dr. Beane," Majul Majul said, surveying my face. "You are ethereal."

"I have yet to use it," I said, "but they say it's better than chloroform."

The next closest town was Cleo Springs, so we camped in a glade beside the Washita River that night. When I got the fire started, Dr. M.M. began to groan and drub his head with his fists. "What's to become of me now?" he moaned in a fresh outburst of grief. "O Indra, why hast thou forsaken me?"

I saw he was in a bad way and was about to offer him some jimson weed seeds, but he hauled a bottle of Parker's Tonic (forty percent alcohol) from his coat pocket and consumed half of it to augment the power of his electric belt. "What, what is to become of me?" he whinnied again.

"Well," I said, "if I was in your moccasins, I'd sure paint the name off this rig, first thing. Second, I'd change my name, and third, I'd visit the towns where you sold those electric belts with a remedy for battery acid burns of the generative organs. Those who have suffered from such an ailment are sure to buy any cure which offers relief, and they will recommend it to others who wish to take precautions against the horrors of such an affliction."

"Ecumenical!" Dr. Majul Majul cried, and he bounded up like his trousers were afire. "Nonpareil!" he ripped, at which Roselle sat straight down on her haunches and bawled.

"The saintly beast approves our plan!" Majul Majul cried, pointing to the chin-whiskered heifer. "Young sir, you have saved my sacred mission! Krishna and the cattle bless you! I see by your frequent references to the flora that you have knowledge of medicinal plants. What specific, if any, would you suggest for acid burns of the generative organs?"

"A combination of basswood bark and the leaves of the prairie dock are pretty good on burns," I said.

Dr. Majul Majul seized my hand and wrung it. "Sir, I implore you, for the sake of those unfortunates afflicted with the corrosion caused by that unscrupulous battery merchant in St. Louis, to join me in this mission of mercy. If you can concoct such a cure, it should go down at two dollars a bottle."

"I get half," I said.

"Less expenses."

"That seems fair."

So we shook hands on it, and Dr. Majul Majul set about preparing our dinner of split beans and condiments, which concoction I suspected of being lethal until I tasted it. It was warming to the inner man and delicious. After this we turned in and slept in benign confidence of awakening.

The next day, while I stripped bark from the local basswood trees and pestled prairie dock, Dr. Majul went to Cleo Springs for paint to hide the evidence of his past crimes, bottles for our cure, and labels for the bottles. He took my horse and I warned him to leave the beast outside of town in case one of the Gospelers happened to be there. He seemed to understand my meaning.

Before Majul Majul left he buried his electric belt paraphernalia, but he insisted on wearing his own, which, he said, had higher-quality batteries than those he'd supplied his clients. He was addicted to the titillating current flowing over his torso and could not give it up, he said. Whenever he took it off he fell ill with one thing or another, which showed me again the power of the human mind over illness. M. Majul promised to come up with a new name for himself, one for our cure, and one for me too if I felt I needed it. I said I'd figure my own name if he didn't mind, but asked him to check around to see if a Mr. Boardman had been heard of in that vicinity, or anyone from Odessa, Texas.

After Majul left, Roselle was particularly frisky, but I think she'd begun to miss the diet to which Tim-oo-leh had treated her. It takes a lot of fodder to keep an animal operational, especially one growing as fast as Roselle.

As I stewed up a mess of basswood bark she kept stalking around watching me with an expression in her eyes much as to say: *Now see here, there's certain messes as to which I draw the line, mashed bark being one of them.*

"Roselle," I said, "this is for the human constitution. When we get to town I'll feed you up fine on alfalfa hay and shucked corn, and we'll load enough in the rig to give you a feeling of confidence that your vittles are not in jeopardy. Meantime, chaw grass."

"Baw, mo!" she grumbled, and she set about nibbling the grass around the base of the trees.

"Sit!" I commanded, and she sat.

"Come!" I said, and she trotted to me.

"Lie down and roll over."

Roselle obeyed with an exasperated sigh. I dismissed her, and she resumed grazing.

But the thing about this was that Alice Beck's drawers were still in my saddlebag and had gone with Majul Majul to Cleo Springs. Roselle had not followed them, and she had not missed them when they were gone.

"You're weaned of Alice Beck's drawers!" I called to Roselle.

She looked up at me, puzzled, as though she too sensed the transformation. Then she tossed her head and continued stoking grass.

I got to wondering if I ought to mark Roselle in some way in case she got lost, but the idea of putting a red-hot branding iron to her hide didn't appeal to me.

When you think about how most calves are treated in their formative months it's no wonder they don't make a play of intelligence for the human kind. I reckon if you took a dog pup, threw a rope around his neck and jerked him off his feet, tied his legs together and hit him with a red-hot iron, castrated him, and doused him with disinfectant, you would have something less than man's best friend as a result. I doubt any dog would hang around for a second helping if he could get away. I don't see him greeting mankind with pleasure or fetching its slippers. I was inclined to think that a dog treated thus would sulk and play dumb and might, given a fair chance, kick you silly.

I was further of the opinion that cattle are no dumber than dogs at the outset, but having been brutalized in their early stages they choose to limit their contact with humanity as much as they can. All the humans I have known would also balk at such treatment. I know I would. My objections would be strenuous. Such treatment would very likely stunt my intelligence. Having suffered it, I would be as distrustful of humankind as an Indian is of a congressman.

I decided to get a bell for Roselle, a painless, more humane, and melodious way to identify her.

Dr. Majul Majul turned up about two o'clock with a can of black paint. He was some the worse for having dosed himself with Gilbert and Parsons Hygienic Whiskey and with Peruna (twenty-eight percent alcohol). He began slopping paint on the rig to erase his previous identity. "We'll have a thousand labels by tomorrow morning," he said convivially.

"That's a thousand dollars apiece," I said, to let him know I had a business head on my neck.

"Less expenses."

"Which, so far, is for bottles and labels."

"Paint and entertainment."

"What entertainment?"

"Why," he said, "I had to gather a few gentlemen of the town to announce our product and get the word in circulation. People are clamoring for our product already. The demand is high."

"The demand for what?" I inquired.

Majul Majul interrupted his painting and looked at me with a puffed-up expression. "Why, for the Budge Budge Acid Burn Cure and Hair Restorative!" he declaimed.

There are some inspirations achieved under the influence of Hygienic Whiskey that don't bear repeating and Budge Budge Acid Burn Cure and Hair Restorative was one of these. I supposed it stacked up fair to Kickapoo Indian Sagwa or Nez Perce Catarrh Snuff, but I wished Majul Majul had given more thought to the name of our product before he spread it around town. Considering that the cure was aimed for the amative organs, the title seemed too specific to me. I would have chosen something like Syrup of Salza De Angelis, if that one had not already been taken. That name had a soothing sound, plus you could buy it without revealing exactly what your ailment was, and in mixed company too.

"Why hair restorative?" I asked. "Basswood bark and prairie dock are of no use to the follicles."

"Here, lad! I polled the bald while in Cleo Springs, and there are many such. The art of medicine is that the cure should catch all. Had I seen a predominance of rheumatism among the populace I would have called our cure the Budge Budge Acid Burn Cure and Rheumatism Reliever. In our trade it is wise to have more than one string to your bow."

I had never seen a bow with two strings and was certain such a rig would only confuse the flight of an arrow. "I expect those labels are already on the press," I said.

"Indeed so," Majul replied. "The printer offered to include a cut of a burning schoolhouse at no extra charge, and he's using red ink."

The connection between a blazing schoolhouse and acid burns of the generative organs was a distant one to my mind, but the deed was done, and I wasn't about to cut into my profits by demanding other names or illustrations. Such are the joys of partnership.

"We are fortunate in several respects," Majul enjoined. "A recent schoolhouse fire nearly claimed several young lives, so the community is acutely conscious of burns and seeking remedies for them. Also there is a trial of multiple murderer, Carl Merkle, in progress, with the prospect of a hanging three days hence. This has drawn the population from far and wide, so we're reasonably certain of covering our costs. Are you sure the stuff will work?"

"I make no guarantee about the hair restorative part," I said, and I returned to pestling prairie dock.

When the black paint on the rig was pretty dry, Majul scribed his new appellation on the side with white chalk. The name, as I made it out, was Dr. Dadu Budge Budge, Burns Specialist.

"When the black is dry I'll lay that on in red," Majul said, surveying his handiwork with bleary appreciation.

"See here, Majul Majul," I asked him, "what is the Indian fascination with double names?"

Majul sat down on a log and took a gulp of Peruna. "Why," he said, "this is a common thing in the Punjab. The name Majul Majul is famous in my father's homeland for oratory and great religious conviction."

"Here it is famous for electric belts," I reminded him.

Majul nodded bleakly. "I took the name Dadu from the town where my Hindu mother was born, on the Hooghly River below Calcutta. Budge is a hamlet in the Punjab where my Sikh father was born. I have embraced both faiths so as not to slight my father or my dear mother. Hence this name, Dadu Budge Budge."

"May I make a suggestion that will cut your task of painting that rig by half?"

He nodded around the Peruna spout.

"Why not make it Dr. Dad Budge, Burns Specialist?"

Majul Majul fought my suggestion for half an hour, but finally the Peruna ate into his resolve and he gave over.

"But I introduced myself all over Cleo Springs as Dr. Budge Budge," he objected.

"I'll tell them you stutter when sober," I said.

I rendered my kettle of basswood bark and prairie dock down to a concentrate and put it in an empty five-gallon jug that had previously contained Hygienic Whiskey.

Majul, meantime, completed his paint job on the rig. By then the Peruna had blurred his vision, so it came out Dr. Dad Budge Burns, Specialist.

Having accomplished this, Dad Burns warmed up the leftover rice and dal, and we ate it. Then he rolled up in a buffalo robe and began to alarm the night-creeping animals with his snores.

BLUE LIGHTNING CHILI CON CARNE.

CLEO SPRINGS.

❖Buy six wind-broke, used-up, runty steers often delivered at night by the Hardesty-Clanton gang. Stun, drain, skin, and gut as for Porterhouse Steak. Dice the steers to one-inch cubes except for intestines and organs, which will be sold to the jail cooks at Fort Smith. Barbecue the beef until well done.

❖Into commercial vats of suitable size pour three tons of washed kidney beans. Add a ton of canned or fresh tomatoes as available. Add a four-pound sack of salt, a ten-pound sack of red chili powder, four pounds of cumin, five gallons of molasses, and one bay leaf. Mix the cooked steer meat into the beans etc. Cover and let simmer three days. Can in five-pound tins and label. This product is nearly always found in chuck wagon larders as a direct test of the manhood of drovers in the cattle states.

❖What they called it I cannot repeat.

CHAPTER THIRTEEN

❖ ❖ ❖

In the morning I decided to release my stolen horse in case it might be recognized by someone in Cleo Springs and lead to my arrest. I threw my saddle and the Sharps into the rig and composed a note, which I attached to the Gospeler's horse's halter.

> *To whom it may concern,*
>
> *This horse was stolen from one of the Gospelers riding with the OHO outfit out of Texas—Matthew, Mark, Luke, or John. They would be happy to get it back, no questions asked.*
>
> *Yours truly,*
> *A repentant thief*

I tied this to the bridle, headed the horse north, and gave him a smart swat. He cantered away, quite surprised, but as I was boarding the rig with Dad Burns the horse came back. I had to smack him and head him off again. He went quite a distance this time, and I supposed he'd gotten the idea he was not wanted. But as we reached the road that fool horse came out of the brush and fell in behind us, looking sorrowful and unjustly accused. I threw stones at him and yelled a choice set of epithets, but he continued following us at a distance. "Git!" I yelled. "Go on!

Get yourself found. I'm done with you. Head for the stable."

I could have hobbled him or tied him to a tree, but I was afraid he might starve before someone located him. At last I insulted him enough so he got the message and ambled away.

Dad Burns put leather to his nag and we were off, Roselle trotting along beside the rig shaking her head as though commenting on the faithlessness of human-kind.

I was nervous about entering Cleo Springs, imagin-ing I would be recognized and apprehended for my past crimes. I mentioned this concern to Dad Burns, who rectified the situation at once. He dragged a length of blue cloth from the rear of the rig and told me to wrap it around my head for a turban. "From now on you are Fasli Akbar," he said.

"Sounds like a skin disease!" I objected.

"It is a respectable Muslim name," Dad Burns said. "And it will broaden our appeal to other varieties of religious persuasion while we're here."

"There are no Muslims in Cleo Springs," I said.

"Good. Then they will have no comparison by which to judge whether or not you are the real thing."

Like fool's gold, there was a glitter of reason in most things Dad Burns said, so I decided to ride along as Fasli Akbar until we sold the cure and I could buy a horse and skin out for Enid with Roselle.

Cleo Springs was a rectangular affair of mostly empty building lots. The town had risen on the hope that the railroad would put a station there. It had not, but the town lingered on, subsisting on bean gardens, some cattle, and a factory, which manufactured Blue Lightning Chili Con Carne. There was a courthouse, a school, a church, and the usual collection of stores. We took a room at the Fairburn House, a two-story board-and-batten hostelry with a false front and jacked-up prices because of the Carl Merkle murder trial. The prospect of a hanging had brought folks from miles around, many of whom were relatives of Merkle's victims, so rooms were at a premium.

Roselle, of course, did not qualify as a guest in this establishment, though she marched right up to the desk with us. We registered as Burns and Akbar, and while Dad Burns carried our gear up to the room, I drove the rig to the livery barn with Roselle. There I hired a stall for Roselle and put my saddle on the gate, thinking Alice Beck's drawers, though less attracting than they had been, would keep Roselle company. I asked the liveryman, a ruddy-faced Irishman called Jack Fetch, to have the rig shafts repaired and do whatever else needed doing to keep it rolling, but on no condition to scratch the paint on its sides.

On my way back to the hotel I ran smack into that fool Gospeler's horse, which sidled up, mooning at me, with the incriminating note on its halter. I skipped back as I had come, ducked into an alley, and ran for the hotel. When I got there Roselle was waiting for me on the front porch.

"Here, dang! You were supposed to stay at the livery barn!"

"Bo!" Roselle said, and she sat down.

"Come!" I commanded.

"Baw!"

171

"You come right now!"

Now it is true that a heifer cannot say "alfalfa" or "shucked corn," but it is equally true that there are ways of communication that are as good as language, and Roselle let me know, clear as crystal, that I had not lived up to my promise of luxurious fodder.

"All right!" I said. "Alfalfa. Shucked corn. I forgot."

Roselle rose and followed me back to the livery barn, and I asked Fetch how Roselle had gotten out of her stall.

"She must have opened the latch and snuck out," Fetch said.

I saw by the expression in Roselle's nigh eye that this was the case, so I gave her a lecture on snucking and put her back in a stall. I served her alfalfa and shucked corn myself, and when I was certain that she was satisfied I returned to the hotel.

When I got there, the blamed Gospeler's horse was standing at the hitch rack. I couldn't believe no one had seen the note on his halter and taken him into custody. He spotted me right off and pranced in my direction. I ran around the hotel, through the back door, and up the stairs to our room, arriving breathless.

"What is it, Fasli?" Dad Burns asked me. "Are you found out?"

"I'm being stalked by that dang Gospeler's horse!"

"Ignore it," Burns said. "In your present guise no one can trace that horse to you." He was diluting my concentrate of basswood bark and prairie dock with alcohol for public consumption. I saw the labels on the dresser and took one up. It was red with a picture of a flaming schoolhouse in the middle and a bunch of kids running out, terror on their faces, pigtails and shirttails ablaze. You could almost smell the searing flesh. The name of our product ran above the flames, and underneath was the standard testimonial saying our stuff would cure everything, external or internal.

Burns wasn't sure of the ratio of concentrate to alcohol and decided to run a test of its curative potency. He removed his electric belt and broke out one of the batteries. "How do the labels strike you?" he asked me.

"Awful," I said.

"Hold out your hand."

I did so without thinking and Burns shed a drop of liquid from the battery on it.

"What's that?" I asked him, for it didn't hurt right off.

"Probably sulfuric acid," he said.

Then I yelped! It was like a snake snapped its fangs into the back of my hand and commenced to chaw. I shook my hand and danced around while Burns dove for the cure. He dashed it on my hand and rubbed it in. "Does it work?" he demanded. "Does it work, Fasli?"

My hand was on fire. I roared and cavorted, and people in the adjacent rooms spilled into the corridor blabbering. I stuck my hand into the pan of concentrate and the pain eased some. "Is it better?" Burns asked.

"Is that what leaked out of your electric belts?" I asked him.

"It is."

"You'd do well to return to the Punjab," I said. "I see now why old Red Beard was so intent on killing you."

I looked at the raw welt on my hand, and my heart went out to the purchasers of Dr. Majul Majul's electric belts. Hanging was too good for Majul.

Burns looked at my hand and shook his head woefully. "It ought to cure in a couple of days," he said.

"If ever," I said. I wrapped my throbbing hand in my bandanna and stepped to the window, sulking. Below in the square I saw two carpenters erecting a gallows platform. Although the jury had not yet gone out, the gallows was being prepared at the taxpayers' expense and would not likely go unused.

Burns had decided forty-three percent alcohol was about right for our cure and was bottling it up when there came a rap at our door. I opened it to reveal a woebegone-looking man wearing smoked glasses and supporting himself on a cane. "Dr. Budge Burns?" he asked in a pained whisper.

Burns set his work aside and transformed into his best professional manner. "Here I am, sir. What may I do for you?"

"Oh, sir!" Smoked Glasses said, and he fell on Burns's breast weeping like a paddled child.

"There, there, my man," Burns said. "You can tell me."

"I saw your rig," Smoked Glasses said, but he was overcome again by a flood of tears.

"Just tell me, sir," Burns said gently. "I am here to help you."

174

Smoked Glasses braved up and shook the tears from behind his glasses. He straightened his shoulders and cleared his throat. "I am Reverend P. Stoner of the Cleo Springs First Baptist Church. My sister, in the town of Beaver Springs, knew I was afflicted by asthma and catarrh and kindly sent me a Majul Majul Electric Belt she'd purchased through the mail, hoping it might improve my condition. The device worked for a time. My cough vanished, and the lung congestion cleared. I felt the healing powers of electricity passing through my body and recommended the device to my parish."

The reverend gulped back another freshet of grief and continued.

"Then one Sunday I was preaching on the horrors of hellfire, which await all unrepentant sinners. My voice was clear and filled with the power of the Lord. I was free of the usual rasping coughs, which had previously threatened my oratorical hold on the parish. I saw the expressions of terror on the faces of the women and children and knew they would never sleep again without a strong dose of abject prayer. I felt the heat of my sermon and was filled by the fire of my own voice when all of a sudden . . . oh, sir, sir!"

Stoner collapsed again, clinging to Burns until finally he slipped to his knees in a watery heap. "Oh," he wailed, "shall I ever be the same? Oh, curse the day I ever strapped Dr. Majul Majul's device from hell to my abdomen. My amatory days are done!"

I excused myself, saying I would return after Dr. Burns had completed his examination. I had no desire to observe the symptoms. My throbbing hand filled me with sympathy for Reverend Stoner. I imagined him ripping off his vestments and clutching his fiery parts while trying to remove the burning belt. I saw him dancing in violent pain and howling as his congregation rose in horror to see their pastor taken by the devil right before their eyes. Acid on the back of a work-hardened hand is one thing; on the generative organs it is quite another. The only cure I could think of for such a case would be to remain immersed to the navel in cold tapioca pudding until the condition righted itself, if ever.

I decided to visit the court and have a glimpse of the murderer, Carl Merkle, whose greater, more heinous crimes might ease my conscience about my own. Outside, on the porch, I looked for the Gospeler's horse. Not seeing him, I made a dash for the gallows platform and ducked under it. When I didn't see the horse from this vantage point I ran for the courthouse and made it without discovery.

The courtroom was filled to capacity, but I managed to wedge in against the back wall and got a fair view of the proceedings. A flinty-looking judge was on the bench, and a lawyer, brandishing a set of spectacles on a ribbon, was addressing the jury, most of whom were picking their ears and waiting for the hanging.

"Carl Merkle says he didn't do it!" the lawyer cawed. "Well, gentlemen of the jury, there are nine people dead, waylaid and killed in remote sites all through this county. Their bodies, abandoned to the elements, were stripped of valuables, some items of which were found in Carl Merkle's possession when he was apprehended."

The lawyer picked up a chain and held it aloft. "A gold necklace," he intoned.

"Oh, my baby, my child!" a woman in the audience cried out, bursting into tears. "My little girl!"

"It's brass!"

The voice boomed out, and I saw Carl Merkle rare up from his place at the prisoner's bar. He was a hairy man with the configuration and brooding truculence of a grizzly bear. His hands were cuffed, and a chain ran from the manacles to shackles on his feet. Two bailiffs planted him back in his chair, and he sat there swinging his head from side to side, mouth slack, dull-witted to the point of insanity. "Brass," he muttered, as if this was a key point in his defense.

"There, you see," the lawyer proclaimed, pointing his pinch-nose glasses at Merkle. "What more proof can you want? There is the very form and picture of a fiendish killer. Look upon him! See his eyes. See in them the man who conspired with himself nunc and tunc to kill these hapless victims, each one of whom died of a broken neck, as we hope Carl Merkle will also die!"

"My child! My child!" the woman wailed.

"In five instances," the lawyer continued, "the victims' necks were broken after they had been shot to death, as though Carl Merkle was practicing his favorite method of killing: to pounce out of the darkness, seize the victim from behind, and snap the spinal cord with a sharp twist! Or perhaps he snapped their necks, then shot them for his added pleasure. Does it matter? Not a whit. We will never know the horrors experienced by these victims, but we can see their killer seated here, and no reasonable man cannot but agree that society can only be served by removing Carl Merkle from it."

This lawyerly formulation was a twister, but I guessed it made sense, and I left the courtroom, certain justice would be done and somewhat relieved that I had not yet sunk to this depth of depravity. Meaning Carl Merkle's, not the lawyer's. I was making my way to the courthouse door when a bulletin board riveted my attention, for in the center of it was a poster: WANTED! WYLIE JACKSON. REWARD $5000.00.

My heart pumped ice water. Five thousand dollars! For that amount of money I'd apprehend myself!

I sidled up to the board and, while pretending to adjust the bandage on my still-burning hand, read the particulars through frozen eyes. Blond hair. Brown eyes. Five feet eleven. Seventeen years old. Gone missing between Odessa, Texas, and Wichita, Kansas. Reward to be paid for information leading to the safe return of the above. Contact Miss Clara Hampton of Odessa, Texas, or Mr. John Boardman of the Box Z Ranch, Waycross, Texas.

At least they wanted me alive.

I stumbled out of the courthouse and bumped straight into that fool Gospeler's nag, which nuzzled up to me so soulful and friendly that any jury in the nation would have picked us for long acquaintances.

"Git!" I said to him from the corner of my mouth.

I saw that someone had removed my note and turned him loose. Obviously no one in Cleo Springs wanted to be caught with this stolen horse long enough to have their credentials examined.

I lit out around the courthouse with that nag clopping after me. I jumped a board fence, ran through two yards, and cut back to the hotel. When I got to the room, Dad Burns looked ill and was dosing himself with Hoofland's German Bitters (twenty-five percent alcohol). The Stoner case had evidently shocked his constitution. He opened his mouth to tell me about it, but I said I wouldn't listen and would leave the room if he spoke of it.

"You are heartless, Fasli."

"Such are the Muslims," I said.

Dad Burns nodded mournfully and swallowed his bitters, and I sat down to contemplate my immediate prospects.

I wasn't entirely certain that Dr. Majul Majul Dadu Budge Budge Burns would not turn me over for the reward if he connected me to the poster. The description on it wasn't much to go by, there being plenty of five-foot-eleven seventeen-year-olds with yellow hair and brown eyes roaming the country. It would take someone who knew my previous incarnation to link me up with that flyer, which had no doubt gone to every sheriff in the country. I hadn't given Majul my true name, so that was safe, and until we sold the cure and split the profits, I was too broke to buy a horse and make my getaway.

I could, of course, resteal the Gospeler's nag, but I

was trying to work my way up from crime into the medical profession, and a doctor on a stolen horse did not conform to the Hippocratic oath, as I understood it. Thank God they had not included Roselle on the reward poster or I would be a cooked dog. Obviously Mr. Boardman did not know I was still traveling with her, which saved me some.

Having concluded my best chance was to sell the cure and reinforce my pocket money, I sat down to compose a letter to my aunt Clara, to put her out of her misery and save her five thousand dollars.

Dear Aunt Clara,

I might as well be dead, but to ease your mind, if it does, I am not. If ever you see Mr. Boardman I wish you'd tell him that my stealing his horse was more or less an accident. I can't decide which, but I left it with the OHO outfit and stole another horse from the Gospelers, which I have also turned loose.

I didn't aim to turn out this way, but once I got to running downhill I couldn't seem to stop. Such is the fate of one born with the blood of a cotton broker in his arteries. I'm trying to slow up before I bottom out and it would help some if you could lift that reward off my head since it will keep me changing my name and identity pretty fast. Also I do not want you to lose such a sum of money if I was ever found. I summered with an Indian and learned a thing or two that will keep me in sorghum and beans, so don't worry about that part of it. Meantime I wish you a happy future with Mr. Eldon Larkin.

> *Your nephew now removed,*
> *Wylie*

SPANISH EGGS.

FAIRBURN HOUSE.

❖I ate this dish and reconstructed it from the flavors.

❖Mince a clove of garlic and fry in pan with one chopped onion. Blend into this one spoon of flour, one can of ripe pitted olives, and a can of tomatoes. Add oregano, chili powder, and salt and mix. Break six eggs into the pan and bake in hot oven until eggs set. Sprinkle with grated cheese and serve.

CHAPTER FOURTEEN

❖ ❖ ❖

That evening Dad Burns and I put on our first pitch for the Budge Budge Acid Burn Cure and Hair Restorative. We used the gallows platform and brought Roselle along to add color to the plea Dad Burns said we would make on behalf of U.S. cattle after we'd sold the cure.

To foil the wanted poster, I'd darkened my face to a suitable India Indian tone with tobacco juice and pinned a glass sparkler on the front of my blue rag turban. The effect was such that I hardly knew myself and felt secure facing that crowd of strangers, any one of whom would have been happy to collect five thousand dollars for my apprehension.

We set some candles out and stacked our wares on a table we'd rented from the hotel. Dad Burns threw a fit of oratory that gathered a crowd, including that cussed Gospeler's horse, which was not put off by my disguise and hung around like he was a member of the family.

Roselle climbed the stairs to the platform and was so pleased with herself that she lay down, rolled over, played dead, and counted to seven with her front hoof, all in quick succession. She got to acting up so bad I was ashamed of her, but when she sat down and gazed at the crowd they all burst out laughing. There is something about a sitting bovine that provokes risibility. A dog, a cat, a bear, even a horse can sit without tickling the funny bone, but a sitting heifer is funny. A sitting cow is funnier still. Sitting is a posture unnatural to bovines, given the underworks with which they are blessed. Being yet an unbred heifer, Roselle had no developed udder, so it wasn't teats folks laughed at. It was that the bony rump works of cows offers no cushion for the sitting posture; consequently the legs spraddle out, and it just looks dumb and awkward and . . . plain funny.

Also Roselle's expression contributed to the humor. She thought she was civilized. There was a wise-eyed look about her that was disconcerting, and her buffalo goatee was another feature that translated into laughter.

"Hey, here's the daughter of old Chief Sitting Bull!" one galoot hollered.

"Bo!" Roselle said.

"Hi golly! Let's send her to Congress!"

Roselle was about to hog the show, but I made her lie down and stay quiet so Doc Burns could take up the pitch.

Burns was in his bitters, but it didn't cut the flow of his language by a hair. The crowd was full of drunks and wisecrackers, some of whom wanted to know if our cure would work on rope burns and volunteered Carl Merkle as a likely customer even though the jury was still out. Others asked why, if our cure grew hair, Doc Burns didn't have any.

"Hair," Burns responded grandly, "is a matter of choice. Those who prefer hair may have it in abundance. Those who don't may shave it off. For my part I only use hair in the winter and scrape it off in the mild seasons to allow the health-giving rays of the sun to nourish and fertilize my brain. This, however, I am frank to confess, presents a hazard to the use of our cure that I mean to warn you about, for I have no intention of misleading the citizens of this community.

"Last summer I dozed off in the direct sun and burned my naked scalp. To cure this I applied our Budge Budge Acid Burn Cure and Hair Restorative, but a secondary result was that hair sprouted on my head, and I was forced to resort to the barber twice a week for relief. When burns occur on parts of the body that are the natural habitat of hair, our cure will settle the burn and increase the production of hair to boot. This is not to say, however, that if you burned your tongue our remedy would grow hair on it; no, sir, for that is not a natural place for hair, likewise the forehead or the heels of your feet and such places."

Burns went on in this wise for quite a spell and when he concluded we sold a hundred and sixty-three bottles of our device before I could make proper change. Then, as sales fell off, Burns raised his arms for silence and announced, "Now, my good friends, my Indian assistant, Dr. Fasli Akbar, straight from Calcutta, will honor us with an address on the evils of eating meat . . . Dr. Fasli Akbar!"

The crowd beat their hands together, but I was not prepared for this. That fool Burns had not told me I was to make a speech. I thought he was going to do it, but I guessed (correctly) that the bitters had sapped his vitality and he'd decided to leave the proselytizing to me.

I stepped up to the lights with Roselle standing at my side for moral support and cleared my throat. "The evils of eating meat," I began, "by Fasli Akbar."

Roselle bobbed her head, and the crowd got quiet as I struggled to organize my thoughts. They did not fall into any pattern, so I launched right off, hoping the inspiration of the moment would keep me afloat.

"Meat," I said, "is a well-known animal substance."

This having met with no contradiction from the crowd, I was encouraged to continue.

"It is found on most varieties of animal life: cows, horses, dogs, cats, sheep, and crocodiles, to name but a few. It is found in even larger quantities on elephants and whales. It is a substance without which not many animals can get along. I have not heard of one that does, so they naturally object to having it taken from them. When it is they usually kick off, which brings me to the object of my discourse.

"Ladies and gentlemen, why should we deprive the animal kingdom of that which it requires to move around in? Would we have the same done to us if the shoe were on the other foot? Not likely. There is hardly a man or woman among us who would sacrifice an arm or a leg to feed the chickens, yet we, on the other hand, are consuming their drumsticks and wings without a thought as to the consequences to us if the situation was reversed. Why is this so? Is it because we have nothing else to eat? Not so! We have corn, succotash, blueberries, apples, and all suchlike fruit of the fields, trees, vines, and bushes in abundance. Plus the animal kingdom is not averse to supplying us with such personally harmless items as eggs and milk, if we could but see our way clear to leaving their meat alone. This strikes me as a fair bargain when you take into account such things as buttermilk, cottage cheese, cream, Swiss cheese, Jack cheese, and fried eggs. The truth, ladies and gentlemen, is that we can all get fat and drunk as we please without recourse to the flesh of the animal kingdom.

"Furthermore, eating meat is a dangerous practice, as anyone can see who has witnessed a cattle drive or observed some poor fool strangling on a chicken bone. Have you ever seen a person strangle to death on a watermelon? No, ma'am! So the message is clear and obvious to those who can read the signs. Leave the animal kingdom in its flesh and confine your appetites to the vegetable world, with milk and eggs thrown in.

"We have all seen cases, too horrible to mention, of people whose innards have been et out by loathsome worms, who break out in putrescent sores, whose blood has been tainted by molecules and worse, who take out in fits and convulsions, all from eating badly cured or undercooked pork chops.

"Have you ever heard the same things said of a persimmon? Not in this world.

"Meat is a killer whether you look at it from the point of view of the donor or the consumer. You'd just as well go after your stomach with a quart of lye as to stuff it with meat.

"Now lastly, ladies and gentlemen, for I see some of you have begun to look green and pukey from the meat you no doubt had at breakfast or supper, for which I recommend a strong dose of ipecac and jalap to throw it out before it consumes your vital organs, I would like to turn your attention to the moral results of eating meat. These are not as obvious as the physical ones, and there are some people who have survived the devouring of flesh for years before they succumb to the inevitability of it. But look closely at them, and what do you find? Think about this carefully.

"Would you like to be trapped in a cabin with one of them? Would you sleep well at night, snowed in, without any vittles, with a known carnivore? Not me. For experience has shown that once a man has tasted meat he is addicted as a tiger to it and not too particular as to its source. I have heard of such men eating shoe leather, pack rats, and rattlesnakes. There is no end to what they'll clap their teeth into once they've started down the crimson path. Ask yourselves, then, if you wouldn't fry up just as nice as a lump of snake or gopher. Sure you would, and juicier!

"So, ladies and gentlemen, the hunger for meat has destroyed the reliability and morals of most men in the country and many women too. If they can't get cow, hog, sheep, or chicken, they'll go right on up or down the line until they can sink their bloody teeth into the first thing that will satisfy their craving, even though a barrel of apples was standing nearby. You know this is so as well as I do.

"What goes first at the boardinghouse table among such folks? The biscuits or the beefsteaks? You know the answer. Beefsteaks! Have you ever heard a biscuit call its mother or cry out in pain? Have you ever felt affection from a biscuit or had it wander over and comfort you in your loneliness and bereavement as animals do?"

At this Roselle nuzzled me, affectionate as a pussycat, and gazed at the audience with an appeal for mercy.

I was so wound up I was about to burst, and Dad Burns was standing behind me, urging me on by clapping his hands and interjecting, "Krishna! Krishna!" every now and again.

"It is not the biscuits that make monsters of us all," I cried. "It is the beefsteaks, the pork chops, and the veal!"

"Krishna. Krishna! Hare Krishna. Hare. Hare!"

"And I vow the time has come for us to stand up for the animal kingdom and cleanse our souls of this gore. I vow the time has come to throw a single tax on meat and do away with this traffic in death and destruction . . ."

"Krishna!" Burns roared. "Krishna Hare!"

". . . to turn our faces away from meat to the ways of peace, love, vegetable plates, milk, eggs, and cheese!"

I was overwhelmed with emotion and might have burst into tears if Dad Burns hadn't rared back and let go with his version of "The Battle Hymn of the Republic" while the crowd joined in with theirs.

> Mine eyes have seen the glory
> Of the vanishing of lard,
> We will trample out the beefsteaks
> With vegetables restored.

Roselle was so thrilled she danced around the platform, and the Gospeler's horse was prancing at the edge of the crowd and whickering "The Vegetable Hymn of the Republic" along with Dad Burns.

> We'll abandon tripe and sausages
> For apples and Swiss chard,
> Vegetarians marching on.
> Glory, glory hallelujah,
> Glory, glory hallelujah!

We sold another forty-eight bottles of the cure and folded up for the night. I saw Roselle to the livery barn, then skipped out the back door to fool the Gospeler's horse, which had followed us. He took up the chase, but I hid under the gallows platform, and when he lost my track I made for the hotel, where I had a glass of pokeweed tea to calm myself. It had been a glorious experience.

Profitable too.

CHEESE SOUFFLÉ.

FAIRBURN HOUSE.

❖This dish was being served at Fairburn House when we arrived. Make a white sauce (three spoons of flour, three of butter, one cup of milk, stir and heat). Add three beaten egg yolks and one cup of grated cheese of your choice (I like cheddar) and stir constantly as cheese melts. Add three beaten egg whites and bake in a bowl insulated in a pan of hot water, fifteen minutes. Garnish with mustard honey and basil.

Chapter Fifteen

❖ ❖ ❖

The next morning I refreshed my swarthy makeup, attached my turban and my sparkler, and went out to buy Roselle a bell. Dad Burns, having proselytized most of the night at the hotel bar, was in a somnolent mood, so I let him snore. I took breakfast with the other guests and was disappointed to see that my lecture the previous evening had not altered their eating habits. Sausages, bacon, and other gore were still on the sideboard, but I contented myself with corn muffins, huckleberry jam, and buttermilk. Breakfast done, I slipped out the back way to avoid the purloined Gospeler's horse. When I scouted the street, the fool horse was nowhere visible.

Taking advantage of this, I ran to the hardware store and bought a collar and cowbell for Roselle. It was a good brass bell with a firm tone, and I judged she would like it once she got accustomed to the sound. Before I left the store I observed the street from the doorway and still couldn't see the Gospeler's horse. This troubled me. When something that has been annoying you stops doing so, it raises questions. Upon whom, I wondered, was that horse now lavishing its affection? Had the horse found an honest man in Cleo Springs, or had it been scooped up for vagrancy?

The town had filled considerably, and the guilty verdict against Carl Merkle had been delivered. The hanging was scheduled for two P.M. so people would have time to finish their picnic lunches. Families from nearby farms and settlements were arriving in wagons, and I judged it was a good time for Dad Burns and me to set up business, which I determined to do once I'd belled Roselle.

I slipped from the hardware store and blended into the traffic, still wary of that tagalong horse, but once again I could not locate him. When I got to the livery barn Roselle was seated by the watering trough waiting for me. Some folks had gathered around and were laughing and conjecturing as to Roselle's lineage, so I told them she was a cattalo, a cross between a buffalo and a longhorn. Some found this to be offensive and huffed off as though I'd suggested crossing humans with gorillas and getting something like Carl Merkle, which, I expect, would be the logical result.

When I attached the bell to Roselle she shied a couple of times, but when she got used to the sound she settled down proud as a steam engine. "Baawooo!" she said, and she tossed her head to ring the bell.

I asked Roselle if she'd seen the horse from which I was a fugitive, and she rang the bell twice. I took this for no, but I didn't think she really meant it. Not on the first try, anyway.

I told Roselle to come, and we walked back to town to find the post office and mail my letter to Aunt Clara so she could strike my name from the genealogy page in our family Bible, thus ending the miserable cotton broker's line. Roselle clanged along beside me, and after I mailed my letter we returned to the hotel, where I intended to resurrect Dad Burns and get to work.

We were crossing the crowded street when all at once a voice from behind us said, "Fetch up there!"

Nothing is more surprising than a vaguely familiar voice aimed at your spine. I stopped dead, hoping it was not who I thought it was, but when I turned around, it was. Standing with his hand resting on the butt of a worn-looking pistol was the Gospeler who had so admired Ruddy Bob. He was grinning at me. "Axel Beane," he said.

I elected to rely on my turban and swarthy complexion for protection. I had no other. "Excuse me, sir," I said, mimicking Dad Burns's Indian whine, "could you direct me to the American consulate, so I can get my visa validated? I seem to have lost my directions."

"Axel Beane with a bandage on his head and tobacco spit on his face," the Gospeler said.

"Fasli Akbar, sir. You seem to be under a miscalculation as to my person. Ask any passerby, sir, who has attended my exhibition, and they will tell you who I am."

"Axel Beane," he insisted.

"Stay, sir. I am a foreigner to your shores. My habitat is India, far across the sea. You have me confused with some other appellation. My mother is a Budge Budge, my father a Dadu. I am a Krishnan and a Sikh from the Punjab."

"You're the same bad liar here as you were on the trail, Wylie Jackson."

"Here! Don't be exercising random names at me.

You have me alternated in your mind with some other person. I know not whereof you speak and bear no resemblance thereto."

"Oh," the Gospeler said with a nasty grin. "Excuse me, Your Highness. Upon closer view I see I have indeed made an error in my phrenology. The thief who stole my horse, which I have just now recovered here in this very town, has a reward of five thousand dollars for the safe return thereof. He travels with a cattalo heifer. You, of course, would not possess such an article about your person, would you?"

His sarcasm was unnecessarily pointed since Roselle was standing right beside me, staring up at the Gospeler with an enrapt expression.

"I don't take your meaning, sir," I said.

"I don't suppose you know that cattalo heifer there at your side, do you?" the Gospeler asked, aiming his finger at Roselle.

"I do not."

"That is not your heifer?"

"She is not, sir."

"Do you deny her?"

"Thrice."

The Gospeler shook his head woefully. "Wylie," he said, "you are a low dog. Come on, I'm taking you in." To enforce this demand he jerked his pistol, and the jig was up.

It was the first, but not the last, time I saw Roselle charge a man with a weapon in his hand. The bell clanged, and from a dead start Roselle hit the Gospeler in the midriff and carried him through the doorway into the Cleo Springs pharmacy. The pistol went

198

off with a thunderous crash and there was the sound of breaking glass and splintering display cases and furnishings. People rushed out of the place wild-eyed, flapping their arms in dismay. Pedestrians on the street took cover. Farm wagons and buggies dispersed.

I ran inside the pharmacy to save Roselle and found the Gospeler crammed into a corner. His pistol lay useless on the floor, and Roselle, head lowered, was about to charge again. "Call her off, Jackson!" the Gospeler croaked. This irritated Roselle, who charged, driving the Gospeler through the flimsy board-and-batten wall into the alley behind the store.

"Roselle!" I yelled.

"Baw!"

"Sit!"

Roselle trampled the Gospeler, who was rolling around gasping for air, his face pale as the underside of a goose. "I give up," he cried when he got some breeze in his lungs.

"Sit!" I commanded again.

Roselle sat on the Gospeler's chest, mashing him into submission.

At this moment the town sheriff, Frank Lesh, turned up and caught me by the ear. A portly man with a handlebar mustache, he was about to announce my arrest, but Roselle upped from the supine Gospeler and charged Lesh, catching him just above the knees and carrying him back into the ruined pharmacy.

"Roselle," I called, running after her. "Roselle! Roselle!"

The brass bell clanged as Lesh rolled off Roselle's

back and thrashed around until he scrambled up on the counter where Roselle couldn't reach him. He clawed for his pistol, but I threw myself in front of Roselle. "Don't draw!" I said. "We give up. She didn't mean it, Sheriff. She saw a gun kill a calf one time, and she gets excited if anyone draws."

Sheriff Lesh considered this claim with his hand on the butt of his pistol. He decided not to draw. "You're under arrest for all this destruction," he said.

"Yes, sir."

"Incarcerate that critter at the livery barn and let's go."

The Gospeler came in through the broken wall. "He's mine, Sheriff Lesh. I was trying to bring him in for you to hold. I got a previous claim to yours."

We walked Roselle to the livery barn. The Gospeler was arguing to establish his claim to me, and Sheriff Lesh, not yet knowing my value, agreed to book me for having stolen the Gospeler's horse.

The last thing I saw before Sheriff Lesh slung me into the calaboose was that danged Gospeler's horse attached to the hitch rack before the jail. The next thing I saw was Carl Merkle, my cellmate.

He greeted me with an undecipherable growl, which I took to mean that one more murder would not signify since the jury had sentenced him to hang.

I caught the bars and offered Sheriff Lesh the opinion that I'd prefer to be held in a different cell.

"There is no other cell."

"Then lash me up to a tree someplace," I begged.

"You're too slippery to be at large," Lesh said. He

slammed and locked the cell, and quiet descended like a calamity.

There were two army cots in the room, and I took the one opposite Merkle's. The first thing I noticed was that Merkle was not shackled, as he had been in the courtroom. The second thing was how he cracked his knuckles as he gazed at me, bobbing his head from side to side in a kind of agreement-negation motion. *Cri-cra-crack* went his knuckles, like snapping spines. *Cri-cra-crack!*

"Howdy," I whispered.

Cri-cra-crack!

Had I cracked my knuckles three times in such a way, all the bones would have been broken.

The Gospeler came down the corridor from the sheriff's office, and I jumped to the bars to greet him. "So," he said, "you're corralled at last."

"Get me out of here," I whispered, trying to roll my eyes in Merkle's direction without moving my head, trying to indicate that my murder was imminent, that I was being sized up as an hors d'oeuvre to a hanging.

Cri-cra-crack!

The Gospeler looked over at Merkle, nodding pleasantly. "Hello, Merkle," he said.

"Hello, Matt," Merkle growled.

That they could be acquainted sent a chill up my spine.

"You've come to a bad end, and I'm sorry for it," the Gospeler said. "One murder might be excused, but nine is swallowing the hog."

"I done worse in the war." *Cri-cra-crack!*

"That's a different situation."

"As the tree is bent, so shall it grow," Merkle said. "All that killing was habit-forming. I liked the hand-to-hand. The bayonet charges."

That Merkle had the ability to form a simple sentence increased my sense of panic, and I appealed to the Gospeler. "Go my bail, and I'll pay you back from the proceeds of my burns cure product."

"No. You're worth five thousand dollars to me right where you stand, Jackson," the Gospeler said, "and I mean to protect my gain. I've sent word to Boardman where to find you, and I expect he'll strike fire from his horseshoes coming to collect you. Why you're worth so much to him I cannot say. Put to the jury, your case would land you on the gallows platform next to Merkle and give the crowd double pleasure for their taxes."

"He wanted dead or alive?" Merkle asked.

"Alive."

At this Merkle rared up, caught me around the neck, and put his free hand on the side of my head. One sharp push and I knew it would be over for me.

The Gospeler knew it too and clearly regretted having revealed my value. "I'll call Sheriff Lesh," he said.

"He won't get here in time," Merkle replied. He shoved my head over to the snapping point, and I knew if he added any pressure my neck would pop like a champagne cork.

"What do you want?" the Gospeler asked.

Merkle let up the pressure some. "Bust me out of here, Matt," he said. "We was in the same outfit once.

Bust me out, and you can collect on this cuss. Otherwise you can stand there and watch your money die."

"How can I do that in broad daylight?" the Gospeler pleaded. "Don't rob me of this grubstake, Merkle."

"I got a plan."

That this hairy villain could plan made my mind spin, plus the fact that he had twisted my head about a hundred and eighty degrees, and I blacked out, dead or unconscious. In my subsequent state I could not distinguish between the two.

When I came around I heard Merkle's knuckles cracking. I refused to open my eyes, preferring blindness to seeing Merkle, seated on his cot, watching me as closely as a falcon prepared to swoop down and snap my neck.

Then I heard Dad Burns come along the corridor. "Fasli! Fasli!" he cried. "I have just discovered your incarceration and have come at once to your aid."

I opened my eyes and there was Dad Burns at the cell door, wringing his pudgy hands.

Merkle glared at Burns. "Who is that article?" he asked me.

"I am Dr. Dadu Budge Budge, Burns Specialist," Burns intoned, rising to his full dignity.

"You got any money riding on this boy?"

"Fasli is my business partner," Burns said.

"What's it worth to you to keep him alive?"

"Hold on, Merkle," I complained. "I can't be sold twice."

"You can be sold as often as I find a buyer! What'll you give to keep him alive, Burns?"

"Why, he is dear to my heart," Burns faltered.
"Cash!"

There are veils in the eyes of man, like transparent lids in the eyes of snakes, which often reveal their inner thoughts. I saw such a veil slide over Dad Burns's eyes, a larcenous glaze that announced his intent as clearly as if it had been spelled out in firecrackers. He was going to take the cure and the cash and decamp.

I rose from my cot and went to him. "Burns," I said, "don't do it."

"Do what?" Burns whined, innocence blossoming in his face like skunk cabbage in a rancid pond.

"Run out on me," I said.

"Never, Fasli, my son!" he cried, trying to pretend this had not occurred to him.

"Burns," I said, "if you abandon me I will tell Reverend P. Stoner that you are Majul Majul, perpetrator of the famous electric belt fiasco. I will suggest he undo the paint on your rig and see beneath it your true identity, and the victims of that device will search you out no matter how deep you bury yourself in the Punjab!"

Dad Burns paled considerably. "What do you want of me, Fasli?" he asked.

"Take Roselle and go to where we camped. Wait there until I come. If I don't come, take Roselle to Agnes Badgley in Enid and inform my family that I am expired."

"I will do it," Burns said, and he started to leave, but Merkle intruded.

"So you're Majul Majul," Merkle said. I was so

annoyed with Burns I'd forgotten Merkle was over-hearing all we said.

"That is a canard," Dad Burns replied bravely.

"I'll just tell Stoner about you when he comes to guide me to God and the gallows."

Burns blanched and appealed to me.

"Unless," Merkle appended.

"What?" Burns begged.

"I saw your pitch from my cell window," Merkle said. "I'd like to be sent off with a double boost, just in case Stoner's line is out of style. In my place two faiths is better than one, so I won't blow your name to Stoner if you'll be here to send me off in the proper Krishnan fashion . . . otherwise . . ." *Cri-cra-crack!*

The sound of Merkle's cracking knuckles convinced Burns to attend the ceremony as a practitioner of the Hindu faith. He departed, promising to return, but I wouldn't have bet the farm on that.

When we were alone Merkle fixed me with a murderous glare. "We better get in motion," he said. "Do what I tell you to do or die."

I assented, having no doubt Merkle meant exactly what he said—that if I attempted to call out, the last sound I'd ever hear would be my neck cracking like Merkle's knuckles.

Merkle rose and rattled the bars furiously, yelling at the top of his lungs. "Sheriff! Sheriff! I want my last wishes! I want the rights of a condemned man!"

Presently Sheriff Lesh came along the corridor with a shotgun under his arm. "Shut up, Merkle! You'll get your due!"

"I want prairie oysters, cigars, some kidneys, and steam beer!" Merkle yelled.

"Anything reasonable," Lesh said. "Now quit bellowing."

"I want soap, a washrag, a towel, and a safety razor so I can meet my maker clean-shaven and neat, as it is my right to do."

"That'll be done. Anything more?" Lesh asked.

"Bring something nice for the boy," Merkle said.

"What would you like, Jackson?" Lesh asked.

A ticket out of that place would have been just fine, but Merkle was gazing at me, and I knew he could break my neck before the shotgun fired. "Oatmeal," I said. Suddenly I had a yearning for oatmeal, for good simple vegetable food to fortify my belief that I'd see another sunrise.

"And put some raisins in it for the lad," Merkle said. "A few nice raisins with cream and brown sugar. How does that sound, boy?"

It sounded good if I would live to eat it.

CONDEMNED MAN'S LAST MEAL.

SHERIFF LESH.

❖Carl Merkel's prodigious appetite for organ meat may have some connection to his murderous disposition. As we ate he told me he had developed a taste for prairie oysters during the lamb castration fests when these amative organs were removed and consumed on the spot after being barbecued. This was braggadocio, as lamb gonads aren't particularly tasty without a deal of preparation as follows.

❖Upset the lamb and remove the gonads with a deft slice of a sharp knife. Split and soak a dozen gonads in salt water. Remove the fibrous lining, veins, and cords.

❖In a fry pan mix a cup of A.1. sauce with cider vinegar, catsup, four sliced onions, brown sugar, celery seed, salt, pepper, nutmeg, and cloves. Add the nuts to this and simmer until reduced. The sauce is good, and the nuts give you something to chew.

❖Merkle also had kidneys, a slice of liver, and a marrow bone.

Chapter Sixteen

❖ ❖ ❖

When Sheriff Lesh and the men he'd deputized for the hanging brought the dinner, there was a mountain of food for Merkle: prairie oysters, kidneys, fried potatoes, two bottles of steam beer, and other things I cared not to look at. There was also soap, washrags, towels, and a safety razor.

I got oatmeal with raisins, cream, and brown sugar.

"You satisfied, Merkle?" Lesh asked.

Merkle demanded cigars. "These are the wishes of a condemned man," he bawled. "I still got rights!"

Sheriff Lesh conceded and sent for cigars, which one of the deputies delivered ten minutes later. Merkle took these and put two cigars in his coffee cup to soak, a taste that turned my stomach.

Having been unconscious when Merkle laid his plan, I wasn't aware of what, if anything, it consisted. I just hoped that when it was sprung I wasn't killed in the crossfire.

As I ate my oatmeal I fell to thinking about cow heaven, which that fool Dad Burns had told me about, and imagined myself up there among those heavenly cattle—cows, bulls, and calves romping in the clouds. Up there I knew the cattle language, and there wasn't any Wichita, just fields of red clover, timothy, meadow fescue, and alfalfa. All the vanished buffalo were there, huge shaggy herds of them rolling by, their hooves drumming to the gentler sound of cowbells. There were Guernseys and Jerseys, short-horns and Aberdeens, zebus and Kerrys, and all kinds of cattle I hadn't heard of or seen but which went back through the ages. And there were maidens, all of whom reminded me of Alice Beck, to milk the cows and comb them down and put their ribbons on. I could hear their contented lowing and bells all through the meadows as calves of every nation splashed in the streams and frolicked at the salt licks. I sat there gazing at parades of cattle all fit and glossy, great deep-chested oxen leading the way, followed by quicker Spanish bulls. The parading cattle were red and black and white and brown, colors of gray and yellow and blue I couldn't believe. My only regret was that I was not one of them because I was stuck even there by my human form and stupidity. But when Roselle showed up she explained to the others that I was all right despite my calf-blasting days. Roselle told them how I'd sworn off killing and had taken to vege-tarianism. She had my speech on the evils of eating meat printed up in cattle to prove my credentials. When they read this, members of all the cattle nations came to welcome me and offer condolences for my human condition. I told them the next time around I'd take my chances as a longhorn, and they said this was fine with them, and to prove there were no hard feelings they let me ride on their backs in the next parade. It was better than any human heaven I had heard about, and I was happy to be there.

I roused from these reveries and found that Carl Merkle had finished his grisly meal and was shaving. I never saw a man so unhandy with a razor. By the time he got through carving the fur off his face and neck he was such a mess of nicks and cuts it looked like he'd walked into a reaper. He yelled for Sheriff Lesh to bring him some adhesive plasters.

By now it was eleven o'clock, and we could hear the hangman testing the drop, using bags of sand equal to Merkle's body weight. I listened to the trap fall over and over and heard rope snap and squeal. It made me squeamish, and I prayed Merkle's escape plan didn't get me killed.

Sheriff Lesh turned up with the plasters, and Merkle fell to the floor, groveling and begging for mercy. "You got the wrong man," he cried. "I'm innocent. I'm too young to die! Don't let them take me, Sheriff! Have mercy on me, please, please!"

I was astonished by Merkle's sudden turn to cowardice. It was disgusting to see him groveling so.

"Here now," Sheriff Lesh said. "Get a grip on yourself. Be a man."

Merkle staggered to his feet, blubbering. "Oh, I want to be, Sheriff Lesh, but I'm scared. I'm a coward. I can't face it. I can't. I can't!"

"You must face it, Merkle," Lesh said.

"Then make it quick, sir. Don't let me see all those people out there! Put the hood over my head here in the cell and rush me through that crowd to my maker. Let this boy witness my end as an example for him to mend his ways. But be quick as you can, sir, or I'll fight and make a fool of myself before all these folks."

"We'll be quick, Merkle," Lesh said.

Merkle caught Sheriff Lesh's hand between the bars and kissed it several times before Lesh could jerk it

211

away. "Oh, thank you, Sheriff. Thank you. Thank you. Rush in and pop the hood on my head. I'll try to be ready."

When Sheriff Lesh had gone, Merkle tore off his clothes and ordered me to do the same or die. He squeezed himself into my buckskin togs, which were elastic enough to admit him if he avoided any sudden movements. He padded me out with strips torn from a blanket and cinched his clothes on me. Then he slapped adhesive plasters on my face and colored it with ketchup.

Merkle took the coffee-soaked cigar and used it to darken his face to a Calcutta tone. He put my blue turban with the sparkler on his head. "How do I look?" he asked.

The transformation might have fooled two blind men and a wobbling drunk, but I didn't expect that was what he wanted to hear. "Perfect," I said.

I saw now it was Merkle's plan to substitute me in his place on the gallows, and I had no enthusiasm for it. When they came for him I was going to yell blue murder and hope to get one jump ahead of Merkle and be rescued before he could snap my neck.

"Now what?" I asked.

"We pray," Merkle said, and he shoved me down on my knees beside the cot. "Bow your head and mumble," he said. Merkle covered the cell window with a blanket to diminish the light, struck fire to a cigar, and commenced puffing like fury, filling the cell with smoke, hoping in this wise to obscure the officer's vision.

Outside, the crowd was getting restive. Some fool

was pounding on a bass drum, and others were letting off firecrackers. I mumbled, and Merkle knelt beside me, still puffing the cigar, warning me between exhalations how quickly he could snap my neck if I tried anything foolish.

We knelt there, side by side, waiting for eternity. Then came the sound of chinking finger cymbals, and the door at the end of the corridor opened.

I caught a glimpse of Reverend P. Stoner, grave as a tombstone, reading from a Bible clutched in his hands, and beside him came Majul Majul Dadu Budge Budge Burns clad in a bedsheet, with a crown of flowers on his hairless head. He was cavorting like a Hindu ecstatic to the sound of brass cymbals on his fingers and chanting, "Krishna, Krishna, Hare, Krishna, Hare, Hare!" And behind them came Sheriff Lesh and the deputies.

"Keep your head down!" Merkle warned, and he chucked the smoking cigar under the cot.

I heard the key in the cell door, and when it opened I made my play. I bolted to my feet. "Don't take me!" I screamed. "Don't—" A black hood was socked over my head. "I'm Wylie Jackson!" I cried as the deputies caught me by the arms and dragged me down the corridor. I fought and struggled, and the finger cymbals rang in my ears like icicles. "No!" I screamed. "No! I'm Fasli Beane . . . Akbar Jackson!"

"Slipped his halter," Sheriff Lesh said.

"Matthew! Mark! Luke! John!" I howled.

Reverend Stoner was reading the Twenty-third Psalm in my ear. "Reverend Stoner!" I yelled through the muffling hood. "Don't let them take me! Dadu, it's Fasli!"

"Come to Jesus, Merkle!" Stoner replied.

"Hare! Hare!" Dad Burns sang.

By now we were outside, and the crowd set up a great cry as the deputies dragged me, screaming and fighting, to the gallows. "Dad Burns!" I howled. "Majul Majul, save me, or I'll tell them who you are. Electric belts!"

"What's that you said?" Reverend Stoner asked.

The finger cymbals stopped.

I broke free for a moment and ran bang into one of the platform corner posts. This stunned me, and the deputies caught me again and dragged me up the steps to the gallows.

"Did you say Majul Majul?" Stoner asked.

"Majul! It's Fasli Akbar!"

"First madman I ever hung," Sheriff Lesh said to Stoner as he fit the noose over my head and snugged it around my neck.

"No, no!" I bleated.

Then it got very quiet, and I couldn't think anymore. I was dead before they sprang the trap. I stood there in all that darkness and silence not wanting to think. No use to start a thought and have it . . . interrupted.

The rope broke.

No, I was on my way, soaring upward to Go-loka. Then I heard the Gospeler's voice. "You got the wrong man, Sheriff Lesh. Carl Merkle just rode out of town. If you hurry you can catch him."

"Impossible," Sheriff Lesh cried.

"Pull off that hood and see. Drop that trap, and I'll sue you to recover my five-thousand-dollar reward. Now that you've been told, hang him if you like, but be prepared to pay me my five thousand."

I protested this suggestion as well as I could through fear and the hood. "Don't hang me! I'm too young to die!"

"Carl Merkle's very words," Lesh said.

"It's Wylie Jackson in here," I howled.

I felt the rope lifted from my neck; then the hood was raised. The light hurt my eyes so I couldn't see for a moment; then I made out the Gospeler standing beside me on the platform. Sheriff Lesh looked closely at me. He yelped and abandoned the platform, running back toward the jail with the deputies behind him, brandishing their pistols.

"You put on a good show, Jackson," the Gospeler said.

"You'd have let them spring that trap!" I accused.

"Not hardly."

"Where's Merkle?"

"To save your life I gave him the horse you stole from me. Merkle is headed for the territory. You still owe me one horse."

The crowd had raised a yell of disappointment at having lost their hanging and split in all directions to form a posse and recover Merkle.

Reverend P. Stoner was staring at me. "You're not Merkle," he said.

"I'm Wylie Jackson, apprehended," I replied.

"Nor are you Fasli Akbar," Stoner said, lucubration working slowly until he concluded that Dr. Dad Burns was probably not Dr. Dad Burns. This led him back to my raving. "You called that dancing feller Majul!" he said. "Majul!"

"I was mistaken."

"Mistaken! Those were your almost dying words!"

At this Reverend P. Stoner clutched his head, uttered a screech, and jumped ten feet from the platform to the ground. I thought he'd broken both his legs, but after a second he dashed away brandishing his Bible. "Majul!" he yelled. "Majul Majul!"

The Gospeler took me firmly by the arm and led me back to the hotel. There I asked the clerk if my partner, Dr. Dad Burns, was about. I intended to warn him not to schedule any medical appointments with Reverend P. Stoner, but the clerk had not seen Burns.

I started for the door, intending to seek Burns and alert him to the possibility that his true identity had been discovered, but the Gospeler had me by the arm.

"Where do you think you're going?" he asked.

I explained my mission, but he would not consider it. "You're pretty fragrant, Jackson," he said. "I promised to keep you in good repair, so let's march upstairs. I'll go find your partner for you."

Since the Gospeler seemed prepared to enforce his request ungently, I acquiesced. Ten minutes later I was in a tub of hot water, scrubbing my hide. The Gospeler wadded up Carl Merkle's pungent clothes and volunteered to find replacements for them and to locate Dad Burns too if I promised not to get lost.

"Unlikely in this garb," I said, and the Gospeler left me to my ablutions.

I hadn't had a bath since the steam plunges with Tim-oo-leh, so the bathwater got pretty nourishing. When I was some shades lighter than I had been as Fasli Akbar, I toweled off and wrapped a blanket around my shoulders. I was attracted to the window by unearthly howls of vengeance, and I saw Reverend P. Stoner riding out of town ahead of a swarm of men and two ladies, followed by a buckboard laden with provisions. I assumed this crowd was part of the posse headed out to recapture Carl Merkle.

The Gospeler returned with the new clothes he'd bought for me out of his own pocket and told me to try them on for size. "You look to be about mine," he said.

"Your what?" I asked.

"Size," he said.

This surprised me since I hadn't been paying much attention to my size with all else that had been going on, but as I put on the pants and shirt I sensed I'd sprung up some and filled out too. That was why Merkle had been able to fool Sheriff Lesh into thinking I was him. I'd grown taller and put on flesh. I'd been thinking of myself as I used to be back in Odessa and was only now catching up to how I was.

I put on a denim jacket that was a bit tight in the shoulders, and the Gospeler said I'd need boots. I'd left my old ones with Tim-oo-leh when I appropriated his moccasins.

"I thought you'd better try those on for yourself," the Gospeler said.

"Say," I asked, "how come you're laying all this out for me?"

"Mr. Boardman told me to." He took a telegram from his shirt pocket and held it out for me to read.

MATT BURDICK. CLEO SPRINGS,
OKLAHOMA TERRITORY: HOLD WYLIE
JACKSON. TEND HIS NEEDS. WILL REIMBURSE
UPON ARRIVAL. JOHN BOARDMAN.

"It's ten words," I said. "And you're Matt Burdick."

"The same."

We shook hands.

"Did you locate my partner?" I asked him.

"Gone," the Gospeler said.

"Gone?"

"He lit out of town before you got to the gallows trap. I checked at the livery barn."

"You see my heifer there?"

"Jack Fetch said Burns took her."

"You mean Dad Burns took Roselle?"

"Fetch said as much."

It flashed on me then that Reverend Stoner's party wasn't after Carl Merkle, it was after Dad Burns, and if that crowd caught him, there would be nothing left to bury but the bullet holes. I lunged for the door, but the Gospeler caught my arm. "Here," he cautioned, "you stay put until Boardman arrives."

"That electric belt posse will kill Roselle and every living thing around Majul Majul!" I cried.

218

"I got no investment in that," the Gospeler said. "Sit down and we'll play checkers until I collect on you." He shoved me toward a chair.

I'd never hit a man in my life. I gave no thought to doing so then, but I hit the Gospeler on the jaw, and it took us both by surprise.

He turned on the heels of his boots like a pivot door, and I caught him again, reversing his direction. His knees struck the floor and he tottered there, looking puzzled. Then he fell forward on his face and lay so still it frightened me. I felt his pulse and knew he'd recover and that I'd better be gone when he did. I rifled his pockets and found twenty-six dollars. I unbelted his pistol and fastened it around my waist. Then I did the lowest thing I was ever called upon to do: I took his boots and hat.

There are some things even a low horse thief is not supposed to do and one of them is to take a man's boots and hat. This is an offense beyond all civilized forgiveness. Steal horses, yes; steal pistols, yes. These are within the realm of low thievery. But to take the hat and boots of a man is a crime unspeakable. I was deeply ashamed of myself but also in a hurry.

When I reached the livery barn, Jack Fetch confirmed that Dad Burns had ripped out of town and taken Roselle with him. I knew Burns had seen what a crowd-pleaser Roselle was and had decided to go it alone with her, believing that in my hysteria I might have betrayed his identity to Reverend P. Stoner, which, as it turned out, I had.

I told Fetch that Mr. Matt Burdick had asked me

to bring his horse to the hotel, and I cinched my saddle on the beast. Having escaped the gallows, lied, stolen, and cheated, I put Burdick's rowels to Gospeler Two and vanished from Cleo Springs knowing I would soon be the object of hot pursuit.

CURRIED HORSE.

UBIQUITOUS.

❖Horse meat is deep red and smoothly textured with almost no marbling or fat content if taken from the larger sections of the beast. It has a sweet flavor and is tender. To disguise its origin it is best to curry horse.

❖Take two and a half pounds of good horse rump. (See recipe for Porterhouse Steaks.) Dice horse into cubes. Braise these in nonhorse fat and hold. Grind into paste a quantity of coriander seed, caraway, cardamom, black pepper, dried hot peppers, green ginger, cumin, etc., or use a prepared curry powder mixed with lard and flour, but this is not as good as fresh.

❖Collect wild onions and whatever other vegetable matter the field offers, such as pigweed, and put into the pot with the horse. Simmer and add the curry paste, stirring slowly. Add raisins and what fruit you may possess. Serve over rice, toast, or boiled potatoes. It is wise to mention something about lamb or beef curry as you pass the plates. The sauce will cover the lie.

❖This dish is often found in low-class boarding-houses and on prison menus.

CHAPTER SEVENTEEN

❖ ❖ ❖

In the next few hours I put as much mileage between myself and Cleo Springs as I could. The influx of fugitives and posses in the pursuit of them that afternoon probably exceeded any similar intrusion into the territory in its entire history. First there was Carl Merkle, the convicted mass killer, running for his life from the posse organized by Sheriff Frank Lesh. Then there was Dad Burns with Roselle, headed for safer climes on the assumption that his connection with the electric belts might have been revealed. Burns was being hunted by Reverend P. Stoner and his electric belt posse, burning with vengeance. Then there was me hoping to save Roselle before the posse overtook Burns. And behind me, I had no doubt, was Matt Burdick and whatever support he could muster, determined to recapture me and earn his five-thousand-dollar reward.

Given how news spread in seemingly isolated areas, it was not unlikely that by noon the next day every renegade Indian, outlaw, and bounty hunter in the territory would take a hand in this game, for pleasure or profit.

I rode fast, crisscrossing the country, hoping to pick up Dad Burns's rig tracks. I knew he could not travel fast towing Roselle and hoped he'd have sense enough to turn her loose for his own safety. How I would find her then I did not know, but I'd rather have her roving free than in proximity to Burns if the electric belt posse found him.

Toward dusk a light snow began to fall, and Gospeler Two, wearied by the long ride, began to flag. I kept looking over my shoulder to see if there were riders behind me, but any rising dust, which usually signals the presence of horsemen, would have been dampened by the snow, and visibility was poor.

I rode on slowly to spare my mount and scanned the country with increasing despair. The silence was oppressive, cold and miserable. The only encouraging thought was that I had to be taken alive to be of value. If I'd had crayon and cardboard I'd have attached a placard to my back: THIS IS WYLIE JACKSON. HE IS WORTH $5,000.00 IF TAKEN ALIVE. DO NOT HARM. HE WILL GO QUIETLY.

I came to a butte, which I knew would give me a better view of the country, and dismounted to lead my horse up a stony defile to the top of it. When I arrived the snow had stopped, and the sun, low on the horizon, shone through the clouds, washing the whitened landscape with a rosy glow. I shaded my eyes and turned slowly, trying to magnify my vision.

As I looked east, Dad Burns's drummer's rig popped up like a black bug crossing a tablecloth. It was about five miles off, too distant for me to make out Burns or to be sure that Roselle wasn't on the far side of the rig.

I started down the forward side of the butte, leading my horse, watching the far-off rig, but suddenly I heard a distant howl and saw a group of riders charge from a grove of trees like pellets from a shotgun. It was the electric belt posse. They were aiming for the rig, brandishing weapons and screeching like the furies of hell.

The posse opened fire with all guns as soon as it came within killing range. Then, to my horror, a four-legged critter appeared from behind the rig. My heart gulped as the beast reared and broke away. Then I saw by its galloping gait that it was a horse, not Roselle.

Surprisingly, Dad Burns rose in his seat and returned the posse's fire. The rig careened as the terrified nag tried to escape the bullets. I had always believed there was a convention in such cases of conflict: that horses, being inoffensive and noncombatant, were generally spared; that the target was the man, not the horse. This illusion was shattered by the electric belt posse, which fired on everything that moved.

Evidently Dad Burns had foreseen trouble and armed himself with two pistols, but he was hopelessly outgunned by rifles and shotguns. He dove into the rig for shelter, but as I had predicted, there was not going to be enough of him left to scoop up for a burial.

The guns boomed as the posse circled the disintegrating rig. The nag fell dead in the traces. Under the impact of all that lead the rig sagged and finally toppled over.

One of the posse brought a can of kerosene from their supply wagon and doused the horse and rig with it. A spark, struck by the continuing barrage of bullets, ignited the kerosene, and the rig blazed up, raising a column of black smoke in the cold air. I remembered Majul Majul's description of Indian burial rites, how the Hindu consigns his dead to the burning ghat and sends his soul aloft in smoke and flame. I imagined Majul Majul Dadu Budge Budge Burns rising thus to Go-loka on this column of smoke and removed my stolen hat to pay my respects to his passing.

As darkness fell the posse continued to shout and howl and shoot into the flames until there was nothing left of the rig, the horse, and the man but ashes. Their vengeance slaked, the posse members turned their weary mounts toward Cleo Springs. They rode away, bowed in the saddle, still grieving their amatory condition, for which no amount of murder could possibly compensate.

I decided to put in for the night and found a sheltered place on the butte. I dared not light a fire, though it was bitter cold, so I eased the cinch on Gospeler Two and wrapped myself in Burdick's slicker. I gazed at the stars and mourned Dad Burns. Had he lived he would have been a powerful voice on behalf of all kine. I vowed to carry on his work and finally fell into a fitful sleep, dreaming of Burns in Go-loka.

At the first tweak of dawn I rose and led Gospeler Two down to the flat. We found a stream and watered ourselves. I let the horse crop some rime-covered grass; then I rode out to inspect the ashes of the rig.

I hadn't gone a mile when I heard hoofbeats and turned, expecting trouble. And lo! what should appear but Gospeler One, trotting in my direction with an

226

expression of fool delight on his face. He had been nicked across the rump by a bullet, which had caused him to break his lead and bolt.

Seeing that incriminating horse upon which, according to Burdick, Carl Merkle had made his escape altered my view of what had happened the evening before.

Merkle, riding Gospeler One, must have come across Dad Burns and decided to throw Sheriff Lesh's posse off the track by continuing his flight in the drummer's rig. He'd broken Burns's neck, cut Roselle loose or killed her for sport, and taken the rig. This scenario did nothing to improve my spirits.

I decided to backtrack and try to find Burns's body and perhaps that of poor Roselle, another innocent beast slaughtered in the rampaging path of mankind. The rig tracks were not hard to follow. Pausing now and again, I could see the imprint of them picked out by the frost. I'd gone five miles almost due north when I came to a spot where prints of a horse's hooves intersected the trail. They matched the hoofprints left by Gospeler One exactly.

I cast about, seeking the bodies of Roselle and Burns without success. About a mile east of the rig tracks I came upon a crowd of hoof marks and another wagon track. These, I was certain, belonged to the electric belt posse and their supply wagon. I guessed then that Dad Burns, hearing the electric belt posse howling through the countryside, had abandoned the rig and taken to his heels.

I rode back to the rig tracks and found the place where Burns had dropped to the ground, untied Roselle so she wouldn't impede the rig, and smacked his horse to drive it off over the plains.

Merkle, finding the empty rig, had expropriated it and sealed his doom.

I could see by Dad Burns's wavering footprints that he had been steeping himself in the Budge Budge Acid Burn Cure and Hair Restorative (forty-three percent alcohol).

Roselle's tracks led in another direction, and on the theory that God takes care of fools and drunkards I left Burns to his destiny and went in search of Roselle.

I hadn't gone an hour, with that fool horse, Gospeler One, trailing along, when I heard the sound of a bell and knew Roselle was close by. I came to a halt and listened. It was broken country, full of gullies and washes, which skewed the direction of sound. I heard the bell again, this time from a place where I hadn't guessed it to be. I went in this direction, but Gospeler One pawed the ground and beckoned with his head. The blamed incriminating horse was asking me to follow him.

I knew Gospeler One was fond of Roselle, and I'd seen the ears of a horse turn nearly all the way around to track the direction of a sound, a trick my ears could not perform, so I let him take the lead. He stalked forward, cautious as a hunting hound, and I can't swear to it but I believe he presently came to a point, one hoof raised, neck stretched, his muzzle aimed into a gully on our left.

I dismounted, approached this place slowly, and came upon a group of Kiowas seated around a campfire consuming Gilbert and Parsons Hygienic Whiskey, one of many concoctions whose sole purpose was to circumvent the laws against selling whiskey to Indians by passing it off as medicine. This crowd had grown quite hilarious under the medical influence and failed to spot me. I took the size of those Kiowas and found it to be a young war party well armed and painted, out to express their exuberance of life the only way they knew.

There wasn't much in the way of recreation on the range, particularly not for young Indians who were born on the tail end of their nation's glory and were being fed government-contract beef. They couldn't even hunt without interference from white agents or troops, and I guessed if I were in their moccasins I'd be pretty sore too, and go out and play the painted savage every Saturday night to any audience I could get.

I saw Roselle tethered to a log and she saw me. Her bell clanged as she tried to pull away and come to my side. Her efforts were pretty determined, and I decided to make my play before she started bowling Kiowas head over heels.

The Kiowas were startled when I stepped forward and spoke to them in Cherokee, probably most of it root and herb talk since those words were practically all I knew. The Kiowas snatched their weapons and tried to look fierce, but one was so far gone on Peruna or some such that he kept giggling, which killed the effect they were trying for. I continued my herbivorous chatter, pointing to Roselle and miming she was mine and that I'd be willing to buy her from them.

One of their number with a lot of red, blue, and

yellow signs on his face spoke trade-post English and decided to take me on. "You one big fool," he said to me, swallowing his voice to make it sound deep and guttural.

"Yes, that is regrettable," I said easily. "How much do you want for that heifer?"

"You one damn crazy white eyes," the Kiowa blustered.

"How would three dollars suit you?"

"Ho!"

"Fine," I said, and I went over and untied Roselle from the log.

At this Red, Blue, and Yellow had to make himself large in the eyes of his six comrades, so he stood up and aimed his rifle at me. "You no take!" he said.

"You said 'ho,'" I said, and I fished the cash I'd filched from Burdick out of my pocket and peeled off three dollars.

"*Ho* don't mean yes!" Multicolored objected.

"*Ho* don't mean no," I said.

"*Ho* means *ho*!"

"Right. Here's your three dollars, chief."

"*Ho* could be yes or no," he said, and he began to look sorry he'd gotten into it. The eyes of his comrades were fixed blearily upon him, and I judged they were all about ready to take a nap.

"I took *ho* for yes," I said.

"No," he said.

"Look here, chief," I said. "I want to make a fair deal, but I don't want to ho ho, yes yes, no no all day with you. How about if we let the heifer decide?"

At this the giggler had a fit, and Red, Blue, and

Yellow shot him a nasty look. "She no know," he said, nodding to Roselle.

"She knows," I said, "for she is a great shaman heifer, a witch cow from Go-loka. Roselle?"

Roselle fastened her attention on me.

"How many Kiowas are there here?" I gestured to the natives around the fire; then, while they waited for her to respond, I secretly showed Roselle seven fingers.

Roselle stared at me, and for a moment I thought she'd forgotten the trick Alice Beck had taught her and that I'd be a candidate for a set of Chauncey Potter's skullcaps.

"How many, Roselle?" I repeated.

To my great relief Roselle scratched seven marks on the ground with her fore hoof.

"She says there are seven," I said to Red, Blue, and Yellow. "How's that agree with your count?"

The giggler let go again, rolling on the ground with medicinal delight.

"Roselle," I said, "what shall we pay these Kiowas to make them happy?"

Again Roselle struck seven.

"All right," I said. "A dollar for each of them." I added four more dollars to the ransom and handed it to the multicolored chief. At first he refused to touch it, but the rest of the party counseled him to take it, and he did so, looking fierce at me. I looked fierce right back, and we stood there locked in fierceness until we couldn't keep it up, and grins started seeping around the edges of our lips. We scowled threateningly, trying to hold off. We made menacing sounds and stalked around one another, but at last the dam

231

burst, and we commenced laughing and flopped down helpless on the ground, clutching our bellies.

The rest of the Kiowas joined in, and you'd have thought we'd struck gold or laughing gas. Tears ran down our faces, because it hurt to be tickled so by human foolishness.

Roselle must have thought us a fine-looking sight because she joined in the fun, lying down, rolling over, and raring up on her rear legs, and when she sat down the Kiowas were once again convulsed. Their gleeful cries and helpless gurgling rebounded through the gullies, and Gospelers One and Two came up to observe us and wait until we recovered our wits.

At last, gasping and wiping tears from my eyes, I got to my feet and shook hands with the Kiowas all around, saying I'd drop in again if I ever came that way and asking them to convey my apologies and felicitations to Tim-oo-leh if they ever ran across him. That I knew the venerable medicine man impressed them so much they offered to give my money back, but I said they should keep it since it was stolen in the first place and warned them to steer clear of the electric belt posse now on its way to Cleo Springs.

"Those folks have suffered depredations near as bad as the Indian nations," I told them, "but they are not as philosophical about it. Bide your time, gentlemen. Bide your time, for I think the white race will undo itself with gadgets. It is their weakness for sprockets and gears and electric currents that in time will incapacitate them for real life. You just stand out of the way and watch."

"Ho! Ho!" Red, Blue, and Yellow said, and I let it go at that.

I boarded Gospeler Two, and the Kiowas waved as I rode off.

Twenty minutes later Gospelers One and Two, Roselle, and I were moving easily over a vast, silent plain under a pewter sky. With the electric belt posse retired, Carl Merkle shot to ashes, Majul Majul once again on his own trail, and Roselle by my side, the territory seemed considerably eased of menace. I still had Matt Burdick to worry about, but since he was out to save and not kill me I was in a joyful mood. The Kiowas had contributed immensely to this change of disposition.

I decided to loop far south, then tip northeast again, hoping to circumnavigate Burdick and reach Enid before the heavy snow began to fall. Getting to Enid had lost much of its importance to me, but a bargain was a bargain, and I had no other destination in mind.

I'd managed thus far to keep Aunt Clara's five-thousand-dollar reward from being claimed, and I intended not to be a drain on the annuity funds provided by her noncombatant cotton-broker brother-in-law. The surest guarantee of that, of course, was to get myself killed and thus avoid those out to collect on me, but this, as yet, seemed a drastic solution to a financial problem.

SHEPHERD'S PIE.

ORTLAND.

❖If a sheep has been downed by a coyote or a wolf, shoot the predator and snatch the sheep carcass. Boil several potatoes. Hide and gut the carcass, preferably a new lamb. Hold the tongue, liver, and heart. Cut away the chewed parts and mince the rest to hash. Heat a Dutch oven. Mash the potatoes, adding a bit of condensed milk, salt, and pepper. Slice wild onions and braise in oven with hashed lamb. Add one can of tomatoes. Mix and flavor. When hash is tender, top with mashed potatoes and bake until brown.

❖Throw leftover carcass to the wolves.

CHAPTER EIGHTEEN

❖ ❖ ❖

Once again I was headed out of Indian territory and determined this time to shed it. Two days later I cut into the Shawnee Trail someplace above Fort Gibson and had turned northeast when my passage was obstructed by a herd of sheep—a sea of sheep, you might say, since they covered about ten acres in one clump.

The Gospelers, Roselle, and I waded into the crowd, and Roselle, who had never seen this variety of beast, thought she had to play with them to get acquainted. She cavorted around, scattering them pretty good, when the shepherd and his sheepdogs got excited and came up to protest. This shepherd wasn't like the ones in the Bible pictures with a crook and beard and flowing robes. This one had a rifle, a slouch hat of Confederate persuasion, one mean eye, and a disposition to match it. "Get that heifer out of my sheep," said he without preamble, "or I am going to add variety to my diet."

"Pardner," I said quietly, "we're moving through your mutton the best we know how. I'm sorry for the disturbance, but this trail is a public passageway presently impeded by your woolies."

"You'd better accommodate your tone to me, sonny, or they're like to find you dead on the ground having been hit by a herd of sheep. I'd just as lief let air through you as I did your cussed brothers at Fredericksburg," Mean Eye countered.

"I am a Texian born and bred," I replied, "and if you'd like to open hostilities, I am your man."

We might have exchanged further words, but our parley was interrupted by a buckboard that came larruping through the sheepman's flock, full speed. The sheep scrambled, jumping on top of one another in their haste to avoid the oncoming horse and wheels. They peeled away like waves at the bow of a ship, and I heard the driver yelling, "Go, Binnacle! Git! Git! Git!" Binnacle, thus addressed, was the handsomest gray gelding I even had the pleasure of seeing, and he had a pace that would have put a drum major to shame. The driver of this vehicle was a gray-bearded article with a voice like a waterfall, wearing a blue frock coat and a pillbox hat with a glossy visor.

Seeing his flock split and scattered as the buckboard bore down on us with no sign of stopping, the sheepman's jaw dropped.

"You there!" the driver bellowed, hauling down to a trot in a lovely maneuver. "You with your tater trap open. Where's the Bigler place?"

The sheepman gulped and batted his meaner eye.

"Oh, it's you, Ortland; I should have known," the driver said, and he hauled Binnacle down to a walk. "Where's the Bigler place? I'm off course here, damn it to bloody hell!"

"Bigler?" Ortland blurted.

"B-I-G-L-E-R! Damn your brain! Do you know the name or do you not?" This was shot over the

238

driver's shoulder because the buckboard was still in motion and picking up speed.

"There's a new family moved in on the Neosho," Ortland called.

"That's the one," the driver replied. "You'd better sort out them sheep, Ortland. I saw a couple of them in there with coccidiosis."

The word spiked my ear. That was what the Chickasaws were suffering from. Coccidiosis. I'd forgotten the word, but there it was, hanging in the air like a sign from heaven.

My plans for Enid were snubbed short, for if there was a chance of my learning something that would save the Chickasaws I had to take it, out of loyalty to my benefactor, Tim-oo-leh. "Who is that man?" I asked the shepherd.

"Dr. Izard McNally," he said.

"Well, I'd better have a word with him." I turned the Gospeler's tail on Ortland and struck out after McNally with Roselle and my spare horse trailing along.

I'd never seen a buckboard so swift and curious as the one Dr. McNally was driving. It seemed to squirm, wriggle, and roll over rocks and potholes like a living thing. There was a pole hanging off the tailgate with canvas, ropes, and pulleys, and I couldn't make sense of it. Dr. McNally kept yelling a stream of nautical instructions to his horse as they sped along. "To the larboard, Binnacle! East by nor'east! Haul away!"

By the time I came up beside the buckboard, Roselle was far behind, and Dr. McNally didn't slacken his pace. He looked over at me, his blue eyes clear as the Caribbean in his weathered face.

"I'd like a word with you, sir!" I called over the sound of his wheels and hooves.

"Septicemia!" he yelled, and he put leather to his horse.

"Just one, sir."

"Osteolipochondroma!" he yelled, and he headed up the Neosho River road without slowing his pace.

"It's about the coccidiosis, sir!" I yelled.

"Stand abaft!" he warned as the road narrowed, and I fell behind. About two miles on we came to a half-log soddy. Dr. McNally wheeled into the yard, snatched a black bag from the seat, and dashed to the door. I followed him, trying to make my case for the Chickasaws.

"Belay that!" he commanded me. "I may need your help. Come on!"

We went into the place, which smelled of mildew and misery. There was a woman hovering over the figure of a girl on the bed. Rings of black exhaustion around the woman's eyes made her look like a sick raccoon.

Dr. McNally dropped on one knee beside the bed.

"Where's Adolph?" the woman whispered bleakly.

"Anesthetized," Dr. McNally said. "You go sit in the fresh air, Mrs. Bigler. I'll look after Cory. She'll be fine."

The woman could hardly move. I helped her to the door, but Dr. McNally snapped me back. "I need you to help me lift the child," he said.

240

Mrs. Bigler went out, and I joined Dr. McNally. The girl on the bed was about fourteen years old. Her skin was pale blue, nearly transparent. She was barely breathing, and the pulse in her neck was beating feebly. I helped Dr. McNally lift her on to the kitchen table, where he stripped her gown down to the waist. I could see her heart struggling beneath the ribs. "Foxglove," I said.

Dr. McNally looked sharp at me. He took a bottle of carbolic solution from his medical bag and swabbed the left side of Cory Bigler's chest. Then he took something like an awl, dipped this in carbolic, and drove it into the girl's chest cavity.

I about swallowed my tongue to keep my lungs from bucking out of my throat.

"Get a basin!" Dr. McNally commanded.

I staggered around and found a large bowl near the stove. It had something in it, but I went to the door and dashed this away.

"Hold it here!" Dr. McNally said, pointing to a place beneath the awl. I did as instructed, and when Dr. McNally withdrew the awl fluid burst out of the wound with such force he had to deflect it into the bowl with his hand.

The girl drew a convulsive breath, and her heart stopped.

Dr. McNally rummaged in his bag and came up with a hypodermic filled with a solution he'd already prepared. He injected Cory and began pounding heavily on her chest.

"Come back here, Cory Bigler!" he demanded. "You don't slip your anchor that easy, my lady. Get

241

that bilge pump thrashing. Fill those bellows and blow a gale!"

The girl drew a convulsive breath, and her heart kicked and began beating. Dr. McNally turned her on her side so the chest cavity could drain. "You must have seen cattle with the bloat," he said to me.

"No."

"Well, you're a cool one, then."

The effusion from the chest cavity filled nearly half the bowl, then stopped. I carried the bowl outside and emptied it away from the house. Cory's mother was seated in the buckboard in shock. I returned to Dr. McNally. "We got another patient outside," I said.

"Oh, we do, do we?" Dr. McNally replied, laying stress on the *we*. "Well, since you seem to have signed on to this crew, you take care of her."

"You got any anemone?"

"No, I don't have any anemone! There's smelling salts in the bag. Will that suit you? Get her in here, and we'll put her to bed. Get something warm into her."

I found the smelling salts in his bag and made for the door. "That girl could use some Seneca snake-root," I said.

Dr. McNally shot me a withering look. "When I ask for your consultation you may split the fee. Now get on deck!"

Roselle was standing by the buckboard when I came out. I took Mrs. Bigler by the arm, but she didn't move. Her eyes were fixed on the horizon, and her face was inert. "Mrs. Bigler," I said softly.

"Cory's dead. That's it, ain't it," she said. Her

voice was close to death itself, as though her lights were blinking out one by one.

"No, Mrs. Bigler. That's not it. Cory is going to be fine."

At that she crumpled over in a fit of weeping she must have been holding back for days. She gasped for breath, and the tears spilled down her face into her hands. I let her go to it awhile; then I stuck the smelling salts to her nose and she snapped up. "Come down now, ma'am," I said. "Come down. You're going to bed and sleep, and when you wake up things are going to be better. You see if I'm not right."

I helped her into the house, put her to bed, and covered her with a blanket. "What was it, Doctor?" she asked me.

"A congestion," I said. "Nothing you need worry about. Just close your eyes and sleep. There now. There, there, that's right. Everything is all right now. Just fine. You sleep. See how fine it is now? Yes, that's right."

She was asleep before I straightened up. Dr. McNally looked at me. "A congestion," he whispered irritably, and he beckoned me to him. "You can't tell aggravated pleurisy from a mainsail! Help me with this tape."

We bandaged Cory Bigler's chest, leaving a rubber drain in the wound in her side. The girl was conscious and scared, but her color had improved. She kept her eyes closed as we worked on her, and I saw she was a pretty girl beneath her pain and anxiety.

"Doctor," Dr. McNally growled at me. "You tell Mrs. Bigler you were a doctor?"

243

"No, sir."

"That's the truth! Help me get her into the other bed." We lifted Cory gently between us and laid her on the second bed, near the kitchen stove. She only weighed about sixty pounds, so thin and frail it seemed to me she floated in our arms. We covered her, and Dr. McNally sat beside her on the bed. "You girl," he said. "Do you hear me, Cory? This is Dr. McNally. Your father sent me from Fort Gibson, and you're going to be all right now. Will you answer me? I know you're tired, but just open your eyes one time and speak to me. Come on, my girl. One time, then you can sleep."

Cory opened her eyes. They were gray flecked with green and were focused on the hereafter, as though she'd caught a glimpse of it when her heart stopped. "I hear you," she said; then she fell into a deep sleep.

Dr. Izard McNally smiled and stood up. He looked at Mrs. Bigler in the other bed and sighed. "Well, we put them both down just fine," he said.

"Where's the man here?" I asked him.

"You're it for a time. Theirs rode into Fort Gibson to get me and caught an aggravated case of whiskey. He didn't believe there was any hope for this girl, and it took the heart out of him. I'll send him on when he's recovered. Now tell me, who the devil are you?"

There it was again—the fool name question. Dr. McNally saw I was struggling with it and went to pack his tools.

"When you make up your mind, let me know," he said. "I judge you're something less than a wholesale killer, and these women need your help. I'd stay, but

I'm scheduled to remove an appendix in the morning and that can't wait. I'm leaving some medicines here so you can look after that girl until Bigler gets back. I'll come the next day or so. Now you water my horse, but lightly, hear, while I write out instructions for their care."

I went out, unhitched Binnacle, and took him down to the bank of the Neosho. Roselle and my two Gospelers came along, and they all drank to get acquainted. When I hitched Binnacle up again I saw that the pole and canvas on the buckboard was some kind of sailing device, which I supposed Dr. McNally used on windy days to propel himself. I'd heard of that nonsense being tried, but this was the first example I'd seen of it.

Dr. McNally came from the house and saw Roselle at my side. "That your heifer, or is she appropriated?" he asked.

"She's on consignment to Enid," I said. "I'm trying to deliver her there."

"You'd better get your compass adjusted, boy. Where did you learn about foxglove being a heart depressant?"

"From a Cherokee, Chief Tim-oo-leh. I spent some time with him learning Indian cures."

Dr. McNally pursed his lips, impressed. "I know him," he said. "Best herbalist in the Indian nations, maybe the whole country. But don't go treating my patients with Seneca snakeroot. You've got a lot to learn."

"I'd like to, sir," I said.

"Like to what?"

"Be a doctor."

Roselle, meantime, had taken it in mind to investigate Dr. McNally and was poking around him. I was afraid she'd butt him off his feet and told her to sit.

Roselle looked at me reproachfully, but she sat, and Dr. McNally burst out laughing, as most folks did when Roselle sat. "She sits!" he said.

"She does. She also lies down, rolls over, plays dead, and counts to ten. Her name is Roselle. Now, Dr. McNally, about the coccidiosis. The Chickasaws are afflicted with it, and I'm supposed to tell them how to get rid of it."

"Coccidiosis is a sheep disease, boy. Humans don't get it. Now, if you're serious about medicine come on to Fort Gibson and we'll talk. I'm the contract army surgeon there, with a practice on the side, and I could use all the help I can get. Keep that tube in Cory's chest open. Keep her warm, feed her lightly, and make her happy someway. That last is most important. You'll find my instructions on the kitchen table with the medicine."

Dr. McNally tapped the visor of his cap and boarded his buckboard. He took up the reins and put his horse in motion. "Home, Binnacle!" he called. "With luck we'll catch the westerlies on the prairie."

Dr. McNally waved and sped away down the Neosho River road.

POPOVERS.

MRS. BIGLER.

❖Popovers are an act of magic. Mine never popped. Mrs. Bigler's never failed to do so. It's in the wrist.

❖She mixed two eggs, one cup of milk, a teaspoon of melted butter, and a quarter teaspoon of salt together, and whisked this into one cup of flour.

❖She poured this into greased custard cups, put them into a hot oven on a cookie sheet, and baked them almost an hour.

❖Eaten with butter and red currant jam.

CHAPTER NINETEEN

❖ ❖ ❖

I spent two days at the Bigler place, during which time I took stock of myself again and found the shelves pretty empty. That first evening I sat on the doorsill listening to the crows cawing in the barren cottonwoods and watching the snow drift lazily in the shafted sunlight. My mounts were in Bigler's shake-built barn, but Roselle was seated at my side, sighing now and again as though she was peeved at me. "We can't run forever," I said to her.

"Mo."

"I could change my name three times a day, but there aren't many like me traveling with a pet heifer who can do tricks. Likely Dr. McNally is already on to my game, and the sheriff, or the army, will come out to collect me."

"Ma."

"Of course I could leave you here and cut out."

Roselle shook her head and counted to seven.

"But I'd be lonesome."

Roselle nodded.

"I guess we'll just have to make a stand."

Roselle stood up.

"When we get to Fort Gibson maybe I'll turn you out with some handsome young bulls. How would that suit you?"

Roselle started to frolic around in that foolish way she had, stiff-legged, tossing her head until I had to laugh, and she came to me and put her head on my shoulder so I would scratch her ears. "Don't slobber," I said. "Dang, but you get juicy!" At this Roselle washed half my face with her tongue. "I'm goin' to swap you for a dog if you don't keep a civil tongue in your head."

"Baw!"

"Baw yourself."

I guessed the time had come for me to admit that I'd given up the plan to deliver Roselle to Enid. I'd been lying to myself about that for some time. When you get to lying to everyone else it's not long before you add yourself to the list. I supposed I could send money to Alice Beck in Monterey, California, to pay for Roselle. There couldn't be so many sardine-canning lawyers in Monterey that a general delivery letter wouldn't reach them sometime.

If there was a way to settle with Mr. Boardman, I'd sure do that too. I knew I had to make a break toward the truth someday and take my licks. The snow thickened and I got cold thinking these thoughts, but at last I concluded I'd better go under my own name and see what came of it. This decided, I went inside, banked the fires, and looked at Cory Bigler, who was sleeping peacefully, as was her mother. I spread my blankets on the table and stretched out for the night.

The next morning Mrs. Bigler was up and looking better now that she saw Cory was going to recover. She was a large, hearty-natured woman of Swedish descent who'd married Adolph Bigler, a German émigré, and produced one child thus far, being Cory. She was one of those women who attack work like it was a foe best taken by surprise. She jumped on it and thrashed it into submission, taking pride in each triumph.

Cory was still sleeping as Mrs. Bigler made breakfast, whispering to me, "How would you like your eggs, Doctor?"

I drew a deep breath and took my first plunge into the truth since I could remember. "See here, Mrs. Bigler," I said. "My name is Wylie Jackson, and I am not a doctor. I'm a common horse thief wanted in three states and the territory."

Mrs. Bigler laughed and slapped her hands together. "Dr. Jackson, you are a skit. Oh, my!"

"They nearly hung me for murder in Cleo Springs last week," I said.

Mrs. Bigler threw up her hands and carried on like this was the funniest thing she'd heard in her life.

"But the Gospeler saved me."

"Oh, Doctor, please don't," Mrs. Bigler gasped.

I saw Cory was awake and trying not to laugh because it hurt her side when she did. "Please, Dr. Jackson," she begged. "Don't go on so. Please don't."

I stopped telling the truth at once to spare Cory the pain of it. Truth, I saw, was something that had to be administered in small doses, or it could damage the patient. "How are you feeling this morning?" I asked her.

"Surprised to be here, more than anything," Cory said. She looked around the room, and everything her eyes touched seemed to shine. It had been something like that for me after I was hung. When they jerked the hood off I couldn't believe the reality of things and how glorious everything looked to me. A common stone had the shine of diamonds to it. And that was how Cory was seeing things, but deeper because she'd gone farther. When her eyes fell on me I felt shining, too. "You saved my life," Cory whispered.

"No, that was Dr. McNally."

"I don't remember too well."

"You don't have to. Best thing for you to do is sleep all you can and to know you're getting well."

Cory nodded, closed her eyes, and was asleep again with a smile on her lips. She'd collected the world and she was happy with it, and I wondered how it could have gotten along without her.

I tried to make myself useful around the house, but Mrs. Bigler protested everything I did as if I was interfering with her battle plans. We spoke in subdued tones so we wouldn't disturb Cory. "Now, Doctor, put down that broom! What kind of thing is that for a doctor to be doing?"

"There's a reward of five thousand dollars on me," I said.

We tussled for the broom, and Mrs. Bigler wrested it from me, laughing and shushing me and pointing to Cory, asleep. "Please stop it," she whispered.

If I picked up a pot or a stick of stovewood, we tussled for that. It got to be a real contest. I'd feint for the water bucket and grab the dishpan. "I'm a sworn vegetarian!"

Each time I tricked her Mrs. Bigler would laugh and beg me to stop being such an all-fired fool. I tricked her off the throw rug in the front room and snatched it up to take outside and shake, but she came right behind me.

"Dr. Jackson! You are not going to shake my rugs. Now you give me that right here. What kind of thing is that to do?"

There were two inches of snow on the ground, and Roselle came romping up from the barn. I ran around the house with Mrs. Bigler chasing me. "Doctor, give me that rug! Why, I'd be shamed for life if anyone saw you shaking my rug!"

Roselle cavorted along with us, kicking up the snow. Mrs. Bigler was behind me, calling, "Give back my rug! You can't take my rug!"

We came around the house a second time, and I ran smack into a big blond man with a pistol aimed at my middle. "Heist 'em!" he said.

I dropped the rug and did so.

"Adolph!" Mrs. Bigler cried. "This is Dr. Jackson!"

The man looked confused, and there was no time to warn him. Roselle lowered her head and charged, hitting Adolph Bigler just at the knees. He went up in the air with a look of astonishment on his face. The pistol fired harmlessly, and Bigler fell in a heap on the snow. I whistled for Roselle, who came to my side, pawing snow, ready to charge again.

Mrs. Bigler fell on her knees beside her husband. "Adolph! Are you all right?"

Bigler was stunned. He tried to swing the pistol on me, but Mrs. Bigler pushed it away. "Adolph! This is Dr. Jackson. He saved our Cory! Is this the thanks we give?"

"He's stealing your rug," Bigler said.

"He's trying to shake it. Imagine, a doctor shaking our rug. You stop him, Adolph. I can't."

Adolph Bigler scrambled to his feet and holstered his pistol. "I saw him running from the house with the rug and you were after him. I thought he was stealing it."

"Why, the idea that Dr. Jackson would steal! You should be ashamed of yourself, Adolph."

"I only steal horses, cattle, and currency," I said. "I did steal a hat and boots once, but that was an emergency."

Mrs. Bigler commenced laughing again. "Oh," she gasped, "he talks a scandal, Adolph. Don't you believe a word he says!"

Adolph looked at Roselle warily. "You'd best corral that creature," he said. "What is it?"

"A cattalo," I told him. "Cross between a buffalo and a longhorn."

Again Mrs. Bigler burst out laughing. "Land, what won't he think of next!"

"Roselle is shy of guns," I explained to Bigler. "She saw a calf shot one time, and she's never forgotten it. It comes in handy if a law officer attempts to arrest me."

"I see how that could be," Bigler said, massaging his bruised rump.

"Don't pay him any mind, Adolph! Now come inside out of this cold and see how Dr. Jackson has done with our Cory."

I took up the rug and flapped the snow off, but Mrs. Bigler snatched it from me. Bigler was loath to turn his back on Roselle. "Will she let us shake hands?" he asked me.

"As long as no guns are involved."

Bigler and I shook hands; then we trooped inside to watch Cory sleeping. To see us standing around the bed looking at her, you would have thought sleeping was the rarest performance in the world. I'd never seen a girl sleep so prettily in all my life. I could have watched her for quite a spell, but she woke up, and I went outside to feed my stock and let her get re-acquainted with her pa.

I stayed again that night and learned more about Dr. Izard McNally. He'd been a surgeon in the Union Navy aboard the U.S.S. *Muscoota,* a blockader, off the coast of Georgia. After the war he'd come west for reasons unknown, at least to Adolph Bigler. Out of his earshot they called him Gizzard Izard, but he was respected as a fine doctor who had pulled a lot of arrowheads and delivered most of the local babies. Cory, whose full name was Coriander Susan Bigler, was one of these, born at Fort Gibson when the family had been living there and Adolph was a sutler.

"When I reached the fort, I was certain Cory was going to die," Bigler said to me. "I told Dr. McNally so, and he roared at me, 'Why, you damned fool, go get drunk, then. Go moan at a whiskey bottle.' I followed his prescription. I was so scared of losing her I couldn't face it." He put his hand on Mrs. Bigler's knee, and his eyes were moist. "I'm sorry, Inger," he whispered. "I just couldn't face it, and I left you here to face it alone."

"Why, Mr. Bigler, there was nothing more you could have done than what you did, my dear."

There were times when I missed my aunt Clara until I thought I'd bust, and this was one of those. Sentiment has come into disrepute among the cog watchers and carnivores. Having benumbed themselves with meat, electricity, and gears, they resent being exposed to feelings, for they see how poor they have become. I, of course, was headed in that direction myself, being a hard-encased liar.

The next morning Dr. Izard McNally appeared at the door. He came in brushing snow from the shoulders of his coat. I helped him out of it, and he stamped his boots to warm his feet. "Had a fair nor'easter," he said, "and Binnacle had to gallop to keep ahead of me. If we didn't have these hills I could have sailed clear to Joplin. That's the trouble with this country, too many paralyzed waves. . . . Well, lad, how's our patient this morning?"

I caught the "our" and saw Mrs. Bigler grin and bob her head at me much as to say I was found out for a doctor no matter what tales I made up.

"Haven't been dosing Cory with masterwort for the coccidiosis, have you?" Dr. McNally asked me.

"I followed your instructions, sir."

Dr. McNally helped Cory sit up, then began thumping the back of her chest and listening. "Here," he said to me, "get your ear down here."

I colored up some but obeyed, and while Dr. McNally thumped I listened and could hear the different timbres from Cory's chest.

"What's your opinion?" Dr. McNally asked me.

256

I had nothing to go on. I removed my ear from Cory's back and nodded sagely. "Absolutely," I said.

If glares could sear I'd have let off smoke.

"Boy," Dr. McNally growled, "there are three sacred words in the English language you'd better learn right quick. Do you have any notion what they are?"

I thought a bit, then shook my head. "I don't know," I said.

"That's right! Now the next time those words flash in your mind, shout them right out. Let's hear it."

"I don't know!"

"Good. The confession of ignorance is the beginning of wisdom. Now, since you don't know, I'll tell you. Her left lung is still partially collapsed, and she's still got fluid." Dr. McNally laid Cory down again and stood up. He nodded us to follow him to the kitchen. "Adolph," he said, "I think you'd better bundle Cory up and bring her to Fort Gibson, where we can keep an eye on her. She's going to need more care than you can offer here, and I want her close by just in case."

Adolph and Inger clung to one another, their faces filled with anxiety, but Dr. McNally continued his diagnosis. "She's running a fever, and she's weak as a kitten."

"Dogwood, indigoweed, boneset," I said.

"Hold your herbs, boy. I'll give her a febrifuge."

"I don't know that one."

Dr. McNally silenced me with a bullet look. "Bring the wagon around, Adolph. Put the cover up. We'll take her bed and all so she won't be jarred about."

Adolph and I went for the wagon. We pulled the

tarp over the hoops, hitched the team, and drove back to the front door of the house. There was a foot of new snow on the ground, which had the blessing, I thought, of cushioning Cory's ride to Fort Gibson.

We covered Cory with blankets, and Mrs. Bigler had already heated bricks and wrapped them in a sheet to keep Cory warm on the journey. After the four of us had lifted the bed and put it in the wagon I was about to ask what was to become of me when Dr. McNally spoke to the Biglers. "Now don't you folks worry," he said. "I'll have a room for Cory made up at my place, and she'll be fine. I know you'd like to stay with her, but sometimes it's easier for a patient to be looked after by outsiders. Lady Pennylunch will do the necessaries, and we'll make out fine. Besides, I've got this woods merchant here to run errands for me."

I took this to mean I was to go, so I ran to the barn and collected my horses and Roselle. When I was saddled up and back at the wagon, Dr. McNally was already scattering snow from his buckboard wheels. Mrs. Bigler was inside the wagon with Cory and Adolph put his plow team to an easy walk.

I followed the wagon with my spare horse and Roselle and saw Mrs. Bigler and Cory smiling at me over the tailgate as we made our way to Fort Gibson.

"I was a Muslim in Cleo Springs," I called to them. "A patent-medicine hawker. My name was Fasli Akbar."

"Oh, pshaw!" Mrs. Bigler cried, waving her hands at me, and Cory grinned like all get-out.

YAM CAKES.

LADY PENNYLUNCH.

❖Lady Pennylunch cooked quickly and served a variety of dishes with effortless composure. I memorized the yam cakes.

❖Boil yams until tender, then skin and mash them. Mix yams with three eggs, a cup of flour, two teaspoons of salt, pepper, and cooking oil. Drop mixture by the spoonful on a sizzling griddle.

❖Serve with butter and honey.

CHAPTER TWENTY

❖   ❖   ❖

Fort Gibson was a busy town located at the junction of the Verdigris, Neosho, and Arkansas Rivers. Steamboats carried freight and passengers up and down the rivers to Fort Smith, Little Rock, New Orleans, Memphis, St. Louis, and Cincinnati, and the sight of river traffic was new to me. For all this there were only about two thousand people resident in the town of tree-lined streets, Victorian houses, a hotel, a train depot, a sheriff's office, and the usual shops and businesses. With the snow falling lightly, it was a pleasant scene as we drove through town with Cory in the wagon. There was snow on the trees and blanketing the yards and the roofs of the houses and shops. The kids were snowballing one another, building forts and snowmen, and their voices rang in the still, cold air.

We arrived about noon, when people were getting their dinner, and I could smell biscuits and carrots and somewhere a raisin pie cooling on a windowsill. It had been so long since I'd had meat that I'd lost the detection of it, but I'm sure there was pot roast too, though I censored that out.

At this time the army still had a small detachment at Fort Gibson to help the U.S. marshals control train robbers, wild bloods, and desperadoes, who took the territory for their playground. When the M.K.&T. railroad got to attracting tourists who wanted the pleasure of being robbed by Bignose Bill, Tracy Starr, or one of the lesser luminaries in the bandido hierarchy, the army took a hand in monitoring this traffic. The idea wasn't to discourage the tourist trade but to regulate the tariff and keep the robberies confined to the Pryor Creek grade on Saturdays, Sundays, and holidays.

City folks thought it was a fine outing to ride the "Katy" and get robbed. They'd buy a weekend ticket, load their pockets with tin watches and Confederate money, and be disappointed if the train wasn't stopped and boarded by some gun-waving galoots. Most times the army was off in the woods close by to prevent the outlaws from expressing their disappointment over the trash emptied into their sacks by passengers who'd come prepared for the show. Paste jewelry and junk was about all they ever got, and the bandits might have quit if the directors of the Katy line hadn't promised them a pension to keep up the act.

The fort proper was about half a mile from town and we drove to it, passing the wood yard and the hay yard and the old, crumbling stockade all sheathed in snow. We turned into the compound, passing the commissary storehouse where Mr. Bigler had worked for a time, and went along officers' row to Dr. McNally's house, which was across from the stone barracks and next to the post hospital. It was a big, comfortable-looking three-story house with a deep front veranda. As we approached, Dr. McNally came out to meet us with an Indian woman at his side. She walked with the grace of a bygone era and had a presence that I could only compare to Tim-oo-leh's. She was a Cherokee, I was to discover, and her name, Lady Pennylunch, derived from the days before the Civil War, when she'd sold hard-boiled eggs to the soldiers for a penny. Her dignity was undeniable, hence the first half of her name. She accepted Penny-lunch and kept her true Indian name in silence.

Four soldiers came to lift Cory from the wagon. Lady Pennylunch introduced herself to Cory and held her hand as we came into the hall and took Cory to her room.

"Go with her if you like," Dr. McNally said to the Biglers. "You, mate, stand by here."

He waited until the Biglers had gone into Cory's room; then he beckoned me into his office, went to the window, and stood there with his back to me. "All right, you'd better tell it all," he said.

"My true name is Wylie Jackson," I began.

"Humph!"

I told him the bones of it straight off. About the drive, Roselle, stealing Mr. Boardman's horse, the OHO anthrax die-up, and so on. I left out the hypo-larium, Fasli Akbar, and the cure since I didn't want to make too big a fool of myself right off.

When I ran down, Dr. McNally turned from the window. "Boardman," he said. "That would be Colo-nel John Boardman, I suppose."

"Yes, sir," I said.

"And you're lying low to spare your aunt Clara from paying the five-thousand-dollar reward for your discovery."

"Yes, sir. I wrote to ask her to withdraw it, but I don't know if she has. When she does I'll give myself up."

"You're a real philanthropist," he said.

"I've never tried that one, sir. Stealing is more my game."

"I know all of the marshals in the territory and most of them owe me a favor. Suppose I arrange to have your stolen horses returned to Matt Burdick without revealing where you are?"

"My hat, pistol, and boots are his, too, sir, and twenty-six dollars. I'm short seven because I had to ransom Roselle from the Kiowas."

"Hat, boots, and Kiowas," Dr. McNally said.

"Yes, sir."

Dr. McNally drew a deep breath and blew it away.

I decided I'd best not mention nearly being hung for Carl Merkle in Cleo Springs.

"I'll see what I can do. Get your stolen horses and that cattalo out from in front of my house. You can put them in the army stables. After dinner come to my study, and we'll talk some more. I find I can only take you in small dosages."

"Thank you, sir," I said, and I bowed myself out of his office.

After I'd sheltered my animals I had dinner with the Biglers in the kitchen. They were sorry to leave Cory but knew it was best, and Lady Pennylunch reassured them.

"She'll be twice the young lady she is now when you see her again," she said.

"I'm sure that's so, Mrs. Pennylunch," Mrs. Bigler replied.

"Lady," Lady Pennylunch corrected, and from this I knew she was not a woman with whom one took liberties in form of address or manners. Her long black hair was pulled back severely in two massive braids. Her eyes were dense black, her skin ruby, and her face, chin, nose, and lips were not shy of size. She wore a plain light blue wool dress, belted at the middle with a worked silver belt inlaid with turquoise and obsidian. She was, to my thinking, the most beautiful, most formidable woman I had ever seen, and I hoped I could live up to her expectations.

After dinner the Biglers thanked me and started back to their home on the Neosho. I stopped in on Cory, who was awake and watching a pair of canaries in a cage on a table beside her bed. "Aren't they nice?" she said to me. "They belong to Lady Pennylunch."

"What are their names?"

"She hasn't told me yet. She said if I watch them long enough I'll know."

"I bet you will."

"Do you have any idea?"

"Not a one. But when I have time I'll come watch them with you. Now I have to meet Dr. McNally."

"I'm glad you're with him, Dr. Jackson."

"Listen, Miss Cory, I'm really not a doctor. I'm a bunch quitter and a renegade."

"Oh, please, Doctor, don't make me laugh."

I tried to think of something that would convince

her and not cause pain but, roving through my past, I couldn't think of anything. I was afraid that if I told Cory about the electric belt posse or the hypolarium she might need stitches. I said goodbye in my best bedside manner and went to Dr. McNally's study.

This was a large book-filled room at the end of the ground-floor hall. There was a standing globe, a telescope, chairs and desks, more books, and some paintings of Indians. Dr. McNally was reading as I came in. He looked up from his book and began to rack my brains as they had never been racked before.

If I thought Dr. McNally was going to coax me into the medical profession I was sorely mistaken. What, he asked me, did I know of chemistry? Latin? German? Anatomy? He asked me to divide three fifths in half, and what was twelve into a hundred and thirty-two?

My negative and failed responses to these questions sank Dr. McNally into a swamp of despondency, but I was on the bottom looking up. After an hour of trying and failing to draw water from my intellectual well, Dr. McNally sighed and stood up. "Well, Jackson," he said, "you're good at leaves, barks, and seeds. You can add some and even subtract. I appreciate your offer to demonstrate chants, rattles, and drums, but I will leave Lady Pennylunch to be the judge of that."

"I'd rather you didn't mention it, sir," I said.

"I see. You are, then, I might say, an unmarked slate. Hard work might leave a mark. Do you care to persist?"

"I do, sir."

Dr. McNally went to a bookcase filled with ominous-looking medical tomes. "Start in the upper left-hand corner and read down to the lower right-hand corner. Go through these books like a weevil through a cotton boll. If any of it takes, we'll talk again. Meantime I'll see you earn your keep in practical pursuits, and you can have the room at the top of the stairs, next to Lady Pennylunch."

"Thank you, sir," I said.

"We'll see if you thank me or not," he said.

I took Wistar's *Anatomy* from the top left-hand corner of the bookcase, went to my room, and read until the words ran together and I fell asleep.

It took me several days to get used to the comforts and discomforts of an orderly existence. At five-thirty in the morning I awoke to the sound of reveille from the fort and twenty minutes later had to stand inspection for Lady Pennylunch. By the end of the week she'd washed and mended my clothes and cut my hair to reveal how dirty the back of my neck could get. If I'd wanted a disguise nothing could have been better than neatness. The first time I caught sight of myself in the mirror I wondered who it was. My eyes were still brown, but the face around them had changed a lot; it was lean and brown where it had been soft and white, and given the right amount of light I could see hair on my top lip, which reminded me of Amos Hypolarium's recommendation about cream and a black cat.

Soon after I settled in, Matt Burdick's two horses and his boots, pistol, and hat vanished. Dr. McNally made an arrangement with one of his marshal friends, but nothing was said of this, and I did not ask about it. I missed the horses since Gospeler One and Two were the best I'd stolen next to Ruddy Bob. I still had my saddle with its secret pouch containing Alice Beck's now-neutralized drawers. Roselle was no longer oriented to them, so they did not represent a threat. Lady Pennylunch said I could use army mounts when I needed transportation, which was not often.

I'd explained my vegetarian convictions, and these were catered to. Lady Pennylunch made burritos stuffed with vegetables in a sauce I could have eaten by the hour, nonstop, and what she did with beans and rice put bacon, chops, and all such slaughter food to shame.

After breakfast Roselle usually strolled up from the stables where she was housed. The dragoons at the fort had made her their mascot when they saw the tricks she could do. Roselle had the run of the place, but her horns were out four inches, and I warned the troopers not to flash a gun in her presence unless they wanted to get picked.

Of course, a couple of men didn't believe me about this. They gave Roselle the test by drawing their guns and were knocked into a snowdrift for their trouble. This increased Roselle's stock, and all the attention she got from the men went to her head. During the morning roll call she'd take her place at the end of the first file, and Sergeant Riggs would bark her name. "Roselle!"

"Mo!"

Then while the men in ranks were stifling their grins Sergeant Riggs would spin on his heel and salute Captain Jacks. "All present and accounted for, sir!"

"Baw!"

"Silence in the ranks!" Captain Jacks would call.

"Mo!"

Roselle gave the men a lot of fun, but I only knew of it secondhand since my time was consumed. Dr. McNally saw to that. "See here, Jackson," he said to me at the end of the second week, "if I'm to be your preceptor you've got to put your time in order. Here's a book of hours, for your diary and notes. From now on you're working twelve hours a day. First watch is seven to noon in the hospital dispensary, where you will dress minor cuts and abrasions and familiarize yourself with standard pharmaceuticals while at the same time reading Cullen's *Materia Medica and Practice* and Quinsey's *Dispensatory.* Second watch, one to four, you will have ward duty at the hospital under the supervision of Lady Pennylunch, who is the finest practical nurse you will ever have the privilege of serving with. Third watch, six to ten, back to the dispensary on call while working on chemistry, dissection, and pathology. I don't want to catch sight of you without a book in your hand, and if I shout a question in your direction you'd better have a ready answer for it."

"Yes, sir!"

"Where's the squamous suture?"

"The head, sir, joining the frontal bone and the parietal."

This surprised him and me. By that time I'd already put so much in my head I didn't expect any of it to come out, but it did.

I followed Dr. McNally's schedule and read medical books until I was drugged with terminology and went around in a daze, snow-blind to the world.

Once in a while I'd slip off to the stables and read to Roselle. " 'This is an operation to establish anastomoses between the systemic and portal venous system to relieve ascites; it consists in opening the abdominal cavity, scrubbing the peritoneum of the liver and spleen and corresponding parts of the parietal peritoneum with a sponge and suturing the omentum within the abdominal wall. . . .' What do you think of that one?"

"Baw!"

"Mustn't forget to take out the sponge."

"Mo!"

"Medical language is almost as tough as cow talk," I said.

Roselle looked disgusted. She didn't see much sense in what I was doing, but having started I couldn't turn back.

Each night before I went to bed I stopped in on Cory, who was much better. She hadn't yet guessed the names of the canaries, but they gave her companionship and hours of entertainment. Reading so much anatomy made it impossible for me not to see through Cory, and while she talked I was rehearsing the positions and functions of her inner organs. She'd been up, I think she said, and walked a bit, and her parents had come to see her twice. Dr. McNally said she'd soon be well, but he wanted her to stay until she was fully recovered with no chance of a relapse. Until the weather improved, perhaps. She loved Lady Pennylunch and wished she could be like her, so beautiful and dignified.

I guess there was room in my brain for some of this, for it came out later, but mainly I was taking on medical facts, and sometimes it frightened me to know that the more I found out the more there was to know. I lost track of real time because I was so engaged hour by hour, my brain swirling like a tornado and sucking up all the medical information around it. Dr. John Hunter's *Blood, Inflammation, and Gun Shot Wounds* got to be light reading for me, and Hamilton's *Obstetrics* was so obvious I thought the man a fool. I'm sure I was crazy much of the time, but I didn't care. When it got too bad I had Roselle to cling to.

Each time I came in contact with Dr. McNally he'd shout a medical term at me. "Choledocholithiasis!"

"Gallstone in the bile duct!"

"Right, Jackson! Carry on."

Dr. McNally kept closer watch on me than I knew. "Jackson," he said to me one afternoon, "man does not live by brain alone!"

"Cerebrum. Corpus callosum. Cerebellum."

"Stow that! Wake up there! What happened to ragwort, Seneca snakeroot, and hepatica?"

"They're in there, sir."

"Someways I liked them better. You're beginning to look at people as though they were ambulatory cadavers for your dissecting eye. It's distinctly unsettling. Your right arm is already longer than your left from carrying a book around. You'd better correct the condition with Gross's two-volume edition on surgery, carried in the left arm to let it resume its original length. Our patient, in case you haven't noticed, is on her feet, and you may have the day off."

I thanked him and picked up Eberle's *Treatise on the Practice of Medicine,* but Dr. McNally snatched it from my hand. "No books today," he said.

A tremor ran through my body. I was being thwarted of an addiction without which I could not exist. Then I remembered there was a book in my room McNally didn't know about, Drake's *Systematic, Historical, Etiological, and Practical Treatise on the Principal Diseases of the Interior Valley of North America as They Appear in the Caucasian, African, Indian, and Esquimaux Varieties of Its Population.* With a whole day to myself I could make it halfway through this tome. But as I reached the door, feeling secure, Dr. McNally said he'd instructed Lady Pennylunch to remove this work from my bedside.

"But Doctor!" I pleaded. "I need it!"

"No," he said sternly. "Rest your eyes."

"What am I supposed to do?"

"Take a walk."

"A walk? Why?"

"Dang, Jackson! You give a person fits! You're all extremes and nothing in the middle! Gather Roselle and Cory and take a walk. It's a brilliant day."

"Just walk?"

"Get out of here!" McNally roared. "It's Christmas!" And he slammed the study door in my face.

BOILED CHRISTMAS FRUITCAKE.

MRS. BIGLER.

❖One cup water, one cup sugar, half cup butter, one cup raisins, one cup currants, one spoon cinnamon, one spoon cloves, one spoon salt. Mix with a little baking powder. Add dates and nuts. Put this mixture on stove and let boil two or three minutes. Set aside to cool, then add two cups flour sifted with one spoon each soda and baking powder. Add lemon extract to suit, mix well and bake one hour in moderate oven.

CHRISTMAS EGGNOG.

SANTA DADU.

❖Separate twelve eggs, add one cup sugar to yolks, and beat until a creamy lemon color. Mix into this two quarts "Waters of Jerusalem." Beat three pints of heavy cream until stiff. Add half a teaspoon salt to egg whites and beat until stiff. Add stiff cream and stiff egg whites to egg yolk mixture. Top with nutmeg and drink until stiff.

Chapter Twenty-one

❖ ❖ ❖

I stood in the hallway trying to catch up with myself. Christmas? Of course it was Christmas, or would be in two days. I knew that. Of course I did, but in the throes of my addiction to medical tomes Christmas hadn't seemed important.

I put my jacket on and went outside. There was three feet of snow on the ground, and I had not seen it get there. The sky was clear, and the sunshine on all that whiteness was blinding. I stumbled along rehearsing symptoms, and to stop this I scooped a handful of snow to wash my face. The cold helped some, and when I found myself at the stables Cory was there talking to Roselle. "Men!" I heard Cory say. "Baw," Roselle replied; then they saw me and stopped talking.

Cory was wearing a long coat, a muffler, and a fur cap about a size too large. Her blond hair tumbled out around it, shinier than I had ever seen. Roselle had grown up and her winter coat was wooly with a buffalo mane over her shoulders. She still looked feminine, but not so youthful and frolicsome as I remembered.

"I'm going Christmas shopping," I said boldly. "How'd you two ladies like to come along?"

"We'd like that, wouldn't we, Roselle?" Cory said.

"Maa!"

We crossed the parade ground over the hard-packed snow and walked to town. I tried whistling to keep the medical terms at bay, but they kept slipping in on me and driving attempts at conversation out of my mind. At last I hit on something and asked Cory if she'd guessed the names of the canaries.

"You and I," she said.

"What?"

"You and I are their names. I never guessed, so Lady Pennylunch told me. I love her for seeing things like that, don't you?"

"Like what?"

"Like how names of things make such a difference and about the way we talk to ourselves about things changes them. When she told me their names I was feeling so sick and blue, but when I heard You and I all that changed. You and I are such wonderful little creatures. I could watch them for hours and hours being happy. Listening to them sing."

"Good medicine," I said.

"The best. How are your studies coming?"

"Fine."

"Mother was so astonished you really weren't a doctor. Now she wonders if all those other things you told her are true."

"What things?" I asked, scowling, trying to remember which crop of lies I'd sprung on Mrs. Bigler or if it was the truth I'd told her.

"About nearly being hung in Cleo Springs."

"That was long ago, when I was Fasli Akbar."

Cory grinned and spoke to Roselle. "You tell me now, Roselle, was he ever Fasli Akbar?"

"Mo," Roselle replied, and she rang her bell twice.

"I was so."

"Mo!"

"Oh, have it your way. Let it go." I wasn't about to get reentangled in my past, which seemed terribly distant, as though it belonged to someone else.

We came to the snow-cushioned town, decorated for the season with a Christmas tree at the main cross street and green, white, and red bunting in the shop windows. People, muffled to the ears, carried Christmas packages in their arms and greeted one another, their smiling faces rosied by the cold. It was perfect. Even the icicles hanging from the eaves looked as if they'd been put there to please a photographer.

I still had eleven dollars of the twenty-six I'd stolen from Matt Burdick and was wondering if I could buy Christmas presents with stolen money and what I'd get Roselle and Cory and Dr. McNally and Lady Pennylunch if I solved this moral problem. I thought I could be forgiven if I found a way, in the future, to return the money to Burdick with interest.

As we came to the center of town I heard a bell ringing and a hearty "Ho, ho, ho!" I saw a fat Santa standing on a wagon beside a lectern made of wooden packing crates. He was ringing a brass cowbell and shouting, "Ho, ho, ho! Meddy Kissymouse! Meddy Kissymouse!"

I knew at once by the twanging mispronunciation that Dr. Majul Majul Dadu Budge Budge Burns had survived his ordeal on the prairie. "Oh, look!" Cory cried. "There's Santa Claus."

He'd stationed himself near the town Christmas tree and wore a red suit and cap trimmed with white cotton and a great white beard that hid all but his

277

eyes. "Ho, ho! Meddy Kissymouse!" he cried. "Meddy Kissymouse!"

Cory caught me by the hand and pulled me toward this apparition, but I knew if Majul Majul et al. saw Roselle he'd recognize me at once. "Hold up," I said to Cory. "Let me park Roselle."

"Let her come, Wylie!"

"No, I don't want her confused by human mythologies."

"Now that is plain stupid, Wylie Jackson. Roselle will understand."

Roselle began to count to fortify this case, but I was firm. "There are times, Miss Cory, when a young lady ought not to come between a man and his beast. I have raised this cattalo and know her predilections. You go ahead, and I'll join you when I have parked Roselle."

Cory fluffed indignantly and marched to the crowd gathering around Santa Majul. I took Roselle to the train station freight platform and told her to lie down and stay.

"Mo!"

"You stay put, you hear me?"

"Bah!"

"I'm not fooling now. Stay! Stay! Stay!"

Roselle lowed and nodded, clanging her bell twice. I still wasn't sure if these bell claps had any significance, but I pointed at her nose and admonished her once more. "You stay!"

"Flumph."

I walked away, glancing back at Roselle warningly;

then I turned the corner and joined the crowd around Dadu Claus.

"Meddy Kissymouse, gentle citizens of Fort Gibson. It is I, your dear Sandy Close, come to bless you at this seasoning and recall to you the presence of kine in the manger." At this he took a rolled poster from one of the packing boxes and spread it open for all the crowd to see. It was a vividly colored portrayal of a haloed baby Jesus in the manger with Mary, the three Wise Men, and Joseph. Shepherds stood about gaping in the wings, angels hovered above, and there were several cows and some sheep among the hay.

Santa waited until all had familiarized themselves with these details; then he pointed to the cows. "Here, dear people, are the sacred cows, present at the birth of your sweet Savior. Now what are we to conclude from this? Do you see any turkeys? Do you see ducks, geese, or chickens? No, there are none such. Is this an oversight, or is this Christmas? Now before I answer that question I would like to tell you about the Waters of Jerusalem, only recently discovered and imported into this Christian nation."

Santa Budge let the poster roll up. He took a bottle of the waters from the crate and raised it aloft. The label bore a red-and-green illustration of a mosque, two palm trees, and a camel. I judged it contained about thirty percent alcohol, and I knew other men in the crowd were of the same opinion.

Fort Gibson was plagued by a particularly virulent Women's Temperance Union, which disallowed the consumption of wine, brandy, gin, or whiskey and all such evil drinks. Only uncouth soldiers drank such beverages, but their weakness was understandable, if not forgiven, because they were under the constant threat of death at the hands of the gangs that punctually robbed the Katy line. Family men, however—clerks, lawyers, real-estate boomers, Methodists, Lutherans, or Baptists—had no such heroic excuse, and they all labored under the unwavering stricture "Lips that touch liquor shall never touch mine!"

Given this choice, the good burghers of Fort Gibson faced the prospect of Christmas without punch, grog, or a sly nip in the woodshed. But here was Santa Majul holding aloft the answer to this bleak prospect, the Waters of Jerusalem.

I had to admire Majul's perspicacity. He had come to know the American spirit.

"Gentlepersons," Majul continued, "in this sacred time, with all its joys and hurry, its carols and inclement weather, it is not surprising one may fall victim to the dread catarrh, which, graduating to pneumonia, may sap the vitality even unto death."

Several men in the audience had already begun coughing to prove their need for the Waters of Jerusalem. Their sneezing and snuffling accompanied Majul, who continued, "The symptoms to you of this disease are known. The dull and heavy headache, confinement of the nasal passages, thick and tenacious mucus, ringing in the ears, dizziness and expectoration of offensive matter . . ."

By now the hacking and coughing, snuffling, and wheezing were epidemic. "Come on, sell the stuff!" a man shouted from the crowd, but Majul rolled on.

"Sweet and tangy, the Waters of Jerusalem are specific to all these complaints and will lift them from you as by magic. You will feel the euphoria of your dear Savior steal upon you and gaze fondly on your beloved ones gathered at your fireside, secure and cured of the catarrh, caroling gaily, eyes twinkling in the firelight, feet tapping to the melodies of Kissy-mouse, at merely one dollar the bottle."

"I'll take five!"

"But before I dispense my limited stock of these fine waters let us consider the kine." At this Santa Burns popped open the poster again and pointed to the cows in the manger.

"To hell with the kine," someone shouted.

"Well, I'm glad Roselle didn't see this," Cory said to me. "Come on, let's go."

"Wait. I want to hear him."

"He's nothing but an old faker, Wylie!"

"How did you guess?"

"I'm not dumb as a fence post. Why are all these men standing around, listening to this rot?"

"They're thirsting for knowledge," I said.

"The cow," Santa Dadu resumed, "present at the birth of Jesus, is a justly sacred creature in all nations and should be so revered. Perhaps the Lord grants us to eat turkeys and geese in celebration of his birth, since they are not here present; I offer no opinion of that, but those of you who are contemplating roast beef should reconsider. Would you eat a Wise Man portrayed here, or the angel? Surely not, yet some among you devour a holy creature present at and sanctified by the birth of Jesus. See how he smiles upon the presence of the kine. See his little hand raised in blessing to all present—all, mind you—and this includes the kine."

"All right! Sell, and we'll eat goose!"

But Dad Burns was soaring to his thesis. "See the Wise Men, heads inclined to the stabled kine. Are they fools? Or do they say, 'Respect and preserve these blessed creatures of our Lord.' "

The men in the crowd had stopped hacking and grown surly. Their feet were cold. They wanted to buy and be gone. Had I been on that wagon I would have warned Dad Burns that he was pushing too far. But once a proselytizer, always a proselytizer. He had to get in his final lick. "Gentlemen and ladies who yet remain, how many of you will join me in a vow with Jesus to nevermore consume the cow? Those of you who come to this Christian persuasion, raise your hands."

Two hands went up.

"Get on with it, Santa!" another man yelled.

"Bless you, gentlemen," Burns intoned, beaming on the men with their hands raised. "For you the Waters of Jerusalem are reduced to fifty cents."

Eight more hands shot up, and I saw that Dad Burns had learned to estimate the tolerance of his audiences.

"And bless you also, dear gentlemen. Ten true men stand here vowing to no longer violate the manger and eat beef. Who will join them? Come, gentlemen, follow their example."

Since most of these men had raised their hands and

taken vows of temperance, which they were anxious now to subvert with the Waters of Jerusalem, I saw they were between a rock and a hard place. Beef or booze?

Santa Burns weighed the temper of that crowd to the ounce and fired his last shot. "Gentlemen," he sighed, "being of such persuasion as I am that kine must be honored among us, as by the baby Jesus, I could not, in conscience, sell the Waters of Jerusalem to those who do not share such a view with me and these ten fine men."

He shook his head woefully and stood a moment in an attitude of prayer; then he raised his arms and shouted, "Christian gentlemen, how many now will come to kine? Let's see your hands. Take the plunge! Be Christian! Avow the cow! Eschew beef! . . . The cattle are lowing, the poor baby wakes, but little Lord Jesus, no crying he makes! . . . Why no crying? Because Jesus loves the cow, gentlemen. It's right there in the carol! Raise up your hands. Feel the holy spirit. Raise your eyes unto the kine and the Waters of Jerusalem are thine for twenty-five cents, one quarter of a dollar! In the spirit of Kissymouse, Christ, and kine we reduce the price for all bold men who will honor Christ and his bovine friends. Come one, come all! Have your money ready, folks. Step right up. Form a line, gentlemen!"

This last burst of oratory carried the crowd. They swept forward waving their hands and probing their pockets. Santa Majul opened his packing-crate lectern and commenced dispensing the Waters of Jerusalem as fast as his hands could move. "Meddy Kissy-mouse!" he cried as he worked. "Meddy, meddy Kissymouse!"

I wanted to buy a bottle of the waters for old times' sake, but the risk of being recognized dissuaded me. Fasli Akbar was a closed book, and I wanted to remember Majul in his triumph. "Meddy Kissymouse, Majul," I whispered. Then I took Cory's hand and we went Christmas shopping.

When we got back to the fort, I put Roselle in her stall, and the materia medica descended upon me once again.

The next chunk of time passed in a haze with pinpoints of detail. Adolph and Inger Bigler came for Christmas, and I felt ashamed for having forgotten to get them a gift, but Mrs. Bigler pshawed my apology. "Why, Dr. Jackson, you gave us Cory back, you and Dr. McNally. What gift could I ever again expect from you?"

I had a new buggy whip with silver fittings for Dr. McNally, a leather-covered autograph book for Cory, and a set of silver napkin rings for Lady Pennylunch, which she used to hold her braids, as I'd hoped she would. Odd I don't remember what I got, only what I gave, which, I guess, is what is meant by the saying "It is better to give than to receive."

There was a New Year's party in the armory, and most of the townsfolk came. This was the time the troopers bedecked Roselle in ribbons with a wreath of flowers around her horns and introduced her to ginger beer. They brought her to the party and told her to sit. Roselle did so and drank ginger beer from a

284

bucket. The troopers were convulsed, but the town ladies didn't take kindly to the posture, and there was some talk of building a pair of trousers for Roselle, as though a yearling heifer's udder was unsightly. After this Roselle demanded a bucket of ginger beer in her stall and refused to answer roll call unless she got it. That blamed cattalo had the whole fort buffaloed.

We square-danced, ate, sang, and welcomed 1883 with squibs, rockets, and firecrackers. At midnight I kissed Cory. Captain Jacks kissed her at 12:01 and again at 12:04, which I might have taken exception to if Captain Jacks hadn't been such a gallant figure in his dress blue uniform complete with sword and medals.

Cory shone like a lighthouse, beaming as she waltzed with every suitable man in the town and the entire army command. Roselle got so nosey and cavortsome I decided she'd had enough excitement for one night and took her to the stable, where we fell asleep like two figures in Majul Majul's manger.

When the snow went I was three quarters of the way through the medical books in Dr. McNally's bookcase and my addiction hadn't slackened. I had to get spectacles, which put me in a class with Eldon Larkin, but I'd given over such prejudices and didn't mind being a four-eyes. My distance vision was fine, but I had no use for it. Close was all I needed.

Then one afternoon Dr. McNally called me to his study and told me to sit down. "Jackson," he said, "I'm sending you to the Sayers-Bolton Medical School in Chicago."

"Chicago!"

"A city," he said.

"I know. Where they have slaughter yards."

"I'll look after Roselle."

"But why? I'm learning fast as I can right here!"

"Because there are advances in medicine that I cannot keep up with myself but which you must know about."

"When?"

"Next month."

"But how can I live?"

"That will be taken care of."

I didn't know what to say, to do. I sat there. Chicago!

"I've written Dr. Bolton about you. He's impressed."

So far away from everything I knew!

"It's a four-year curriculum."

Forever!

"What do you say?"

"Thank you, Dr. McNally."

I rose and left the study reeling inwardly. I had never contemplated such an abrupt change in the course of my life. Well, not change, really, but displacement, being uprooted and sent off so far. A month. I had a month. I held this thought for comfort and tried to think what to do.

TOAD-IN-THE-HOLE.

CORY BIGLER.

❖Take a cup of dark flour and a pinch of salt. Mix. Add one egg. Mix. Add cup of milk and a little more. Mix. Put six sausages in a greased pan, brown slightly. Pour batter over sausages and bake until batter rises. Reduce heat and bake until golden brown.

Chapter Twenty-two

❖   ❖   ❖

One day while I was drifting around in a bemused way trying to sort out the functions of the pancreas I came onto the porch and found Cory there. She wore a light cotton dress and a blue bonnet and had a bead purse in her hand.

"Hello," I said to her. "Where you going?"

"Home tomorrow. I have to get my ticket. Dad is going to meet the train at the Neosho bridge."

"I'll go with you," I said.

"Home?" she asked.

"To the train depot."

She didn't object, so we walked down the steps and over the parade ground. It was a clear, warm day, and the flag was limp. Roselle saw us and humped up from beside the flagstaff, where she'd been snoozing. She fell in beside us, her bell clanging as she walked.

The memory of the first time I saw Roselle came up strong. It seemed long ago, and she was changed. I sank my fingers into the fur of her humpy shoulders and felt her movement and her warmth. She'd been my cure and savior, and I was going to miss her in Chicago. "We'll have to get a big place to keep her on," I said.

"Baw," Roselle said.

"I've been meaning to ask Captain Jacks if we could take one of these houses on the row when I get back, but I haven't gotten around to it yet."

"Are you talking to me?" Cory asked.

"Why, sure, who else?" I said.

"I never know. Most times you talk like you were asleep or somewhere else."

"If we could have one of these houses it would be best for Roselle and me too, for I mean to come back here and work with Dr. McNally. Just feel how fat Roselle has gotten! It's the ginger beer. Just feel!"

Cory put her hand on Roselle close to mine, and we walked along with Roselle plodding contentedly between us. Way off we heard the whistle of the Katy line locomotive.

"Must be getting robbed," I said. "Saturday, ain't it?"

"Yes, it's Saturday," Cory said.

"Crazy what people do for entertainment," I said.

"You could use some."

"By then you'll be a good practical nurse. Not that you'd have to work, of course. I don't stand by women working when there's kids in the house, but nursing is useful to know. Have you ever seen coccidia under the microscope? They're something! Dr. Mc-Nally showed me a section of rabbit liver that was full of them. *Coccidium cuniculi.* I wrote a paper on them for Tim-oo-leh and sent it off. It was in Cherokee, too, and Lady Pennylunch said it was pretty good. Did you know there's no medical school in this whole territory?"

"No, I didn't," Cory said.

"That's why I have to go to Chicago, or I wouldn't."

"I see."

"I guess we could do our honeymoon there," I said.

"Are you and Roselle planning to get married or something?" Cory asked.

Well, I had to bust out laughing at that. It was the first time I'd ever heard Cory say a joke. But when I looked over at her I could see even with my glasses on that she was mad! "You and me, Cory," I said. "What's wrong?"

She removed her hand from Roselle's back and turned on me. "Wylie Jackson," she stormed, "this is the first mention to me of any such fool notion! Just because you've taken my temperature and thumped my chest don't mean you own me! I am not going to any honeymoon with you in Chicago or any other place I know of! I'm going home tomorrow, and I'll be perfectly happy not to see you again!"

"Cory! You don't mean that!"

"I do!" she said, and she burst into tears and ran right down the main street, past Lowe's Hotel and the barbershop, headed for the depot like she was going to take the train for home right then.

Roselle looked up at me and shook her head. "I'll be darned," I said. "I musta forgot to ask her."

I set off fast to catch Cory and apologize. I called, but she wouldn't stop. When I got to the depot the train was pulling in and all the robbery victims spilled out on the platform to regale each other with the horrors of the trip. Sheriff Hannegan, whose office was next to the depot, took complaints on his note-pad, nodding seriously as though he was not going to toss this information in the trash can the minute the passengers were gone. Young women were clinging to

291

their escorts and pretending to have the vapors, which required a lot of support. The men were all claiming it was Bignose Bill who had held them up and describing his vicious appearance, his deadly blue, brown, black eyes, his shaggy close-cropped hair and clean-shaven beard.

I couldn't see Cory in the crowd, but I did see a familiar figure drop from the caboose and head for town. He was togged out pretty rough, so I thought he was probably one of Bignose Bill's troop of actor-bandits come up after the show to see how much soda pop he could get for a tin watch. He had all the props on him, a black slouch hat, a low-slung gun belt, and a set of spurs that gave a nasty jingle to his walk. As he turned the corner I caught sight of his face. It was Zeb Zeff. I would have known his hide in a tanning yard.

Curiously, I was so intent on finding Cory, Zee-Zee's presence in town did not alarm me. I thought that someway all that was done and over with, that surely by now my aunt Clara had withdrawn her reward and given me up for lost.

The conductor announced the departure of the train, and the passengers flocked aboard, continuing to console one another over their narrow escape from death and violation. Then I saw Cory standing inside the station, still crying.

I went inside.

"Go away!" she said as I came up to her.

"Cory, it was all so clear in my mind from the first, I just took for granted it was the same for you, too."

"I don't know anything about you. Nothing at all!"

"I'm just me," I said. "Wylie Jackson, orphaned liar, horse thief, and medicine man."

"That's not funny anymore," she said.

"I wasn't aiming for it to be."

She took a handkerchief from her purse and dried her eyes. "Why," she said in a crumbling sort of way, "why, it would be like living with a sleepwalker!"

"I'll wake up in a year or so, Cory," I said.

"The way you go around looking at people like you were seeing them from inside out is not decent! You're doing it right now!"

"I'm looking in your eyes, Cory, and I see you're mad, but you don't mean it."

"Don't tell me what I mean!" she flashed. "Don't you ever tell me what I mean as long as you live!"

Well, right there she confessed she didn't mean it since she'd supposed I'd be around to provoke her for some time to come. I grinned.

Cory knew she'd flawed the game and scowled. "You might ask at least," she said.

"All right," I said, and I was about to do so when she interrupted me again.

"Well, not in any dumb train depot in broad daylight when I'm still mad!" she said. "Your head is so full of medical terms you don't have the sense of a polecat."

"Polecats are wily," I said.

"Fine, marry one of them and take it to Chicago!" Cory said, and she flounced out of the depot so spiky it made me proud to be acquainted.

"I love you, Cory Bigler," I called after her.

She stopped then just beyond the door and smiled a little in the way she had that was better than all the smiles I had ever seen. "Ask me tonight then, Wylie," she said so softly I hardly heard her.

"I will," I said, and I went out to her and we started back to the fort.

Roselle lumbered up from where she'd been lying in the shade beside the depot and followed along, her bell ringing so it made me think of a church wedding. I wondered if Cory would let Roselle be a bridesmaid, and the vision of it made me laugh aloud.

"What now?" Cory asked.

"Nothing," I said, but the idea of Roselle at the wedding, decked out in flowers, made me bust out laughing again, and Roselle moved up to see what it was about. I hung on her neck with tears running down my cheeks.

"Wylie Jackson, you are a fool!" Cory said, but she was laughing too just because I was.

"Indeed he is."

I knew that voice, of course. It was ZeeZee's. I looked up and found him standing on the porch of Lowe's Hotel with his thumbs in his gun belt, teetering to and fro like a Katy line bandido. He didn't scare me; *annoyed* is more the word. It surprised me some that he'd become a tin-watch lifter, but a lot of troubles had gone under bridges since we last parted company, and I supposed ZeeZee had had his share.

"I thought it was you," he said.

"You were right."

"There's a handy amount on your head, Jackson."

"No, the statute of limitations has run out on that, ZeeZee."

"Suppose we step around to the sheriff's office and find out."

"You want to take the time?"

"I got plenty."

Cory was looking worried, but I winked at her and said how ZeeZee was an old friend of mine and for her to take Roselle and go back to the fort.

"Are you sure, Wylie?" she asked.

"Why, we rode the Circle Six together, ain't that right, ZeeZee? Tell the lady."

"We rode the Circle Six," ZeeZee said.

Cory started away slowly, and I gave Roselle a push in her direction. "Go on," I said. "Go with Cory."

Roselle hunched up, and her head dropped. Then it happened, the thing I'd often worried about. Roselle charged up the Lowe's Hotel steps, and I saw that that fool ZeeZee, acting his Katy-line role, had drawn his pistol.

I yelled a warning, but Roselle hit ZeeZee hard at the knees and knocked him back against the wall. He rolled away, surprised and frightened, and started to get up, but Roselle hit him again.

I ran up the steps as ZeeZee fired his first shot. That stopped me, and things went slow from then on. I saw ZeeZee turning on his knees, aiming to fire again. I tried to call out, but my voice was gone. Roselle charged ZeeZee again, horns lowered, slow, oh, so slow that I could make out every muscle and tendon in her body. The second shot came like ice in my brain. ZeeZee fired one more time, then dove over the porch railing like a lazy dream and ran up the street.

Cory screamed. It was a high, despairing sound that went on forever and tore me all through.

Roselle turned and came down the steps of the hotel, but as she hit the ground one leg collapsed under her, then the other went, and she fell on her chest heavily. I saw the wounds in her throat and neck, gushing blood.

I dropped and caught Roselle's head in my arms. Cory was there too, at my side.

"Get help," I said. "Hurry!"

"Are you shot?" she asked.

"No!" I yelled at her. "Run, damn it! Run!"

Cory went white, like I'd slapped her. Then she sprang up and ran toward the fort.

There were people around us now, and I asked for something to staunch Roselle's wounds. I was shaking, sick with fear. I had nothing to work with.

Someone brought towels, and I wrapped these around Roselle. They turned red fast. I told myself over and over: *Pull yourself together! Pull yourself together!* But I was falling apart. The cotton broker's blood had taken over.

I told Roselle she'd be all right. "It's all right, all right, all right," I said, but the tears were coursing down my face so I couldn't see. I wanted her pain, but I didn't know how to get it. I didn't want to think what those three bullets had done to her. That's what I should have been doing, but all I could do was hold her and watch her eyes and say over and over: "It's all right, all right, all right, Roselle."

Someone came to say ZeeZee had been arrested.

A woman came from the hotel with a pan of water, and I splashed some on Roselle's muzzle. She was fevered, but her eyes stayed as clear and peaceful as they had always been, just as they were when Tim-oo-leh appeared. There was no fear in her, none at all.

"Roselle," I whispered. "Roselle. Roselle."

Troopers from the fort began to arrive, and finally Dr. McNally himself showed up. He came to us and knelt in the street. "What have you done for her?" he asked.

"Held her," I said, and I broke into tears.

Sergeant Riggs came and wanted to take me away.

"No!" I said.

"You're no good here, Jackson!" Dr. McNally said roughly.

"I'm trying to be," I said.

"Move aside and let me see her wounds. Sergeant Riggs, help him up."

Dr. McNally laid Roselle's head sideways on the street.

Sergeant Riggs pulled me to my feet. When Dr. McNally saw Roselle's streaming wounds he said, "Oh," but he went to work. "Maybe," he said. "Maybe."

But I wasn't such a big fool as that.

PIGWEED GREENS.

WYLIE JACKSON.

❖Gather new pigweed leaves and rinse. Add tumbleweed sprouts if available. Steam greens in closed pan until tender. Drain and fry in butter. Add salt and vinegar and serve. A woeful dish.

Chapter Twenty-three

❖ ❖ ❖

When the troopers heard about Roselle they flocked into town from the fort and swarmed around Lowe's Hotel. There was a lot of rough talk about what was going to happen to ZeeZee if Roselle didn't live. Sheriff Hannegan got nervous about it and decided to move ZeeZee out of town. He might not have made it if Captain Jacks hadn't ordered the troopers back to the fort.

I shook Sergeant Riggs off and walked back myself, but I stayed clear of the men. I was too distraught to listen to them or talk to anyone, so I went along the riverbank and cut over the fields. When I got to the fort I went to Roselle's stall and sat there trying to collect myself, but her bucket of ginger beer busted me up again, and I put my head on my arms and bawled. All my medical knowledge had come to nothing, to nothing, nothing! When Roselle needed me most I'd failed her. I might as well have killed her myself, the way I behaved, and I knew I could never trust myself with anyone's life in my hands. Books are one thing, blood is another. I'd learned a lot of big words and pored over medical illustrations, but when faced with a real emergency I was still a Fasli Akbar and had about as much right to be a doctor as a cotton broker.

I heard a sound, and Cory was in the doorway of the stable. How long she'd been there I did not know.

301

Whatever time it was added to my shame and self-disgust. I stood up and turned away, trying to compose my face. I hoped she hadn't seen me crying. I heard her come up behind me and couldn't bear her presence.

"Wylie?"

"Go away, Cory. Please," I said.

"Wylie, I know how you must feel."

That snapped me, and I spun around on Cory. I felt the whiteness in my face and the rage in my lungs and heart. "You'll never know how I feel!" I cried. "Don't say you know how I feel! You don't know anything about it!"

Cory blanched and backed away as though I had struck her, and I felt I might do so because my arms were jumping and my fists were clenched. "Wylie!" she gasped.

"Go! Go! Just get out!"

Cory turned then and ran, and I thought, *My God, here is another crime I have committed, and perhaps the worst of all.*

I felt so sick I wanted to vomit and couldn't. All that evil, vile-minded anger and stupid incompetence was going to fester in my stomach forever.

I had to get out of there, to run from myself, to be away.

I got my saddle and put it on an army horse, the fourth one I'd stolen. *So let them hang me. It would be a relief,* I thought. *They should have sprung the trap in Cleo Springs.*

I mounted and hit the parade ground at a gallop, but no one hailed me. Good riddance, no doubt, is what they thought. When I was three miles out of town I slowed my pace and rode along the Arkansas River toward Fort Smith, which was the likeliest place Hannegan would take ZeeZee. *I'll live to kill him* was my thought; after that nothing mattered.

I rode over the Ozark Plateau, then southeast through the Boston Mountains. I figured to camp the night someplace, read the sky, and think. I was in no great hurry to kill ZeeZee. That I would do so was inevitable, a foregone conclusion. I knew I'd kill him, and it didn't matter if it was this year or the next. When darkness came I found a place to camp on the Arkansas River. I hobbled my horse and let him graze; then I rolled out and lay down with my head on the saddle.

I was alone.

I had never really been alone while Roselle was with me, and it was an awful feeling. Worse than Wichita.

The stars came out one at a time, and I saw a million of them appear. I dozed off once and had a dream, one of those quick kinds where everything is crystal clear and so real that you're left with the smell of it.

In the dream I'd ridden up to a hog-farm saloon way off in the flat somewhere. It was the dead of night. I parked my horse at the hitch rack, and there was a U.S.I.C.-branded mule at the rack. United States Inspected and Condemned is what that brand meant. I knew this because it was branded also on my heart. U.S.I.C.

When I stepped inside the place there'd been a gunfight. A pair of smear-faced women were frozen in place against the wall. The lantern wick was faulty so the light kept going up and down. There was a whiskey barrel with two bullet holes in it standing on a sawhorse bar. The proprietor of the place had his arms around the barrel with his fingers stuck in the holes while two rough-looking desperadoes were whittling pegs out of a broken chair leg to plug the barrel and save the whiskey.

Zeb Zeff lay facedown on the packed dirt floor, groaning and shedding blood.

They all knew me for a doctor, so when they got the whiskey barrel plugged they rolled ZeeZee over and plunked him down on the felt-covered poker table and told me to see what I could do.

All I had was a pocket case of instruments—lancets, probes, surgical scissors, things like that. I stripped ZeeZee to the waist and saw he'd been struck on the left side just below the fourth rib. The bullet had been deflected downward and was lodged in the kidney or spleen. The damage was extensive, the bleeding profuse, and I didn't give him much chance.

I hated him, of course, for killing Roselle.

He looked up at me and said, "Oh"; then he closed his eyes, prepared to die.

Suddenly the dismal saloon was full of people crowding around, men and women watching me work on ZeeZee. They were making bets whether he would live or not. They stood there with money in their hands, and the odds got longer as the green felt soaked up his blood. I worked to save him. I tried hard in that dim, flickering light to keep ZeeZee alive. I really tried.

But I woke up not knowing if I had succeeded.

The night air was cool on my face, and I looked up, not at the stars but at all the spaces between them where the darkness went on forever, and it frightened me. I pressed back against the firmness of the earth. I had the feeling that I might fall off and spin away through the darkness and never be found. I picked up a small stone and held it in front of my eyes to block out the sky. I took shelter behind that stone, and it felt alive in my hand.

A stone.

It was more alive to me than all that empty space and empty time, more alive than all the darkness and unknown.

A stone.

It was in the chain of existence Tim-oo-leh had told me about. The stone was changing a little bit each second, being transformed into particles, returning to earth, and the waters would carry it to the sea, where it would rise as rain and come home again on the wings of birds and the clouds. So it would also be with me. *Brother stone,* I thought. Then I did a funny thing. I kissed that stone and put it back where I'd found it, and I felt less alone.

The next morning I wasn't so dead set on killing ZeeZee as I had been the night before. The stone and the dream had leached my rage, but I decided to ride on to Fort Smith anyhow. I had never seen Judge I. C. Parker's court and thought I'd have a look at the man known throughout the territory as the hanging judge. His score to this time was about fifty executions, condemned men hung in groups up to six at a time.

I'd heard he supplied anatomy classes as far off as Detroit with subjects for dissection.

It was a brisk morning, fresh and dew-washed. I saddled up and rode slowly along the Arkansas River, listening to the waters distribute the stones to the sea. The memory of how I'd treated Cory dimmed my eyes, and Roselle's death was a lump in my heart that killing ZeeZee could not dissolve.

That Cory might forgive me didn't enter my mind, because I could not forgive myself for how I'd treated her and for how I'd failed Roselle.

Not wanting to face all the grief, I'd reverted to type and run. It was what I did best. I'd run out on the Circle Six and Tim-oo-leh and everyone else who came in my path.

I reached Fort Smith near noon and located Parker's court, which was in the Federal Barracks. There was a new three-story brick jail adjacent to it filled with prisoners waiting for trial. They were gathered at the barred windows with a view of the gallows yard, and I guessed they were feeling about as miserable as I was. I tethered my horse and when I entered the courthouse Sheriff Hannegan plucked my sleeve. "Jackson," he said, "I don't want more trouble about this."

"Do I look like trouble?" I asked him, but my anger at ZeeZee was coming up again.

"Looks don't always signify," Hannegan said. "Zeff has pled guilty. Judge Parker will clear the case this morning. I want that to be the end of it."

"This morning?"

"That's what I said."

"This ought to be Sunday," I said.

Hannegan nodded. "It is. The judge has a crowded calendar. On Sunday he sentences those who have pled guilty. Calls it Sabbath justice."

"Nice," I said.

"Better than keeping prisoners waiting in the lockup for trial."

"And provides entertainment for the after-church crowd."

"That too."

I went into the courtroom and took a seat in the back row. Judge Parker was on the bench. I'd heard him referred to as "Hell on the Border Parker" and expected a roaring, gavel-rapping showman, but the man on the bench was quiet and intense. A large man, beyond sixty, with a big spade beard. He took case records from the bailiff and spoke to the prisoners in a considerate manner when they were brought from the jail. His sentences seemed moderate enough, and he asked each time if the prisoner agreed that justice had been done or if he wanted to be bound over for a jury trial. Without exception the prisoners accepted Judge Parker's sentence and looked contrite.

I sat through about ten such cases, drunks, assault and battery, breaking and entering. Spectators came and went. I was hungry and getting drowsy when Sheriff Hannegan marched in with ZeeZee.

I sat forward to catch every word, but there weren't many to catch. Judge Parker read the charge, then looked down from the bench at ZeeZee, who stood there with a hangdog look on his face. My hatred of him boiled up.

"Do you plead guilty to this charge?" Judge Parker asked.

"Yes, sir, Your Honor," ZeeZee replied.

"Fifty dollars and costs," Judge Parker said.

I couldn't believe it! I bolted up, shouting, "Fifty dollars!" I made my way down the aisle to the bench. "Fifty dollars!" I shouted again.

Sheriff Hannegan spoke to Parker. ZeeZee saw me and stiffened up, ready to fight.

"Will you approach the bench, Mr. Jackson," Judge Parker said.

"I am approached!"

"You're Mr. Wylie Jackson, owner of the . . . cattalo, is it?"

"I am and her name was Roselle!"

"You object to my decision in this case."

"I do." I looked at ZeeZee, and if he'd winced or smirked I'd have gone for him right then even if I died for it.

Judge Parker frowned at the papers before him, then looked at me again. "I've awarded you about twice fair market value, Mr. Jackson," he said.

That got me hard. "Market value!" I exclaimed. "What has market value got to do with anything? I don't sell my friends! There's damned little friendship going for sale that I can see, and what can be bought ain't worth a sneeze. Oh, I suppose you could buy Zeb Zeff's friendship, but who'd want it? Sure not me!"

"I'll have order if you please, young man," Judge Parker said, and he rapped his gavel.

"You could buy Zeff's friendship for two Yankee dollars and a tin whistle!"

"Mr. Jackson, if you continue I'll cite you for contempt."

"Cite away, Judge," I said, "because if you walked me up here to take fifty dollars for Roselle then I am in contempt of this court in a large quantity. I'd rather be in contempt of this court than of myself, you can bet. You can jug me, or hang me, damn it, but you can't make me sell Roselle for fifty dollars!"

"Mr. Jackson!"

"There may be no law to cover the case, but I'll tell you one thing, Judge Parker, it's not property law. If so then you'd better put a price on every man, woman, and child in Arkansas because not half of them could show the loyalty, the heart, or the wisdom Roselle had. ZeeZee sure can't! You weigh him up for me, Judge Parker, quote me a fair market price, and I'll take him off your hands right now. About four dollars and sixteen cents should do it. But I'll go as high as five if there's a premium on gopher snake!"

Judge Parker was beating a tattoo on the bench with the gavel. The bailiff was moving toward me. "You are in contempt of this court!" Judge Parker proclaimed.

"On that we have agreed, Your Honor," I shouted. "And also I am in contempt of this yellow-bellied, low, cringing counterfeit train robber and grease-gutted carnivore who killed my Roselle!"

"That cattalo attacked me!" ZeeZee put in.

I turned on ZeeZee fists clenched, face flaming. "You pulled the gun! You aimed! You fired!"

"Bailiff!" Judge Parker called. "Sheriff Hannegan!"

"I was scared!" ZeeZee cried.

"You're scared of butterflies! You're scared of chipmunks!"

The bailiff took my arm.

ZeeZee pointed at me and called to Judge Parker. "He's a wanted man, Judge! There's a reward out on him!"

That set me off. I broke away from the bailiff and rushed ZeeZee. The spectators bounded up. Chairs toppled.

I heard Judge Parker's gavel beating. I hit ZeeZee twice, snapping his head over, but he came back hard and caught me a stunning blow on the ear. We grappled; then Hannegan wrenched ZeeZee away and the bailiff caught me.

"You'll pay, ZeeZee!" I cried.

"That's what I'm trying to do, God damn you!"

The bailiff and Sheriff Hannegan forced us into chairs, and after a bit the excitement died down. The spectators retrieved their seats, and a hush fell over the court.

Judge Parker looked down at us, and his eyes were harsh as lead. "You are both remanded to custody," he said, "for a continuance of this case at the convenience of this court." He struck his gavel once. Sheriff Hannegan hoisted me off my chair and shoved me roughly toward the door that led to the famous Fort Smith jail.

OXJOINT JAIL STEW.

FORT SMITH.

❖This dish was served twice in four days to the inmates of the Fort Smith jail. I do not know the chef. I analyzed the contents thus:

❖Steer tails acquired from the Blue Lightning Chili factory, skinned and jointed. Potatoes and carrots, washed slightly. Red onions, halved. Flour to thicken the broth and obscure the contents. A suspicion of beef heart, tongue, and tripe. Salt and peppercorns. Boil until meat hangs off the bone. Serve lukewarm with whole-wheat rolls.

❖Serves a hundred and fifty men. I ate the roll.

CHAPTER TWENTY-FOUR

❖ ❖ ❖

My cell was on the second floor. ZeeZee had been housed upstairs, which was just as well since we'd have felt obliged to cuss and threaten each other, which would probably have bored the hardened criminals and murderers waiting to come to the rope. Since I'd been cellmates with Carl Merkle, these cases seemed tame enough to me. I glowered and told them I'd been the mass killer Merkle's pal, which impressed them so they gave me plenty of roping room and spoke when spoken to.

The man who shared my cell, William Perkins, was waiting to be tried for having robbed a bank of a hundred and sixteen dollars, in the course of which he'd shot and killed a lady teller. It had been an accident, he said, and I believed him but doubted this defense would save his neck. He had a busted ranch out in Dakota, where his wife and five kids were waiting for him to come home. He hadn't notified them of his case and thought it better not to. His spirits were about as bright as mine.

The food was bad, and we weren't let out for exercise. The beds were inhabited by varieties of wildlife left by previous occupants, and the prison swarmed with the ghosts of those who had gone before. When they slept the prisoners, dreaming of their demise, had night sweats, and the place was damp with their apprehensions and regrets.

That night I perspired and dreamed with them.

In the morning Sheriff Hannegan came to see me. "Well," he said, "you walked yourself into it, Jackson."

"That's so."

"You're wanted in Odessa, Texas."

"I know that."

"I've sent a wire to let them know where you can be found."

"I suppose you did."

"Any message you'd like to send to Fort Gibson? I'm on my way back."

I thought about it and Hannegan waited. What was there to say? I'd run my string. If I sent apologies they would fill a book. "Tell them to forget me," I said.

Sheriff Hannegan nodded. "Well, good luck," he said, and he was gone.

I sat on my cot with my elbows on my knees and stared at my feet. I seemed not able to take a grip on anything. Every thought I had was a problem, a failure, a regret. Aunt Clara. Alice Beck. Cory. Dr. McNally. Chauncey Potter. Tim-oo-leh. Lady Pennylunch. John Boardman. There wasn't a person I could recall that I had not let down or betrayed, most of all Roselle.

The prison guards were overworked and underpaid. They extracted minor bribes for minor favors and expressed their fear of being attacked by a show of brutality. Infractions of discipline brought the club, and the first time I was hit across the shoulders for stepping out of line during cell inspection I had an insight

314

into prison life I've never forgotten. The blow hurt and surprised me, but it informed me I was alive and still had feeling. I saw that many of the prisoners invited being hit just to be sure they had not gone brute dumb. They had no rancor for the guards who beat them and who understood that sometimes a blow was a gift to a despondent man.

Given Judge Parker's crowded calendar, I expected my trial would be a long time coming. I turned my mind away from the past with all its ensnaring dreams and concentrated on becoming a hardened prisoner, for I believed I would spend several years in this instruction.

On the sixth day I heard the guard jingling down the corridor, and the key rattled in my cell door lock. I sat up on my cot and there was Mr. John Boardman. His eyes were hard, as they had always been. I stood up and shot back what fire I had, which wasn't much. At least I was more on a level with him, having put on about three inches of length since last we met. His lips were still stitched up, straight and thin as the edge of a rule. His hard-planed face was tan as moccasin leather, and I saw there was a minnie-ball nick in his ear I hadn't noticed before. I braced myself for a roar, but when he spoke it was temperate. "Judge Parker won't let me go bail, but I've got your case moved up for tomorrow."

"Fine with me," I said.

"Is there a place we can talk?" Boardman asked the guard.

"Visiting room," the guard said, and he beckoned me out of the cell with his club.

315

Boardman walked beside me down the corridor. I felt the weight of his presence drawing me to him, so I had to step away to avoid bumping his shoulder. We went down a short flight of stairs to a room in the basement of the building. There was a heavy wire mesh door, which the guard unlocked, and we went inside. There were two chairs and a table in the place. The guard locked the gate and told us to take our time.

"I'm not going anywhere," I said.

The guard left us standing there. "Mind if I sit down?" Boardman asked.

The request surprised me. "It's federal property, I guess."

"For a time it wasn't," he said, and he eased down on one of the chairs beside the table. It was a weary movement, almost pained. He gestured me to sit. I did so, and we faced each other over the table, about four feet apart. For a time Boardman studied his hands as though trying to make up his mind who they answered to. "If General Van Dorn had won at Pea Ridge it might not be yet," he said.

"I wouldn't know about that."

"You weren't born then." Boardman sighed and looked up at me. "I thought we ought to talk," he said.

"I'm sorry I stole your damned horse and ran. I had a reason that I don't plan to share, so there it is."

"This is not about a horse," he said.

"Well, whatever it's about, I'll do my time."

"I came to tell you something that should make sense to you now when it might not have before."

"Fire away."

He bridled up a bit at my sharpness, and I was sorry for it. I had no call to be so hard. "Go on, then," I said.

He tipped back and gazed off over my head, frowning, as he decided how to begin. At last he cleared his throat and spoke in a reflective way. "You know, during a battle, you never see it all. You catch a glimpse here, a glimpse there, and you try to put it together from the bits and pieces, but half the time you're wrong, or unlucky, I'm not sure which. From where I stood that day at Pea Ridge I thought we'd licked the Yankees hollow. I was with General Pike, and we saw our Creeks and Cherokees overrun the Union line and capture their batteries. We'd rolled up their right flank. It was a clean, sure victory, and I thought we'd march on to Mississippi to join Johnston and stop U. S. Grant cold. What I didn't see was two regiments of Union troops that had not yet been committed to the battle. When they charged us we scattered and ran like partridges, and we never got to Shiloh. So, you see bits and pieces and try to guess the rest, and sometimes you guess wrong."

"What has this to do with me?" I asked.

He frowned and shook his head. "I'm trying to get there," he said. "I don't know how else to go at it."

"Take your time. I got plenty."

He nodded soberly and went on. "After that defeat I was transferred and attached to the defense of Vicksburg. There I met a fine young woman, just a girl, really, and we saw each other often. Her brother, later killed, was fighting with Beauregard. Her father was

317

an Episcopalian minister, a force for steadiness in the community but a bit of a fanatic about some things, as aren't we all."

"You speaking of me and Roselle?"

"No, I wasn't talking of that." He met my eyes, and the spikes weren't so rusty and hard as I remembered them being. "The girl I was speaking of and I fell in love," Boardman continued. "I thought I could not do without her. She felt the same about me and was afraid I'd be transferred or killed, as so many had been. I don't mean to say she was weak. Just the opposite, and she was determined to follow her heart in spite of any counsel I had to oppose it, and I can't say I offered much. I didn't want to lose a precious second of whatever time there was for us."

Listening to Mr. Boardman talk this way revised my opinion of him. I stared at him as I had one time in my youth when I saw a butterfly emerge from a cocoon. Not that Boardman was a butterfly! But he was coming out in such an unexpected way I thought of that as he continued speaking.

"There wasn't much time, as it turned out. Vicksburg came under siege. Grant had us pinned against the river, and he brought up a great power of cannon and mortars to bombard us. We were hammered night and day. Night and day. I was with the artillery, counterfiring, and she'd come to me with food. I told her to stay away, out of danger, but there was no safe place in Vicksburg. Mortar shells fell at all hours and rolled down the city streets, or crashed through houses and buildings. Her house was destroyed, and her sister was killed in such an attack. The people moved into

318

caves and dugouts. They lived on mule meat and turnips. Gopher town, the Yankees called it. The mortar shells fell day and night, day and night, and no one in all Vicksburg could be sure if their next breath wouldn't be their last. In such circumstances things happen. She and I clung to each other, and I tried to ease her fear. We loved each other, you see."

I felt something cold along the back of my neck and stood up. There was a casement window above my head, and I could see the feet of people passing in the street. "This is about the reward and the telegram you sent Matt Burdick, isn't it?"

"No, it's about your father," he said, "and your mother."

"The dead cotton broker whose mess I am."

"Not a cotton broker. Hear me out."

"Don't come telling me all I know is a lie! I won't have it. My aunt Clara is not a liar!"

"No."

"Did she marry Eldon Larkin?"

"No."

"Well, that's a blessing."

"Will you hear me out?"

I sat down again at the table, but I was angry now and not much willing to listen. As far as I cared Boardman could stuff himself back into his cocoon.

"The night before Vicksburg surrendered, I escaped. It was my duty . . . my military duty to escape. I didn't know then that I had a greater one. I got through the Union lines and went on to Alabama and Tennessee, losing all the way. Losing. Losing. Without knowing what I'd lost. My name appeared in

319

the Yankee casualty reports several times. I was reported dead. The Yankees purposely reported officers dead to confuse our Confederate commanders and cause grief at home. I was replaced three times by officers who were surprised to find me alive. Our communications and records were bad, so the Yanks took advantage of that. We lost in '64 and '65 until there was nothing left to lose, and finally it was over. After the surrender I went to Vicksburg, but Clara had gone. Some said she'd gone to Memphis."

"Aunt Clara?" I asked.

"I didn't find her in Memphis or any other place I looked. Finally I married the widow of my adjutant, Captain Zeff, killed at Chancellorsville, and we came to Texas, me, my wife, and her son, Zeb."

"Are you talking about Aunt Clara?" I demanded.

"She's your mother, Wylie."

I shook my head, a terse jerk of denial, but I knew as sure as sunrise it was true. Having been told, I knew. And I was so angry I could have killed him. I wanted to tear the furniture apart. "And I suppose you're my father!"

"Yes," he said.

I knew this was also true because I hated him. He must have seen it working in my face and eyes. He was very still, waiting for my rage to break, and I knew if I struck him across the face he'd take it. He'd sit and take it. I felt the power in my arm and hand and wanted to hear the impact as I slapped that waiting expression off his face. I wanted to hurl all the curses I knew into his eyes and watch him take it and triumph over him and taunt him and hurt him as hard as I'd hurt when ZeeZee killed Roselle. I wanted to call him a low, sneaking coward, for this was the secret of my life, which he'd had no right to keep. But I couldn't do it. I couldn't even speak.

"Can I go on?"

Our hands were the same. His and mine. I had begun to see the planes of his face in mine. In another year I might have known it myself without his telling me.

"Can I go on?"

She had been a mother to me, but lying, always lying. And why? Wedlock. Well, of course wedlock. In her pride she could not admit having a child, being unwed. For her pride she had denied and deceived me and made a criminal of me, and I despised her nearly as much as I did him.

"Wylie?"

"You two are a pair," I snapped.

"Wylie, I know this comes as—"

I jumped to my feet, overturning my chair. I was livid. "You know nothing, Boardman! Don't tell me your pitiful little story. I can tell it to you, for God's sake. Do you think I'm a fool? Miss Clara Hampton got pregnant by you. Hurrah! She read the false casualty report that you were dead. Oh, woe! To preserve her Southern dignity and spare her Episcopalian father the shame of it all she fled the family rubble in Vicksburg and had me in Memphis, using a false name, of course. Jackson, the cotton broker. Then she set out bravely to support me, a woman alone in a hostile world. Organ music! We know the story, of course. Poor little match girl! Charlady with a heart of gold!"

"Stop it!" Boardman's voice boomed over me, but I was his son with no more to fear from him.

"Ohhh," I said, "wouldn't that be nice? To stop it and start all over again. Let's do that, shall we? Let's forget anything has been said and keep it as it was, a lie from beginning to end."

Boardman rose then, and I stepped back, expecting a blow, but he went to the door and called the guard. When the guard opened the gate, Boardman looked back at me. He was very calm, very large in his spirit. "Think it over," he said quietly; then he went up the steps and was gone.

Back in my cell with no one upon whom to vent my anger, I was forced into myself. I made up many stories of Clara Hampton and John Boardman, some of these as hateful and degrading as I could think of. But as darkness came and the prisoners fell into their night-sweat sleep, my rage abated, as it had for ZeeZee some days before.

Piccalilli.

WYLIE JACKSON.

❖Eight pounds of green tomatoes, one head of cabbage, two dried onions, three large peeled cucumbers, two green peppers; chop and run through grinder. Place in stone crock with one-half cup salt. Let stand one night. In morning drain liquid and add boiling syrup made of one and a half quarts vinegar and two pounds of sugar. Boil thirty minutes and let cool.

Chapter Twenty-five

❖ ❖ ❖

After breakfast the next morning the guard came and took me again to the visiting room. John Boardman was already there, standing with his back to the casement window above his head. When the guard shut the gate and went up the steps we remained standing, observing one another.

"Well," Boardman said at last, "I can't suppose you think much of me."

"I'm the one in jail," I said.

"I'd like to sit down."

"Help yourself."

He sat again at the table. I remained standing, stiff and again belligerent.

"Had I known where to find her . . . ," he began.

"Happy ending," I said.

He bucked slightly at that. "We can leave it as is if you like, Jackson," he said. "There are only three of us who know. Not another soul."

"I'd like to think about that."

"Fine," he said. "Anything else you'd like to know?"

"When did you see each other again, after the war?"

He scowled at the tabletop. His voice was low and gravelly, distant as Rome. "Four years later, in Houston," he said. "Such a day. Rain slanting down and the sky like smeared tar."

"I don't need all that," I said.

He looked up at me then, angrily. "If I'd had you as a child you wouldn't be so quick with your mouth."

"Whip it out of me, would you?"

"I may yet."

"Your style."

"You want to listen or not? We have a court date. After that you can make up your mind. I'm going back to Clara."

"Tell me," I said.

"In Houston. I crossed the street and she was coming the other way. We met each other face-to-face. It was a shock to both of us. For her I'd come to life. For me, well, it was Vicksburg." He frowned and stared at the wall; then he came back. "We caught each other and those four years vanished."

I remembered now living in a place Aunt—my mother—called the "ishy house." I was four years old. The "ishy house" was a small place, board and batten with a hard-packed dirt yard, and I remembered having a cat called Sandy. That must have been in Houston.

"I'd married Zenobia by then," Boardman continued, "and started the Box Z ranch. I admired Zenobia, loved her, but not as I loved Clara. I offered to leave Zenobia, but Clara refused and she was right. Love remembered is hard to judge, harder yet to re-create. Well, you don't need a lecture. The short of it was that Clara moved to Odessa and I made an arrangement through Mr. Beck so you would be looked after."

"The cotton broker's annuity," I said.

"Yes."

"Then Mr. Beck knows too! You said only the three of us know about this."

"Beck only knows there was an annuity from Mr. Jackson, the cotton broker. That's all he knows."

"Must have been hard keeping all those lies afloat."

Boardman ignored the barb. "Clara and I talked about when to tell you. I wanted to early on, but Clara thought not. There were reasons for it. Private things."

"I thought we'd got beyond that."

"What?"

"Privacy. Another name for lies, isn't it?"

He looked at me, his rust eyes hard again. "I've taken more from you than from any man in my life, Jackson."

"The name is Boardman now, isn't it?"

"If you think you can make it so," Boardman snapped.

"I'm not so all-fired eager about it."

Boardman stormed over and glared at me. "I'll tell you once, don't push me anymore. Don't do it. I did the best I knew how for you. Clara too. It may not suit you, but don't push me once again. Clara felt if we told you it would all come out, which it would have, and Zenobia would have suffered when she hadn't ought to. Maybe that's hard for you to understand."

"I see it," I said. "But why in damnation did you choose a cotton broker as my father?"

He looked at me blankly. "It made sense the money should come from someone who had some."

"It plagued me all my life with the idea I'd been spawned by a damned noncombatant coward! Why didn't you just smother me in my crib?"

"Your father was no coward!"

"How was I to know that? Eliot P. Jackson, the well-read, gentlemanly, dead cotton broker, made me a sissy pants from the git-go!"

"Clara thought some refinement wouldn't hurt you."

"I been runnin' from that danged ghostly cotton broker since I was six years old."

"No need to run anymore, is there?"

"I expect not."

"That's it, then. When Zenobia passed away and the drive came up, Clara and I agreed you should go along so we could get to know each other. When I came back without you Clara about fractured my skull with a stick of stovewood. She'd raised you sixteen years without a hitch and I lost you in three weeks."

"Mad, was she?"

"As a wolverine! Chased me off the place."

"Did she!" I said, grinning.

"I was sure you'd be found, but as time went on I got concerned and posted a reward to locate you and began telling Clara about where you'd been seen, which she only half believed but pretended to for my sake."

"Looks like lying is in our blood."

"No. It's coping. When I got the wire from Burdick I showed it to Clara and lit out to pick you up in Cleo Springs. When I got there you'd skipped again. No one had a clue. Some Kiowas had seen you headed west with that cattalo of yours and that's what threw me off. I took it in mind you were going to California to get out of the weather and to see Alice Beck in Monterey."

"Why would you think that?"

"It's something I might have done. Clara and I went to Monterey hoping to find you there."

"How are the Becks?" I asked.

"Well enough. Sardines are plentiful. The cannery is doing fine and the law business is too. Alice was pretty upset about your being lost and not getting Roselle to Enid. When we came back to Odessa, Clara had a letter from Dr. McNally. A long letter saying how hard you were working. You were doing so well we decided not to interfere just then. Knowing you were safe was enough for Clara. She thought all this business might be too much of a shock and upset your studies. We decided to wait and tell you before you went to medical school in Chicago. Then we got the wire from Dr. McNally about Roselle and saying you'd skipped out again. So, that's it," Boardman concluded. He took out his watch. "We're due in court," he said. "I'll see you there."

The guard took me back to my cell, where I stayed until it was time to appear before Judge Parker. I thought about whether to continue my life as Jackson, the cotton broker's son, or switch over to Boardman. I wasn't yet sure about this, but by now Jackson seemed as false to me as Axel Beane or Fasli Akbar. I was thinking about this when the guard came with ZeeZee and said it was time for court.

ZeeZee and I were marched up to the bench and Judge Parker looked down at us, scowling. "Well," he said at last, "I've reviewed this matter and taken some recommendations on it. I've decided to put you two desperadoes on probation for ninety days, during which time you will report once a week to the closest peace officer in the county where you reside. He in turn will file a report with me. God help you if those reports don't come. Further, you will each find gainful employment, which in your case, Mr. Zeff, does not include being a playtime bandit on the Katy line. You are to give up that dubious occupation at once. If you want to go on the stage be sure it is a stationary one. You, Mr. Jackson, will return the horse you stole from the army stables at Fort Gibson, give over this predilection you have for stealing horseflesh, and hereafter confine your transportation to bicycles. Does either of you have any objection or anything to say?"

"No, sir," ZeeZee and I chorused.

"The final condition of this very lenient judgment is that you shake hands and promise not to make trouble for each other now and forever."

ZeeZee and I looked at each other.

"Do you understand me?" Judge Parker growled.

"Yes, sir," we said.

"Then shake hands."

Boardman was standing behind us with the bailiff.

ZeeZee and I both knew how it was going to be. We brushed our palms on the seats of our pants to dry

330

them; then we slapped hands and began to squeeze. We plastered false smiles on our faces and put every ounce of muscle we possessed into that grip. We pumped our arms up and down and the flesh of our fingers was ground to the bone. If we'd had rings on, blood would have run from our hands like juice from a wine press.

"I sure am sorry I called you them names, ZeeZee," I said.

"I didn't mean to kill that cattalo, Jackson."

Sweat popped up on our brows. Our eyes stood out, but we kept the grins in place and the pressure on, waiting for the other's hand to weaken so we could crush the knuckles to a pulp.

"Just a misunderstanding all around," I said.

"That's it sure, Wylie, old horse," ZeeZee said.

The cords and muscles of our arms were taut as bridge cables and our teeth were clenched fit to bust.

Judge Parker rapped his gavel. "That's enough," he said.

"It's sure good to see you again, ZeeZee," I said.

"Wouldn't have missed it for the world!"

ZeeZee slapped the last bit of his strength into his grip and I was just able to match it. We hung there white-faced, waiting to see who had the endurance.

"Bailiff!" Judge Parker said sharply. "Separate those men!"

The bailiff came between us and after several attempts managed to wrench our hands apart.

"We were just getting friendly, Judge," ZeeZee said.

I nodded in agreement, but my hand was so mashed and sore I didn't think it would be usable for a week.

The bailiff laid two documents on the table for us to sign. They were our probation papers, he said. ZeeZee and I managed to scratch our names with our throbbing hands and Judge Parker came down from the bench. "Well, gentlemen," he said, "I wish you good luck." He offered his hand and I took it first. Parker's grip dropped me to my knees and brought tears to my eyes. ZeeZee fell next and we knelt there like penitent sinners, nursing our hands and trying not to whimper.

"Bailiff, where is that telegram that came for Mr. Jackson?" Judge Parker asked.

The bailiff took a telegram from the bench and gave it to the judge who handed it to me. "Came this morning," he said.

Boardman pulled ZeeZee and me to our feet as I opened the telegram with my teeth. It was five words:

ROSELLE ON THE MEND. MCNALLY.

Boardman and ZeeZee read it over my shoulder.

"Why, damn! That's good!" ZeeZee exclaimed.

I was too overtaken by surprise to speak or move until Boardman took me by the arm. "Come on, boy! Let's go!"

ZeeZee and I saddled up fast as our mashed hands would permit and shot out of Fort Smith with Boardman riding between us. It was a clear, sunny day with visions of grace and glory as far as one could see. I looked aside and saw my shadow fleeting over the earth and oh! oh! that day I was a sunshine rider!

ZeeZee let out a yip now and again and Boardman let off a rebel yell such as I had never heard. I looked over at him, riding beside me in that cannonball way he had, and I thought: *Why, that's my old man!* And I let out a holler that picked my horse right off the ground.

WELLESLEY LOVE CAKE.

AUNT CLARA.

❖Cream one-fourth cup butter and add one-half cup of sugar while beating gradually. Beat yolks of two eggs and add one-half cup sugar while beating. Combine with one-half cup of milk and one and a half cups flour and two and a half teaspoons baking powder. Add beaten whites of two eggs, four ounces of melted baker's chocolate, and one-fourth teaspoon of vanilla. Mix and bake forty minutes in moderate oven.

Frosting.

❖Pour two cups sugar into one-third cup boiling water. Stir until dissolved and boil without stirring until it threads, then pour slowly into the whites of two eggs beaten stiff. Place this pan in a pan of boiling water and stir constantly until it becomes creamy. Beat and top cake when cool and cover with melted chocolate.

Chapter Twenty-six

❖ ❖ ❖

Thank you. Thank you, ladies and gentlemen. Please subside. Thank you very much.

As always, I am grateful to your honored president for his flattering introduction and for calling me forth each year to powwow with the graduating class of Sayers-Bolton Medical School. His kind reference to the little book of my early adventures, which still has a place in your library and is even checked out now and again, makes me feel that the blot I spilled on American literature may be indelible. Those of you who have read it know my shame and glory. Born a bastard, I was lifted above that condition when my parents married, in 1884. My dear mother, Aunt Clara, and I were reconciled and I forgave her for inventing the cotton-broker father who so badly warped my early character. That same year I came to Sayers-Bolton to commence my formal education.

I expect the purpose of having me here is to demonstrate how far medical science has progressed since I matriculated at this venerable institution. Well, I don't mind the comparison. All I need do is load my pipe with sumac leaves and willow bark and it all comes back to me clear as the water in our limestone well. There is no doubt that medicine has changed. None whatsoever in my mind.

It used to be when you saw a man lying in the road with a broken leg you'd get down and give him a

337

hand. No more. Too dangerous. If the leg don't set right, he'll sue you. He may anyway. A dog or a cat, on the other hand, won't sue you even once, which is why I now confine my medical attention to the animal species. They make grateful patients and aren't as likely to waste your talent by running off and killing each other wholesale, as is the human kind. I set a dog's leg last month and he's taken to bringing my evening paper up on the porch. His master sued me, of course, but I settled out of court for thirty-six dollars.

Indeed, medicine has changed. We now have all these quick-fix inoculations and an armamentarium of pills and chemicals that we could not have imagined in the old days. Why, last week a man came to see me from New York. Called himself a folklorist, so I knew right off he was in the government. Said he wanted to talk with me about Indian medicine, but he was too pale and weak to formulate his questions. Appears he had a common cold when he left New York and his doctor loaded him up on antibiotics in such strength that it killed all the bacteria in his system. I rushed him to bed and saved his life with buttermilk, which got the bacteria going again. To administer buttermilk you don't need a hypodermic; an ordinary glass will do the trick. Out our way buttermilk is about twelve cents a quart, but if you add some coloring to it and put it in a fancy bottle you might get the price up to a dollar and a half without bending your conscience any.

On the whole, the profession is about as risky as it ever was. I had an example the other day of its terrors.

338

I was at lunch with some members of the American Medical Association in Topeka, in a public restaurant. Nice place, too, except we found access to the street was impeded by tables, chairs, and some floral decorations. A little girl across the room commenced choking on a chicken bone and the fool headwaiter stampeded us by crying out: "Is there a doctor in the house?"

One of our members suffered a cracked rib in the crush through the door to the street. We concealed ourselves in a nearby alleyway and hired a boy to pay our bill and bring us our hats and medical bags. When the boy came back he said the chef had stuck his finger down the child's throat and saved her.

It's these unexpected interruptions of convivial luncheons you have to look out for. You can never be sure when you'll be ambushed by your calling. One way to avoid this is to stay away from restaurants where they serve fish, chicken, or anything with small bones in it. A hash parlor is usually safe, or a chili joint if the crackers aren't too crisp. Being a vegetarian, I'm usually all right where I eat, but to be on the safe side I always identify myself as a certified public accountant; that way you get the deference due a professional man and if someone has fits at the next table you are not called upon to participate.

Advances in the profession have been wonderful. I remember the time I took Tim-oo-leh (a Cherokee herbalist, for those of you who have not yet learned to read) to the first medical convention held in Oklahoma and introduced him to the miracle of the X-ray machine. We showed that venerable aborigine an

X-ray plate of a boy's stomach, which contained a belt buckle. Tim-oo-leh was astounded! The radiologist in charge of the contraption explained how the picture had enabled the surgeons to locate the buckle and operate successfully to remove it.

Tim-oo-leh wanted to know how the belt buckle had got inside the boy. He went right to the root of the matter, you see. The radiologist informed Tim-oo-leh that the boy had swallowed the buckle. "Why?" Tim-oo-leh asked. The radiologist said this was immaterial to the case. The point, he said, was that the X-ray picture enabled the surgeons to cut the boy open with a minimum of fuss and extract the iron buckle. Tim-oo-leh was even more astonished to think they'd cut the lad open when all the case required was to feed him a wad of moss, which would have encased the buckle and allowed it to pass harmlessly through the system. "Ah," the radiologist countered, "but what if it had been an open jackknife or a bottle of prussic acid?"

At this, of course, Tim-oo-leh was confounded. We went into the convention hall, where he delivered his lecture on Indian pharmacology, which he concluded with a sincere plea that American children be instructed by their elders not to swallow everything they are exposed to. He recited a long list of things not to be swallowed, including derringers, broken glass, rusty bolts, and barbed wire. Indians, he said, appeared to have an instinct protecting them against such hazards which white children did not possess.

I took Tim-oo-leh's advice seriously and to protect my children and grandchildren I keep a log of things not to be swallowed chained to the main beam of our house. This book has grown heavier each year, including, as it does, all presidential statements and the promises of local candidates running for office. We have only recently added such items as store-bought bread and other foodstuffs that we find are chock-full of hazardous preservatives designed to guarantee a quick turnover of the consumer population. It is possible now, thanks to science, to bake a loaf of bread that will stand on the market shelf longer than anyone who eats it can possibly live. Yes, we have come a long way indeed.

I see your able proctor has brought up written questions, which I promised to answer if the medical sophistication they contain is not beyond my capacity. Ah, here we are, one word and a question mark. Roselle?

I'm pleased you asked, for it fills me with apprehension if no one asks what happened to Roselle. The last time a graduating class failed to ask about her there was an epidemic in Europe called the Great War. I put that down to a rampant disrespect for life, for all life, for ahimsa, which I detected in 1912.

When she was fully recovered from her wounds we took Roselle to my father's ranch, the Box Z, near Waycross. There she lived to reproduce just as I did, but she was better at it. She had nine offspring. I had only four. Of course, I was constrained to limit my procreative activities to one member of the opposing sex, but Roselle was promiscuous. I lectured her about this, which may be why our relationship cooled.

"Bah!" she said.

Roselle lived twelve years, then passed away to my euphemism for death, Wichita, which we all have taken an oath to forestall as long and as humanely as possible.

We still have cattalo on our place. We keep them to preserve the breed, and because Alice loves them. That's Alice Beck as was.

I guess I forgot to say that Alice and her parents came to my folks' wedding, and dang if Roselle didn't recognize Alice and kick up like a crazy fool, prancing and counting, rolling over and sitting down. Alice was so thrilled to see Roselle that when I asked her to marry me she said she would and she did two years later.

Some people are surprised that I didn't marry Cory Bigler. All I can say is that Cory had better sense than to take up with a galoot who treated her so badly. While I was studying here at Bolton Hall Cory up and married Captain Jacks. The two kisses they shared on New Year's Eve, 1883, must have stayed with them. Captain Jacks—now General Jacks, U.S. Army retired—and Cory are still together, abiding in Dallas, Texas.

ZeeZee? Why, he got to be an actor. You want to see him, go to the film collection at the Museum of Modern Art in New York and ask them to run *The Great Train Robbery*. You'll see a full-head close-up of ZeeZee pointing a revolver right at you, just as he used to do on the Katy line. After a sparse career as a thespian ZeeZee decided to eat regular and opened a barbershop in Tishomingo.

Well, I could go on for hours, but I see you're

getting restive, anxious to roll out and cure the world, and I don't mean to detain you from it. If you pass through Fort Gibson stop in. Alice is always pleased to see folks from the old academy and if the wind is up I'll take you for a sail in Dr. McNally's buggy. It beats the internal combustion engine all to hell for bringing you close to your creator.

So, ladies and gentlemen, congratulations on the completion of your medical studies. I wish you good internships and welcome you to a profession that is fast approaching the oldest in the world.

No, no! Don't stand up! I dislike standing ovations. I'm just a hard-case old horse-and-buggy doctor who sometimes hears the Kiowas laughing at our gadgets and waiting for us to swallow ourselves to extinction. I hope it don't happen and the best way I know to prevent it is to send you on your way.

Goodbye. Goodbye, and God bless you all!

ABOUT THE AUTHOR

Ric Lynden Hardman, born in Seattle, has been a freelance writer all his adult life, with time out for two college degrees and a hitch in the Marine Corps. He lives in California with his wife and two children and is currently writing *Moonlight Rider: The Second Vegetarian Western.*